I NEVER SAID
I LOVE YOU

A Novel

SARAH MAGEE

For Viola, Maureen, and Khemara,
friends across the years and miles.
Thank you for the memories.

PART I: FRIENDS

~

LISS

"A̲ʜ, Mꜱ. Lᴀʀᴋɪɴ, it's so nice to have you with us again," said the flight attendant, handing me a warm towel. "Janelle" her nametag read.

It had been entirely too long since I had settled in here, 2A, my preferred seat on these transpacific flights. I used to travel to Asia six times a year. Now it had been – what? some two full years? Better not to study the question too closely.

I smiled despite myself, crinkling my eyes, all Janelle and her crewmates would be able to see for the next fourteen hours, at least until I slipped my eye mask into place where it would meet the purple polka dot mask that I wore overtop the snug N95. I wondered how I had ever felt like "a little hamster rocketing about inside an empty wheel, thunking and clunking from side to side as the wheel churns through the clouds," as I had written a friend at the height of my pandemic malaise.

Walking down the jet bridge today felt like coming home, and I could not imagine tiring of travel again, not now and not in the future. I would not even mind if the flight were delayed, such was my ecstasy at being back on a plane. Instinctively, I checked my watch and modified the thought. *Slightly* delayed.

I fiddled with my watch, toggling absently between the calendar, the weather, and the activity tracker. The cabin door was still open. I could yet change my mind, I thought half-seriously.

"Is Seoul your final destination today?" Janelle asked, bringing my attention into focus again.

"Not really."

3

Janelle raised her eyebrows; the Asia-Pacific was just reopening and still not too many passengers were headed out on these flights. What few travelers were traveling abroad were giddy with their plans. The couple in the seats behind me had been chattering excitedly about the long-delayed tour of East Asia they were finally embarking on since they stowed their bags, and an older Korean couple in the adjoining center seats was traveling home after seeing their granddaughter here in the U.S. for the first time. She was already two years old.

Since I couldn't believe my own plans, though, I couldn't begin to explain them to a flight attendant. I pinched myself: not a dream.

Janelle took my jacket and continued up the aisle, while I settled in, intent on dulling my mind against the next twenty-four hours, the whole idea of this trip, everything in the past two decades that had led me to take my seat on this flight in the first place.

"Ladies and gentlemen, this is Captain Douglas and I would like to personally welcome you aboard Delta Airlines Flight 159 with non-stop service from Detroit to Seoul…"

Even after the longest travel hiatus of my life, I could mouth the announcement along with the captain.

I settled snuggly into the nest I had made, all those glorious pillows and blankets, and dug out the fat, pink notebook that was never far from my reach and rested it against my knees. Something in the action reminded me of the evening I decided to send Nao Kao that first, fateful message. I must have sat in bed for hours that night, legal pad on my lap, a firm, straight line dividing the page into two columns. Pros on the left, cons on the right. The page was blank. After almost nineteen years, so was my mind.

Enough forgetting.

The images flooded my mind: a lighthouse, a camera, an overturned canoe. Books. Little white containers of fried rice and Pad Thai, the ones with the delicate metal handles. Crumbling towers against the unbroken blue sky. Picnic baskets and Shaggy and that smile, always that smile, broad and guileless, the gift of a contented man. All of this I remembered that night, as I had remembered it hours earlier, the afternoon sun arcing low, the shadows creeping across the hardwood floor as I took in the pictures spread before me.

I struggled to reconcile that the bright-faced girl gazing at me from the fading stack of photos was, in fact, me.

For the first time in almost two decades, I thought of him. I weighed my options: pitching the pebble into the pond, or laying it back softly on the shore, where the water might lap gently, but no ripples would spread.

Dear Nao Kao, I wrote.

It was as far as I got. Forget about a shot in the dark. If ever anything could be described as a bolt from the blue, this was it.

I checked again that my seatbelt was securely fastened, as the engines thrummed and the wheels spun. The big bird which would carry me to the other side of the earth roared down the runway and lifted into the air. I wondered again if I had been wrong to ever hit send – a butterfly's wings, and all that. I inhaled deeply, focusing on the act of breathing; I was, I knew, as ready for this as I would ever be.

∞ ∞ ∞ ∞ ∞

"I WANT TO go to Laos."

I blinked a few times.

"Sorry. I think you were frozen."

She wasn't. Neither the picture nor the audio could have been clearer, but the words coming through Zoom did not compute. It was the spring of 2020 and for the past several weeks we had been mired in pandemic, those terrifying early days when borders slammed shut without notice and we scrubbed our groceries before shelving them and lowered our eyes and crossed the street when we encountered another human on our morning runs.

My colleagues and I had been working tirelessly as day bled into night, Friday somehow immediately into Monday, to repatriate students and faculty from places a lot less distant than Southeast Asia, although some from there, too, and now this student had somehow finagled precious minutes on my calendar to tell me that she wanted to travel to Laos, to one of the least developed countries in Asia. I adjusted my screen and drew an unsteady breath. This was my seventh Zoom call of the day; maybe I was hearing things.

"Laos," she repeated carefully. "I want to study in Laos. Not now," she chuckled, the absurdity of the conversation perhaps catching up with her, "but when this is over. I know it won't be easy, so I thought I could start planning now."

"Laos?" I repeated. "We don't have any programs in Laos." I articulated the statement slowly, hoping she might catch my meaning.

"Yes, but I heard from a friend that you helped her find a way to study in Sri Lanka, where there were no programs either. This is important to me. See each of my parents left as children..."

Laos. Her face flickered, her words animated, her hands fluttered near her eyes, but I was no longer with her.

∞ ∞ ∞ ∞ ∞

"NAO KAO. NAO Kao Inthavong."

I had spent my life being packed around the world on my parents' various sabbaticals, befriending locals in all the far-flung corners of the world, but even to my globally-attuned ears, the name was unusual. I turned to look. Like me, he was younger than most of the other students in the class. Pan-Asian, relatively non-descript, save for wearing blue jeans and long sleeves despite the mercury hovering around ninety degrees. Kind eyes behind thick glasses. Thin. No, more like wiry. Or scrappy. Unsmiling, but then the international students often were. Flashing the pearly whites at every opportunity is a decidedly American trait.

"Say that again," the professor asked.

"Please call me Nao Kao."

I hated these first day of class exercises, the name, rank, serial number monotony of it, and never more so than when the professor projected such obvious earnestness for us to amalgamate ourselves into one big, happy family. Unlike some students who wanted to share their life story from the first day, who were already speaking of happy hours to come, I sat quietly, hands folded into my lap, just waiting for this exercise to end.

"And where are you from, Nao Kao?"

"Laos."

The professor flicked her eyebrows quickly, but moved on.

I have often wondered if it might have all been different if, like the rest of them, I had not known Laos from Latvia. In another life, I might have been the one to ask whether Laos wasn't one of those countries near Russia, the ones that used to be part of the Soviet Union. Or, at a minimum, I simply might not have cared, absently filing Nao Kao's homeland in my mind as another obscure land to be named and forgotten.

But whether from a forced march through the frigid ooze of North Sea mud at low tide, my hosts determined to show me a good time despite myself, or my encounters with man-eating mosquitos and man-hating monkeys in South America, my identity as a globalist was already forged by the time I entered grad school in the fall of 2000. Whether it was the cumulative effect of these hijinks, the international hallmates I had befriended all through college, or merely how I was wired, I can say only that if ever the stars foretold eventual friendship, this was it.

Not that I had many friends that year. Never mind that I had grown up in Ann Arbor just a few miles from campus, that I had spent four years haunting the stacks and study spaces of the UGLi, or that I had spent more hours laughing and lounging in the Diag than any other first-year grad student. I had, in fact, once been hired to give a private tour to the daughter of an A-list celebrity who was contemplating exchanging the sunshine of California for the zest and zeal of the Maize and Blue.

Now I was a graduate student, and the friends I made through undergrad were all graduated and gone; my future was waiting for me to find it, surely elsewhere, and I felt like a transient. I kept my nose in my books and staked out the farthest corner of the law library. The law library was a far cry from the relative hustle and bustle of the undergraduate library, where laughter often reverberated and joviality reigned among the volumes. No, the law library was a place so quiet, but into whose high vaulted ceiling every sound reverberated, that even a whisper echoed, and you could hear the person three tables over scratching notes onto a legal pad. I worked there one summer in high school, wearing heels for the first time simply because I delighted in the click of them bouncing off the flagstone floor and through the cavernous hall.

By the time my first semester of graduate school ended, I had succeeded in distancing myself from my cohort such that they didn't even invite me to the end-of-semester bar crawl.

"Are you coming?" Nao Kao asked, before he realized I was unaware of the plans. He and I often sat together in class, sometimes lingering after to finish our conversations. Those snatches of conversation before we vacated our seats when the next students arrived were the extent of my social life. Despite the fact that he wasn't even a full member of the cohort, that he was only taking education courses as a cognate, he was eager for the opportunity to socialize with the others, even if some of them thought he was born in the USSR. Nao Kao bore no grudges.

I thought back to my twenty-first birthday a couple of years earlier, the surprise party a handful of well-meaning if misguided friends had thrown at Pizza House, my strident opposition to so much as a mention of my birthday that ended with me stalking out onto Church Street on the coldest night of the year. I had timed my exit poorly and collided with the waiter bearing the large tray of sticky pink daiquiris to our table. Sweet, alcoholic lava flowed over my friends, across the table, and pooled under their feet and on the floor. Months of repentance followed.

"You'll have more fun without me, I promise."

"You won't do it just for the show will you? Because you really do not care what the others think, is that right?"

He looked at me quizzically, as though truly seeing me for the first time.

That might have been obvious from my parries in class, my aversion to *collegiality* as the faculty so often referred to the need to pretend we all liked one another, from the way I rolled my eyes when a classmate suggested balancing a departmental budget by purchasing fewer pens and less copy paper.

Suddenly it dawned on me what a revelation this must be. What a revelation *I* must be. Asian societies are collectivist: the good of the group supersedes that of the individual, full stop. The squeaky wheel might get the grease here, but in Asia, it is the nail that sticks up that gets hammered down.

"No, no, it's just, I mean, I'm not interested. It's not my thing," I stammered.

"Other people, you mean. We are not your thing," Nao Kao teased me, and I smiled—laughed—despite myself.

He moved his hand and a flash of light caught me by surprise. Our many conversations during and after class had hewed entirely to the academic, I realized, not the personal, and despite the months of shared classes, this was the first time I noticed his wedding ring, that simple band of gold that delineated a bright line in relationships all the world over.

"I miss them."

I had stared a beat too long; perhaps Nao Kao had misinterpreted my surprise at my own obliviousness for surprise at his personal life. But now I met his eyes. Waited.

"My wife. My kids, twin babies," he smiled slightly, as though remembering something. "Turning one next month. Ah, but this was the only way though. A better life for all of us in the end and it's only a short time."

Two years did not seem such a short time to me to be away from a wife and little babies, but for once I held my tongue.

"I'd love to see a picture sometime. If you don't mind, that is."

He pulled a worn photograph out of his wallet, and as he passed it to me, I realized how often he must take it out and remember. A young woman with a faint smile and a baby on each hip gazed back at me.

"Boys or girls? Or one of each?"

"Girls, both. What a surprise." He shook his head lightly, as though remembering the first time he heard that news, maybe, or even the surprise when they were born.

"Do you talk to them often?"

"I try to call every other week. It's not so cheap, you know," his nervous laughter hiding what was clearly no laughing matter.

"Well, I hope you get to speak with them over break. Maybe tell them about the snow?"

Oh, the inanity! I could converse for hours if the subject was academic, but five minutes of small talk about anything personal was evidently more than I could handle.

He laughed, though, probably imagining the impossibility of describing snow to little babies whose world was bounded by the mountains and jungles of Southeast Asia.

"Enjoy your break, Liss. And Merry Christmas."

Only then did it occur to me how lonely he must be. I should make a point to be friendlier next semester.

9

NAO KAO

AMERICANS OFTEN THINK all Asian countries – all Asian people – are the same, but they're not. We're not. On an intellectual level, I knew that before I arrived at Chulalongkorn as an eighteen-year-old, but I felt it there for the first time. Nothing in Laos prepared me for the bustling metropolis that was Bangkok. I adapted. I learned to squeeze my motorbike through the least opening, to elbow my way through the crush at the most popular market stalls, to take plain white rice with my meals rather than the sticky rice of home.

Of course, the U.S. would be a bigger adaptation, but exactly how big did not hit me until my flight landed and I encountered my first American. She was a gruff and belligerent customs agent, who shouted and swore liberally. "Fucking students," she spat in my direction, in response to my question about the customs form. I blushed, certain every other officer in hearing distance was staring at me, the cause of such a fierce rebuke. Glancing around, I realized no one had so much as looked in my direction.

In Ann Arbor, the culture shock multiplied. Professors wore sweatshirts and sandals – even shorts! – to teach class. Living alone for the first time, I navigated warehouse-sized grocery stores with forty kinds of peanut butter and thirty kinds of hot dogs, with an entire aisle of noodles and rice, but none that tasted of home. The biggest surprise, though, was the students, the way they comported themselves with one another, the boys and girls always looking, laughing, touching. They would sling their arms over one another or offer one another an enthusiastic squeeze, akin to a hug, but not quite, in hello and in good-bye, in the middle of story, or walking across campus.

Such casual contact between men and women in Laos was completely unknown. I tried to explain it when I called home, but I could not find the words. In Laos, boys and girls did not touch until they were virtually betrothed. There was certainly no translation for the hook-up culture that pervaded from Thursday until Sunday here. Nor could I explain so much else I did not understand about this place where I had come to succeed at all costs. How quickly I found myself adrift from the friends and family waiting for news at home.

Northwoods was dominated by international students, most of them married, many with children in tow. My neighbors quickly became my friends, but hailing from the likes of Lebanon, Ghana, and the Philippines, they were no more able to puzzle out the quirks of tipping practices in restaurants or why the sales tax was not included in the price marked on the goods on the shelves than I was. None of us could begin to understand the obsession with football or the importance of The Game, which, collectively, we finally understood referred to Michigan versus Ohio State. We were both a part of America and apart from America.

"Are all of your friends foreigners?" my mom asked once over the crackle of a poor connection.

"Mostly," I conceded, and it was true.

Melissa Miller, Liss, was an enigma more than a friend. We often sat next to one another and in class she could alternate between stony-faced silence and jolly good humor in the course of a single discussion. Despite myself, I admired the completely unselfconscious way she spoke up in class and how she questioned what the rest of us frequently accepted at face value. She was not above rolling her eyes at particularly insipid remarks, even those proffered by the professor. After class we might linger, and she'd chat happily, her eyes laughing as her words spilled out in irreverent or self-deprecating bursts, a million miles removed from the modest reserve Laotian girls learned from birth. No one would ever mistake Liss for one of those demure women who had peopled my world thus far. Still, it was through these conversations that I first began to understand this new, strange country that was to be my home for the next two years.

All the same, I would not call her a friend. I was pretty sure she didn't have friends.

LISS

THEY DON'T TELL you about the ice cream cart in first class. All the times you're sitting in coach, dreaming about what happens "up front," and you don't even know the half of it. It is not just the five-course meals or the pillows and blankets by Westin or the bottomless beverage service. It is not even the fact that they let you keep your window shade open if that is what you want. No, the nec plus ultra of first class, the pièce de resistance, at least of Delta One, is the dessert cart laden with all the makings of an ice cream sundae at forty thousand feet, to be eaten, no less, with a dainty heart-shaped spoon.

Too many pandemic-laced nights I had dreamed of that cart rattling up the aisle, the choice of hot fudge or caramel or *both* causing drool to spill onto my pillow as I gloried, however unconsciously, in the before times. A small square of brownie, a scoop of vanilla, caramel, hot fudge, whipped cream, and a wafer straw is as close to heaven as a flight on a commercial airline can take you.

Actually, the brownie comes separately. But in first class, you are allowed as many desserts as you want, and if you ask for the brownie, it is an easy enough feat to transfer the ice cream from its own little ceramic dish before asking the flight attendant to ladle on the toppings. All of this Janelle did happily, ice cream onto brownie, hot fudge and caramel drizzled over the little vanilla mounds, a dollop of whipped cream, and then the wafer drilling into it all. Bliss.

I introduced Nao Kao to ice cream, I remembered. He, a twenty-five-year-old, fully-fledged adult, had never known the pleasure of such cold sweetness. I lost count of how many times I goaded him into indulging in my favorite treat during that golden summer. Stucchi's was closer, but the Washtenaw Dairy was better – richer and creamier – and it is possible I tasted every flavor at both that summer.

Those ice cream runs, the backdrop of that honeyed summer, were one of the few memories that rang clear in my mind. Of the present and the recent past, I could talk for hours: it was as though everything I had not told Nao Kao for so many years was at last slipped of its surly bonds. I told him about earning my PhD, and the program director who had all but asked me to leave the program after determining that "my disposition was better suited to arguing cases in a courtroom than the collegial exchange of ideas in academia."

He told me he never liked her since the time she wore a tank top and shorts to teach class, something that still shocked him, and a story which his colleagues in Laos never could entirely believe. He looked forward to gossiping about old professors we had once known when we met, he added, and I realized he took it for granted that we would meet again one day in real life, and not merely as text bubbles on screens. Of the fact that such gossiping should take place under the stars, and that this detail was stated not as an afterthought, but as an integral component of the act, I could make – or chose to make – neither heads nor tails. As I recall, I changed the subject.

I told him of my globe-hopping ways, of how such continual travel simultaneously fueled me and exhausted me. He told me about the rewards of his work, and about his escapes from the demands of it: hikes through the jungle in which he forded rapids and kept a wary eye for ground leeches, those pestilential annelids that could even chew through socks. The hundreds of kilometers he had ridden on a succession of motorcycles, fast and shiny and made for jumping and dirt biking in his younger days, sleeker and more sensible – though still fast – as the years accumulated. The time he tumbled down the side of a cliff, his fall broken only by the vines that snagged and tore the skin until he landed bruised and bloodied, but largely intact in the squelching mud. "My punishment for playing half naked," he'd texted, and I ignored the temptation to take the bait and ask "Which half?"

I told him about Jake, how easy it had been to slip back into a relationship with him, how marriage was the logical next step, how I managed to keep up the façade until I could not: like Hemingway described bankruptcy – gradual and then sudden. Maybe it was the fact that he had already borne the brunt of the worst of me, this man who had once been my closest friend, but with Nao Kao there was no pretense, only things my brain simply refused to recall – and even now, after hundreds of hours of conversation, I was still coming to terms with the gaping holes in my memory.

∞ ∞ ∞ ∞ ∞

"LISS, HONEY, DAD and I are going to invite a few of the international students in our departments on New Year's Day. Is there anyone in your program we should invite?"

"Mmmm," I looked up from my reading.

13

"Liss, please, I don't know why you come home if you're just going to keep your nose in your book all afternoon."

"Laundry," I sighed, and my mom laughed.

Even though it could be an ordeal to schlep my dirties home, it still beat washing clothes in the dingy laundry room in the basement of my building. Which is to say nothing of the quarters I was saving or the fact that the clothes actually dried in the prescribed time. I looked forward to my own washer and dryer – in unit – with almost as much fervor as I looked forward to earning a fulltime paycheck.

"I said, we're inviting international students to a New Year's open house. Do you know anyone we should include?"

My parents met as graduate students at Michigan State when my mom was studying for her doctorate in European history and my dad was working on his in forestry. I was born not long after my mom defended her dissertation, during which I had kicked her repeatedly in the ribs, as she liked to remind me. They had been lucky to find positions together at Michigan, where my mom had been in the College of Literature, Science, and the Arts and my dad in at the School of Natural Resources and the Environment ever since.

Their sabbaticals weren't my only exposure to the wider world. Since before I could walk, my parents had welcomed international students into our home almost every holiday. They relished laying the table with American classics from fried chicken, hunks of buttery cornbread, macaroni cooked with fresh cream and mounds of sharp yellow cheese, and bowls of strawberries sticky with their own syrup buried beneath mounds of freshly whipped cream in summer, to perfectly golden turkeys with pillowy mashed potatoes, green beans specked with salt and glistening with butter, and homemade apple pies at Thanksgiving. Among her other attributes, my mother was a magnificent cook.

From New Zealand and Russia, Haiti and Colombia, China, Israel, and Italy our guests came, not a few of them now lifelong friends whose homes I had shared, whose children I knew, whose stories I loved. My parents spoke five languages between them, six if you counted English, and more than once they had translated official documents in the service of obtaining one or another vital record from far-flung government entities.

"Is Theo coming?" My older brother was home from Beijing where he was studying at the Hopkins-Nanjing Center and I was eager to spend as much time with him as I could. Once he returned to China, it figured to be a year before I would see him again.

"He'd better! I'm planning to introduce him to some of the students I've invited."

I rolled my eyes.

"You mean the girls. You're trying to set him up again," I said accusingly.

"Well I'd much rather he marries a nice girl who wants to stay in the U.S. than one who lives in China and will keep him there!"

"Did it ever occur to you he might want to stay in China, regardless of whether he finds a girl there?"

My mother narrowed her eyes at me. We had mined this territory before.

"Anyway, I think there's a guy from Laos in the public policy school we could invite. Nao Kao. He's taking a couple of education classes, too."

"What did he do for Thanksgiving?"

I shrugged.

"You could have invited him here, Liss!"

"Sorry," I mumbled, aware of never entirely living up to my parents' sociable ideals.

We hosted a baker's dozen of international students on New Year's Day 2001, and though it was well after the ball had dropped, and the gathering was billed as an open house rather than a party, my mom had bright, shiny hats and noisemakers for all, along with her usual assortment of muffins and soups. Some half-dozen of each filled the buffet, sweet and savory muffins from corn to cranberry–white chocolate, and soups that ranged from chili teeming with peppers, onions, and wild venison to shiitake mushroom to her special, velvety creamy tomato, but the vat of Hoppin John dominated it all.

"Eating black eyed peas on New Year's will bring you good luck," my mother drawled, enlightening our guests on the Southern tradition with which she had grown up. Even after decades in the north, her words still poured out like warm honey when she wanted them to.

"Your parents do this every year?" Nao Kao asked between bites of piping hot Hoppin John, into which he had splashed half a bottle of Tabasco. Even my mother's Cajun forebears would be impressed.

"Every holiday, basically. Usually not Christmas. But otherwise, yes."

"This is why you knew where Laos was?"

"Among other reasons."

My mom wandered over to join us.

"Thank you for inviting me, Dr. Miller. You have a lovely home." Nao Kao proffered his hand.

"Please, call me Rachael. It's Rachael Zick, actually. Why should women have to change their names just because they marry?"

I saw the wheels turn, as Nao Kao debated whether or how he was supposed to respond. Rhetorical questions stumped him.

"Mom, Nao Kao is from Laos. Do we know anyone else from Laos?" He looked at me gratefully.

"Now that you mention it, I don't think we do. How wonderful! Please, won't you tell us a bit about your country?"

"The ancient name for Laos, Lan Xang, means Kingdom of a Million Elephants," Nao Kao began. "For hundreds of years, this Kingdom was one of the largest in Southeast Asia."

In choosing history as a starting point, I knew my mom would be in his thrall for as long as he cared to speak.

∞　∞　∞　∞　∞

I WOULD BE hard pressed today to tell you a single class I took, book I read, or professor who inspired me in that second semester of graduate school. If fall is the sweet brassy sounds of a marching band at practice and the roar of one hundred thousand fans on a crisp Saturday afternoon, the Goodyear Blimp circling overhead, winter in Ann Arbor is a bleak time, when the snows fall early and the ponds freeze hard. If the snows are slightly later now, twenty years ago, the snow was piled at the curbs by December, and a hard, black crust covered the diamond shimmer before winter semester started in January. Leaden skies ruled the days, night falling before one even thought to put supper on, though the blackness offered a welcome respite from the inescapable gunmetal gray of the year's first quarter. A bluebird sky is a rare sight in Michigan between those long, dark months from November to March.

After my parents' New Year's open house, Nao Kao and I began to spend more time together. He reveled in the snow, as only one raised amidst the unbroken lushness of Southeast Asia might. Weather – the wait five minutes and it will change, four seasons in the span of four hours weather – was a novelty to him. He delighted in tromping through the blanket of white, packing his first snowballs, rolling his first snowmen, and admiring the angel-shaped print his limbs etched into the snow. For the first time since I was a kid, I saw the beauty and the magic in the fresh-fallen snow, the miracle that a snowflake represented to one who hadn't grown up taking for granted that winter meant white.

"Each snowflake is unique," I told Nao Kao as we rolled snowballs in the Law Quad.

"Each one? Someone has checked?"

I rolled my eyes at his need to question everything I said.

"At least according to the people who know about these things. Or, you can have it your own way and they can all be the same."

He tried to catch a few on his fingertips to compare.

"You're supposed to catch them on your tongue, you know?"

"But if you catch it on your tongue, won't it melt before you can compare it to another one?"

My eyes flashed and I blinked a few times. It never failed: Nao Kao always found the fallacy in any logic – admittedly, mine had been weak – and called it out. Whereas the habit would have been irritating in most people, I found it almost endearing in him.

"I guess, uh, I guess if you wanted to compare them, well, then, yes, I suppose you should catch them on your finger," I stammered. "But if your goal is only to catch a snowflake – like a kid enjoying winter, Nao Kao, then you should do it my way."

I stuck out my tongue and expertly caught a flake on the quivering tip.

Nao Kao looked at me dubiously, then tentatively poked his tongue between his lips.

"Not like that! All the way! And point it!" I instructed.

He did so, to no avail.

"It's not hard," I chastised him gently, "stand still and a snowflake will land on it. It shouldn't take more than a minute."

He pointed his tongue again, glancing at me for approval. Ever impatient, the moment had passed.

"I'm cold, Nao Kao. Let's go."

"I will practice," he promised, solemnly, hilariously. "You will see."

I laughed at his earnestness and bid him good night. A more thoughtful friend might have offered hot chocolate – or at least advice on drying hats and scarves and especially mittens – before watching him clamber onto the bus.

Mornings after a snowfall, he would wake early, bundle himself into his warmest layers and trudge through campus with his trusty camera, capturing the tranquility of so much pristine whiteness. Often it seemed that the worse the weather, the brighter he smiled, cheerily leading class discussions on Maslow's hierarchy of needs or the Morrill Act, which was all the more amazing to me since unlike me, for whom education was my field of study, education policy was only Nao Kao's cognate.

He reveled, too, in the transition of power that winter, the inauguration of a new president. I neither watched nor celebrated as the man who had been referred to derisively on campus all fall as "the shrub," swore his oath to preserve, protect, and defend the Constitution of the United States of America. Nao Kao both watched and celebrated though, but not because of any special allegiance to George W. Bush.

He was enamored of the transition of power, the smooth and steady way in which control of the state – the fate of it, even – passed between the hands of two diametrically-opposed men at a prescribed hour on a prescribed day quadrennially. From a geopolitical standpoint, Southeast Asia is a tough neighborhood, dominated by coups, strongmen, and authoritarianism of many stripes. Such an overt display of democracy was the stuff of lore there and Nao Kao drank it down to the last, glistening drop.

It must have been around this time that he found my haunt in the law library. At first, he would come and study, asking occasionally my opinion on a journal article or two, his whispers rising through the rafters, drawing hard stares and ire from the law students occupying the nearby chairs. He thought I spent too much time there, telling me so as sunlight gained on darkness and tentative birdsong filled the air.

When he decided he had had enough of these bookish habits, he would show up with a container of takeout, luring me away to the Union, where we swapped stories of the lives we had led. For all my worldliness, I was oblivious to the expense those little white boxes represented to him, to what those hours tucked in the big wooden booths in the Union basement cost him.

We would laugh about my misadventures in Rio and Rome as we devoured cartons of Pad Thai, or I would try to explain why the local

Meijer carried forty-seven varieties of orange juice but not one of black vinegar as we made quick work of a pile of fried rice. The owner of the little Thai place in the Union food court was a family friend; she would often supplement our takeout with the higher-end fare from her restaurant. Soon mounds of soft, rubbery squid, their suction cups working against the tongue, or steaming bowls of spicy Tom Yum Goong heaping with shrimp, became regular parts of our dinners. I knew, though, that it rankled Nao Kao to accept Khaliya's generosity and I never did take her up on her offer that we be her guests at her Kerrytown restaurant.

Generally, I talked and he listened, a steady stream of chattery opinions as we studied or slurped noodles.

"Nao Kao, did you see the headline in *The Michigan Daily* today? The one about the Law School ruling? It seems like a bad loss for the U."

"Nao Kao, did I tell you about the time the Brazilian customs office confiscated a box of textbooks my dad was shipping and then harassed him for months about coming to São Paulo to bid on it at auction?"

"Nao Kao, which do you think is the better movie: *American Beauty* or *American Pie*?"

"Nao Kao, do you know that scene in *Ferris Bueller*...."

"Did you see the state is considering slashing funds for colleges and universities....

"Are you going to resell your textbooks? I'm trying to decide if I should keep any of mine..."

Occasionally I was rewarded with more than a chuckle, a raised eyebrow, or an mmm-hmmm.

"What do you think about the Naked Mile? You've heard of it, right, and that last year the police cracked down on the runners? I don't think they're going to do it this year."

"The Naked Mile? Remind me again about that." I still only had half of his attention as he skimmed through a stack of journal articles.

"It started, I don't know, probably ten or fifteen years ago. A bunch of guys decided to celebrate the end of the semester by stripping naked and running through campus."

Nao Kao snapped his head up.

"Say that again. They were naked? Entirely?" His words rang with the sounds of scandal and disbelief.

"Buck naked, Nao Kao. Birthday suits."

"And they can do that? It is legal?"

"I guess so. I think it might be like Hash Bash — it's not exactly legal, but…" I shrugged, thinking how to explain the vagaries of not only American culture but ultra-liberal Ann Arbor to someone who had grown up under communism.

"The police have said no one even called the cops. It's like people were just used to seeing naked men running around town or something. But then it got too big, you know? Thousands of spectators began to arrive after women started running –"

"Women also do this thing?" Alarm and consternation filled Nao Kao's voice; I imagine he was considering the possibility that his daughters might engage in such mischief twenty years from now, should they ever fall under the influence of a pack of wayward Americans.

"Well not anymore. Like I said, the cops cracked down last year and…" I sensed palpable relief that law and order had been restored and Nao Kao relaxed his shoulders and returned his full attention to the articles spread before him.

∞ ∞ ∞ ∞ ∞

RETICENT, ALMOST TACITURN, by nature, I couldn't help but feel lucky on those occasions when Nao Kao would throw in a few words about life in Laos. He would tell me of the Lao people's relationships with the water and soil, the intimate connection with the land, the belief that the river was like a person and must be treated with the same warm kinship. He explained that, whether for reasons entirely mythical or partially historical, the whole of the ancient kingdom of Champasak was considered cursed by illegitimate pregnancy, with every woman expected to sacrifice a buffalo every year. "Actually," Nao Kao added, almost as an afterthought, "in some villages unmarried mothers were expected to sacrifice a buffalo for their sins until quite recently." When I discovered that "quite recently" extended through my school years, I thanked my lucky stars that come what may – or what perceived sins – in my life, no animal sacrifice would be expected of me.

My favorite stories were the ones that offered color and texture about his own life. If I was fortunate, Nao Kao might tell me of the market days when he helped his parents, carefully balancing baskets of such unfamiliar foods to me as mung beans or galangal root, as well as the ubiquitous rice, atop his head as they made their way down the roads, muddy or dusty, depending on the season.

He told me of the jackfruit trees, where the fruits easily reached twenty pounds, and tamarind trees whose unassuming, brown pods yielded sweet, tangy pulp. He told me about the first time he saw an airplane, about the aid workers who had sparked his interest in the wider world, about the bout of childhood malaria that nearly killed him. After he told me of the flooding rains that washed much of life away one wet season when he was in high school, he apologized for boring me with so much detail.

"Why would you say that?" I asked, exasperation heavy in my voice.

"I guess I'm just not used to talking about myself so much."

"You should practice more often, Nao Kao. You always make me do the heavy lifting in our conversations," I said, only half-joking.

He looked at me and shrugged. Maybe it was the continuous years of warfare he'd absorbed from birth until adolescence, the stacks of grenades outside his school, the ones the children had played with, not understanding the realness of the danger, but which they had all survived, or maybe no more explanation was needed beyond an understanding that we – each and every one of us who has tread upon this earth – are who we are, but Nao Kao Inthavong was the most placid soul I had ever known.

On the first day of spring, I cajoled him into spinning the Cube with me.

"It spins?" Nao Kao asked, looking out the Union windows. It took me a moment to realize he was referring to the Cube, such a fixture of the landscape it was to me.

"Ah, the Cube! Yes, of course. You haven't ever spun it?" I shouldn't have been surprised that Nao Kao had never spun the Cube. All through undergrad, I'd dragged hapless dates this way. The only one who knew about the Cube was the one who lived in West Quad and passed it on his way to Angell Hall three times each week.

"I used to spin it all the time as a kid. Especially in the summer. My parents would bring us down here, my brother and me, and we'd race round and round until we were dizzy."

I mustn't have been more than three or four the first time I reached up and put my weight into making it turn. The Cube was a hulk of black metal that changed with the weather, freezing in winter and searing in summer. On a day like this, the ground squishy, the sky bright, spring just beginning to play peek-a-boo, it would be cold and slick beneath our palms.

21

As we pushed it around, gaining momentum and growing dizzy as it rotated on its base, Nao Kao began to tell me more about Laos – and how his parents fled from the communists.

"War was not new to Laos, you know. By the time of the American Vietnam War, that is. Always our neighbors were plundering the country, making war in the region. Actually, it is only the French who created Laos as a country, when they wished to consolidate it into a single, governable entity at the end of the nineteenth century. Mostly, it did not matter. We are an agrarian society, even today. Who is in power, the language of administration, it is as the Chinese say about heaven and the emperor. You know this proverb?"

I did not.

"Heaven is high and the emperor is far away."

"Heaven is high and the emperor is far away," I repeated.

"Yes. Or, sometimes, and maybe more appropriate to Laos, 'the mountains are high and the emperor is far away.' Either way, the meaning is that central authority retains little control over local affairs. For most Lao, especially those living outside of the cities, it did not matter who was nominally in charge. A bowl of rice in the belly, this mattered. Not the rest."

"Okay," I said after a beat of silence, unsure whether the story had reached its apogee.

"The Vietnamese began to use Laos as a sanctuary in the early sixties. Of course, the U.S. followed with their bombs. Your bombs."

Nao Kao let the line he had drawn between us sink in for a moment.

"So. The U.S. began bombing Laos in 1964. This did not stop until 1975. Actually, few people realize this, but Laos was one of the most heavily bombed countries in history, anywhere in the world. Of course, all of this, all of these bombs raining onto Laos, it was a violation of the Geneva agreements, but as they say, all is fair in love and war."

He stepped back from the Cube, which continued to twirl slowly, its movement governed by the laws of science and the universe, and walked over to one of the concrete benches. He sat heavily, concentrating, I could tell, on what came next.

"No one in Laos was unscathed by so much war, so many bombs. The entire country was the battleground, but at least for us, when the war ended, unlike in Vietnam or in Cambodia, the communists came into power peacefully. But my family, my parents, they were educated. A target for the communists, you see. So, never mind that my sister

22

was not even two years old, that my mom was many months pregnant with me, they fled to Thailand. To a refugee camp. And that is where I was born, just a couple of months later. Actually, today is my birthday. This story that I have told you, it is only twenty-five years in the past. History is still recent in Laos, you see."

My mind spun with so much information. This was by far the most Nao Kao had ever spoken at once; how anyone with these stories inside himself found interesting my mundane tales about high school in America or summer tennis camps escaped me. And yet, Nao Kao egged me on, my middle class, middle America existence as surreal to him as life in a refugee camp was to me.

I made the only response I could conceive of at the time, the one concrete fact I could latch onto.

"It's your birthday!" I practically shouted. "Happy birthday, Nao Kao! Now, quick, we should go to Stucchi's! You get a free scoop on your birthday!"

Whatever he expected me to say in response to the heaviness of what he had shared with me, urging him to indulge in ice cream, and on a day when spring was only still a promise, was certainly not it. Surprise shone momentarily in his eyes before his laughter filled the chilly evening air.

"You are a mischievous one, aren't you?" he replied. "But, come on, we better go if we are going to have our ice cream before they close."

∞ ∞ ∞ ∞ ∞

NAO KAO LIKED that after so many years on campus, first as a faculty kid and then a bonafide undergrad, I knew every nook and cranny the campus had to offer. I had opinions and advice aplenty, which I shared frequently and adamantly. If he was going to eat on Central Campus, he should eat at South Quad and not West Quad. A quiet corner at Border's was almost as good as the library and offered the advantage of more interesting reading material if you needed a break from your coursework. Yes, he could take a book off the shelf and read a few pages, as long as he was careful not to break the binding before he put it back.

He laughed when I told him that he could ask to sample three flavors at Stucchi's before settling on one, but that the fourth would draw condemnation. He must try an omelet at Mr. Greek's and the raisin toast at Angelo's and by all means he could not be a proper and respectable Wolverine until he had purchased at least one t-shirt from Steve and Barry's.

My repertoire of undergraduate misadventures was as far from his experience as dengue fever was from mine. Of all the misadventures, his favorite was sneaking a boy onto the roof of that Virgin Vault, Martha Cook, and making out under the stars to the sounds of the hall director pounding on the door behind us.

"Whatever gave you that idea?" Nao Kao asked with disbelief.

I shrugged.

"The window opened out onto the roof. The question is, why did no one have the idea before me?"

"Because they followed the rules."

I laughed. "Maybe. The girls there do like their rules. But, more likely, they just didn't get caught."

"Because they didn't have the idea to string twinkle lights around the dormer window!" I added after a beat, the full extent of this particular misdeed now revealed.

This elicited the sounds of Nao Kao's laughter that I so enjoyed, his glee spilling forth a pitch higher than his speaking voice.

"Were you always so naughty?" he asked, mock admonishment in his voice.

"What you call naughty, I call high-spirited. And, yes, of course I've always been this way! You can't learn such impishness – you're either born this way or you're not!"

Whether in wonder, disbelief, or perhaps even admiration, Nao Kao could only shake his head.

"What is your wife like?" I asked suddenly, realizing that whatever stories of home Nao Kao shared never included the shy-looking woman I'd glimpsed in the photo.

He looked at me contemplatively, considering, I assumed, which virtues he might first extol. Funny, I expected him to say, or charming or brilliant or delightful or simply lovely. Instead he simply shrugged and said, blandly, "She's a nice girl. Normal." I didn't think to ask until later what constituted "normal." Not that he would have answered.

Oh, but those story nights were a welcome distraction from the rest of my life that winter, and especially the rapidly deteriorating relationship with which I had limped into grad school.

"Is Jake the one you sneaked onto the dormitory roof?" Nao Kao asked one night over noodles at the Union.

Jake Larkin was decidedly not the boy I had sneaked through the dormer window. No, Jake was a sober and stable type, a teetotaler and early bird who yearned for little beyond a quiet life. A rule follower to the last, the mere idea would have horrified him. Easy on the eyes with long, luscious lashes and copious curls to match my own, he was a year older than I was and, wanting to stay in Ann Arbor rather than return home to Evanston, he had applied to the School of Public Policy, where he spent one semester before deciding it wasn't for him. For another six months, mom and dad paid all the bills and he had all the fun before they ultimately decided that Jake could find himself just as well in the shadow of the Windy City. Had he remained a student of public policy, he and Nao Kao might have taken classes together, an idea that amused me tremendously.

Jake left Ann Arbor without us properly breaking up, though it was clear we were headed in that direction, especially once he accepted a job that would keep him in the city, for the world was my oyster and I certainly was not about to limit my job search to Chicagoland in the name of a mediocre relationship. He and I had been together—in our on-again, off-again fashion, at least— for almost three years, which I was stunned to learn was the same amount of time that Nao Kao had been with his wife. From first encounter to wedded bliss had been a mere matter of months, according to the timeline I'd overheard him sharing with another student, but when I tried to pin down the details, Nao Kao brushed me off.

"We met, we liked each other well enough, we married."

"And we'd both grown up as refugees, so it was good to have a shared experience," he added, almost as an afterthought.

A nice girl. Normal. I remembered.

Whether it was love at first sight or merely a desire for the comforts of another body, or some point in between, only Nao Kao could know.

Thinking back to the worn picture he had pulled from his wallet, the wife and babies always at his side, yet, inconceivably far away, I did not raise the subject again. When we spoke of Nao Kao's life in Laos, we spoke instead of the country's history, and especially of the Vietnam War, the war's legacy there, and Nao Kao's frustration that no one here even seemed to know Laos existed, let alone that it had been bombed to smithereens by American forces intent on punishing the Viet Cong.

"So much war," Nao Kao would remind me, tracing this history of warfare backwards through civilization. "Always, the factions were warring, especially with those in Thailand and Vietnam, to whom we were a vassal state. Of course, we are dependent on our neighbors, too, for any trade. Laos is landlocked. Either down the rivers or overland, but whatever comes in or goes out must pass through neighboring lands."

"Tell me about the elephants," I requested, wanting to know more about the pachyderms, which had leant their name to the ancient kingdom. Certainly, I wanted to hear about them more than the bombs which Nao Kao had so clearly designated as American. *Your bombs*, he had said, more than once, and while I knew he did not hold me, personally, responsible, I still felt the sting.

"Ah, the elephant. It is our national animal, you know. It is the symbol of prosperity, and it represents the strength of Laos." He paused, "Ironic, isn't it, since we are not so strong." He winked, as was his habit when he wanted to make sure his listener understood he spoke in jest. With Nao Kao, even the serious could be fun.

"But why is it the national animal?" I asked. "Only because there are so many?"

"No, no, Liss. It is because of Buddhism, la. In Buddhism, the color of the elephant represents luck and peace and wealth. So, it is a very good thing to be like the elephant. If you visit Laos, you can see the image of the elephants everywhere, in the pagodas and the temples, even on the former flag of the country, the one before communism. That was the three-headed elephant, to represent the three former kingdoms that make up the country today: Vientiane, Luang Prabang, and Champasak."

"And were there one million elephants in Laos?" I asked, incredulously.

"This I do not know, but I doubt it very seriously. The land is too small for quite so many, I think. Maybe a few thousand. Today a few hundred." Diminished, I understood tacitly, like so much else in Nao Kao's beloved homeland.

As he spoke of the elephants and Buddhism and the ancient kingdom at the root of the modern-day country, his eyes shone and his hands twirled and spun through space, animating his speech. He spoke with pride, too, of what this American education would bring not only to him and to his family, but to his country. Nao Kao looked forward to his role in advancing Laos's development, and his passion for good governance and how he might bring such practices to bear knew few bounds.

Although Nao Kao tried to shrug off how many times he was asked to repeat where he was from, how many students – graduate students, no less – asked, literally, where in the world this place even was, his spirit sparked when he spoke of home. In contrast, his shoulders slumped and his brow furrowed when he spoke of the state of education here. It depressed him, frankly, that so many bright, young things had reached the apex of the American educational system without a stronger grasp – arguably, in some cases, without any grasp – on world affairs or geography.

"You aren't a real American," he teased me on occasion, taken aback by a knowledge of global events that exceeded not only that of the other American students he encountered – but sometimes that of the professors, too.

I had not visited Laos, but I could find it on a map and that counted for something. I was, Nao Kao told me, the only student – the only *American* student – he knew to whom he had not had to offer an impromptu geography lesson describing the location of his beloved homeland wedged between Thailand and Vietnam. Often even that description drew blank stares or embarrassed smiles. When I told him of a friend from undergrad, a girl who had graduated at the top of her class in high school and studied economics and political science at Michigan, who now worked for a think tank in DC, but who did not know Kansas from Kentucky on a map of the United States, Nao Kao could only shake his head vigorously in disbelief.

"Do you know U Thant?" he asked when I told him this, and I admitted I did not.

"He is the former Secretary General of the United Nations. From Myanmar. And he said once something which every boy and girl in my school learned by heart. 'The truth, the central stupendous truth, about developed economies is that they can have – in anything but the shortest run – the kind and scale of resources they decide to have.' Such magnificent possibility! For years this idea captured my imagination. But here, in America, sometimes I cannot help but wonder how this is possible – and for how much longer?"

For we both knew the central, stupendous truth now was how little those in the developed economy, at least the American economy, knew of the wider world. Eventually, there would be a price to pay for such ignorance.

NAO KAO

"WOULD YOU LIKE to come for dinner next Friday?" Rachael Zick asked as I wrapped up my New Year's Day lesson on Laotian history. Most of the other guests had already departed from her open house.

I paused a beat too long, uncertain how to respond to such an unexpected invitation.

"We often host students for dinner, Nao Kao. But it's an invitation, not an obligation," she added.

"That's very kind of you, thanks. Yes, I'd be happy to join you."

"Wonderful!" Rachael beamed, her face lighting up unexpectedly. "And why don't you see if you can convince Liss to come that night, too."

She walked away before I could respond, leaving me to think what an odd family they seemed to be.

"Ugh, dinner at home," Liss groaned, when I asked her.

I waited, having learned in class that a prolonged pause could lead to a modification of her initial position.

"Fine, I'll come. But only because you asked nicely."

I couldn't tell whether she was genuinely pouting or putting me on, but when she met me at the bus stop, her eyes sparkled with mischief.

"Oh, Nao Kao," she said, drawing out the vowels, "there might just be a little trouble tonight."

She didn't sound like she minded.

She kept a quick pace, the heels of her boots smacking a steady beat against the sidewalk, shoveled and salted, but still patchy with ice. I tread carefully, the rubber soles of my shoes no guarantee against a winter injury.

"Nao Kao, come in, how nice to see you," Liss's parents greeted me in chorus.

I turned to make space for Liss and noted the twinkle of mischief had hardened into a steely glint.

"Nao Kao has just been telling me about his childhood job helping his parents sell produce at their market stall. I told him I knew you'd be interested, too."

The truth of her statement depending on your definition of the word "just." I had told her about this earlier in the week, but she met my quizzical expression with a flat, even one of her own.

"Please," I read on her face, and so I obliged.

Liss was animated throughout dinner, never allowing the conversation to falter, prodding me in her efforts.

"How do you see Laos's economy developing over the next decade?" she would ask. "What are the biggest environmental threats?"

"Where in the U.S. have you traveled? Where do you most hope to visit before you leave?"

Only as we put on our coats to leave, did I begin to understand.

"Where's Jake?" Rachael asked Liss, before we could slide out the door, and in the heaviness that settled around us, I understood that this was the question Liss had been dodging since we arrived.

"Liss?"

I was watching a battle of two steel-willed women, the likes of which I had never seen because the likes of whom I had never known.

"Not here," Liss answered finally, and I saw by her expression that Rachael Zick had won.

∞ ∞ ∞ ∞ ∞

"WHO IS JAKE?" I asked a few weeks later, as we studied in the Union.

A storm cloud crossed Liss's face as she arched her brows and pursed her lips. She sighed audibly as she did so, and I thought again how unlike anyone I had every known she was.

"My boyfriend," she finally replied, then grabbed a mound of noodles with her chopsticks and shoved them all into her mouth. The subject was closed.

I reconsidered my observation of a moment before. In the months I'd gotten to know her, this was the first I was learning of Jake. Clearly this was someone who could keep her own counsel, who knew as much about discretion as any well-bred Laotian.

She stared at me, daring me to ask more questions.

"Would he mind if I took your picture?"

"What?"

"I mean, Liss, if you became one of my subjects for my photography?"

"All the pictures you're always taking on campus? The ones for your photography class? What's that to do with me?"

"I've been focusing on landscapes, yes. But later this semester we will practice portraits. Will you do it?"

She shrugged, non-committally.

"Why not?"

"I'm not photogenic. You'll get better pictures with someone else."

"I'll have more fun with you, la."

She smirked.

"You win, Nao Kao. Anyway, it's not my grade. And as for Jake, no, he wouldn't mind. But he also won't know because he's left Ann Arbor and we're about to break up."

My heart jumped.

LISS

First class is discreet, with seats too widely spaced for chitchat even if one might be so inclined. That was seldom the case even in the before times – no need of a hoodie and headphones to telegraph to your neighbor up front that small talk is not your thing. These days, after what feels like a lifetime of warnings of stranger-danger-of-the-infectious-variety, no one is inclined to make small talk with their seatmate anyway. The chatter of smug men sharing their successes is no more.

I flicked on the tv, remembering that the last time I flew, I'd binged on the *Downton Abbey* movie, once, twice, three times in the mental fog of thirty-eight thousand feet as I flew back home from Shanghai. Surely, in the hundreds of choices catalogued in Delta Studio I could find something to serve as a similar narcotic.

Big Bang Theory. Curb Your Enthusiasm. Friends. Friends! Ha! Nao Kao told me I looked like Jennifer Aniston once. Our hair alone made for a laughable comparison – she, the woman who popularized The Rachel, and me with my tangle of red. Nicole Kidman I might have understood. Instead, I had accused him of thinking all white girls of a certain age looked alike.

"Only the pretty ones," he replied, and perhaps I should have known then that the game was up: the emperor was not the only one who was far away.

I reminded him of that recently, a single line of text pinging around the planet and received only a telltale laughing sticker in return.

"Dammit, Nao Kao," I'd replied, "don't mock me with those stickers."

I checked the time. Still another ten hours to Seoul.

I used to read voraciously on these transpacific runs, as much as three books on some flights, but I could not have concentrated on anything more serious than Dr. Seuss on this flight. Not that Seuss would have been a bad choice. You can learn a lot from the good doctor, I mused as Phoebe sang about her smelly cat.

My personal favorite Seuss book is *Oh, the Places You'll Go!*, which I have gifted to more than one recent graduate over the years with the observation that it is no more and no less than the handbook for life. Who better than Seuss to remind the young and ambitious – or even, maybe especially, the not-so-young and ambitious – that you'll no sooner be amongst the high fliers and soaring heights than you will fall back to earth.

Bang-ups, Dr. Seuss will have you know, and hang-ups, can happen to you. The *can* might be my only quibble: will. most. definitely. Yes: bang-ups and hang-ups will absolutely, positively happen to you. That is more like it.

In that case, you may be headed, he fears, toward a most useless place. Connoisseurs of Seuss will know that I am not making this up. The most useless place is The Waiting Place. It is here, in this waiting place, where the masses are, as the name implies, just waiting: for trains and planes to come or go, for the rains to pass or a decision at last, or maybe just for a second chance. Everyone is just waiting.

It sounded a lot like the pandemic life, and even more like this flight. Waiting to see what – or, more to the point, who – was waiting for me.

I turned my attention back to *Friends*; if I squinted hard enough, I could almost see myself in Jennifer Aniston.

∞　∞　∞　∞　∞

TOO MANY TIMES to count I had tried to reconstruct the series of events that led me here, to the places I never expected to go, places – literal and figurative – I had so successfully obliterated from my memory that I could not have told anyone for love or money that they ever existed at all. Nao Kao. Laos.

It beggared belief to think it was a straight line from one student looking for a way to study abroad in her family's ancestral home to Nao Kao Inthavong. No, that would be too simple, and yet, there is no denying that without that request, those six little words, *I want to go to Laos*, I might yet have continued to exist in blissful ignorance of either Laos or a particular Laotian.

The universe works in mysterious ways, though, and had I dodged the study abroad bullet, I almost assuredly would have still been hit by the one fired at me shortly thereafter, the request to design and teach a course on current events in Southeast Asia. To say nothing of the dusty boxes I hefted from the depths of my closet in the midst of a cleaning binge. I recognized them immediately as the ones I had packed away two decades earlier. Clearly, the universe had determined that certain memories had languished long enough. It was time to dust them off and breathe them back to life.

And so, only days after speaking with the earnest undergrad intent on studying in Laos, a country that had not crossed my mind for going on twenty years, my cleaning frenzy yielded the papers, the textbooks and, yes, the photos that I never expected to see again. A treasure trove by any other name would be as sweet.

∞ ∞ ∞ ∞ ∞

I HAVE ALWAYS hated the word *muse*. Rodin had a muse. Renoir, too. I had seen just what that meant the first time I visited the sun dappled house-cum-museum in Cagnes-sur-mer.

However many pictures Nao Kao might have taken – whichever way he posed me against the gentle slopes of the wave field, or in the crush of late blooms in the Arb, or with my palms pressed tight against the black of the Cube, or, I remembered now, as I held the fading image, mid-cartwheel on Madison, illuminated by the sulphurous orange glow of the streetlights and the shimmering whiteness of the moon, both of us returning to my apartment after a late night printing run to the Fishbowl – yes, however many pictures there were, I was not his *muse*.

"The play of the lighting was so good," he replied immediately when I asked if he remembered all of the photo sessions he had insisted upon. I was momentarily stunned to think the lighting is what he remembered. I shouldn't have been surprised. He had become a professional photographer, even if only on the side.

It was during one of those "shoots," as he insisted on terming them even then, that we touched for the first time. It is odd to remember now, when I consider how regular touch is – or used to be. Hands shaken at receptions, a touch on the forearm to garner someone's attention, a hug with a friend, a stray hair gently brushed from a colleague's shoulder. Yet Nao Kao and I had never touched, not so much as our fingers brushing.

He asked me to wear a scarf that day. It must have been in May and I remember that the scarf was ridiculous in the warmth of late spring, not to mention that he wanted it to lie just so. The scarf was the color of emeralds, something to offset the masses of red curls that swirled to my shoulders and to accentuate the deep green of my eyes. The scarf had its own ideas about how to lie, and as those ideas were not in harmony with the photographer's sensibilities, this necessitated regular adjustment on his part. Nao Kao's fingers lightly brushed against my collar bone each time he set it into place.

"You've got a flyaway one," he had said softly, almost as to himself, brushing my hair into place, his fingers hesitating just a moment too long. "Can't let that ruin the shot."

He adjusted the scarf again and placed his hands on either side of my face tilting my chin just so. I felt like I was having my senior pictures taken again, though I doubt my heart had beaten so hard then.

"Yes," he said quietly, almost to himself, "I think this will be the best one."

He waited for a cloud to float into a position where it partially obscured the sun.

"Now look down with your eyes and smile just a little," he said.

He began clicking away, a small smile illuminating his face.

It was okay. This was my friend Nao Kao. Happily married, and with two darling babies to boot.

∞ ∞ ∞ ∞ ∞

SURELY, I HADN'T sat there on the floor of my home office, holding that picture, the word *muse* echoing through the contours of my mind for as long as it felt. At some point in that frozen moment, a little voice from deep within piped up, suggesting enough time had passed, suggesting that I finally do I what I ought to have done years before. Whether it was two minutes or twenty hardly matters.

As I repacked the box a little piece of paper fluttered by, nearly translucent, but the beautiful script was still legible. I had only ever known one person who could write like that, and Nao Kao always did recommend good books. I jotted the title in my notebook before repacking the lot and returning it heavily to the back of the shelf where it had sat, unsuspecting, for all these years.

∞ ∞ ∞ ∞ ∞

AT ITS HEART, a code is but a communication designed to be seen and understood only by the parties involved.

I read a book on codebreaking once and was fascinated by the notion that any two people can and do develop codes in how they communicate and that the more intimate the communication, the more encoded it becomes. Messages shrouded in mystery, except to the recipient.

Sometimes, though, even to the recipient.

I thought of how my communication with Nao Kao had evolved in the time since we first reconnected. After nearly two decades, we had plenty of the mundane to recall, so much life lived since we'd last exchanged stories, to say nothing of the universal hue and cry of lives altered by pandemic on either side of the globe.

"Where's the most interesting place you've traveled?" might greet me when I checked my phone in the morning, the hopping off point for a conversation to last the week.

"I'm craving Mexican," I'd write, and then query, "what's your favorite food?"

Nao Kao would regale me with stories from his childhood, the miles he walked or rode on his bike, the novelty of the telephone in his father's office.

Later, I tried to identify exactly when the conversation shifted, but the change was too subtle for me to finger precisely. Extended conversations on philosophy and politics and parenting gave way to a series of images, usually sent in the wee hours while I slept. Stray cats and dogs in a nearby park that he'd quasi-adopted. A field of wildflowers in peak bloom or the gnarled trunk of a towering tree. Monks in saffron, birds in flight. By the time I truly noticed, the transformation was complete; I was left with a paucity of words.

I think that is when I noticed, too, though, how frequently the photos arrived. Quickly I lost count of how many mornings I woke up to one or two or three or four pictures of his day. The university at first light or his kids riding their bikes. A temple, a train, a cup of tea. Sunset from a balcony, or the morning mist rising from the mountains.

Laos had been the last country in Asia to report a single case of COVID-19, and even deep into the second year of pandemic registered only a few score cases. Nao Kao suspected underreporting, but except for the occasional scare, usually a migrant worker returning home, there was no denying that COVID was virtually non-existent there. Nao Kao was not confined to his living room. A waterfall. A wooden bench. Morning mists suspended from a valley floor.

On their own, any one of these pictures was a mystery. They say a picture is worth a thousand words, but it matters tremendously whether six of them are "I think you might like this," or "wishing you were here with me."

Without the guideposts, I was lost. If there was a larger message, it fizzled in the echoes of time and space and culture. Only months later, did I begin to suspect that the pattern – the message – was woven into their cumulative total: I believe you might like this. I am sharing with you.

Not infrequently had I rolled the marble of his remark in what I still think of as the early days of our conversation, the days when much of what we discussed revolved around piecing together the past. When I revealed that one of the prongs of what had happened was connected to my mom, he seemed surprised, and maybe a little hurt.

"I remember your parents fondly, the New Year's party, the times they invited me to join you all for dinner. I liked her. She didn't like me?"

"Oh, she liked you just fine then," I assured him. "But that was before well, you know…" I still could not bring myself to put words to all that had transpired.

"Would that bother her so much?"

"Only because, as I'm sure she would have told you herself, that is not the way she raised me."

Being Rachael Zick's daughter was often its own trial. When your mother has received a Genius Grant, when she is fluent in four languages and conversant in three more, when she commands a lecture hall as easily as a Scottie dog, and has the great and good of the world at her fingertips, with a contact list – her digital rolodex – that was the stuff of fairy tales, it goes without saying that lessons abound. Half the members of her audience might not have realized they were in her thrall, but my mother's mastery of the iron fist in the velvet glove was never lost on me. The formidable and illustrious Rachael Zick scared the hell out of me, and she and I both knew it.

"Just make sure she doesn't grill you about texting some weirdo over in Laos," Nao Kao replied, ignoring my moralistic barb.

At the time it was his self-deprecation that struck me, especially since Nao Kao Inthavong was one of the least weird people I knew. Much later I wondered if he already realized – or decided – what I only slowly came to understand: the conversation was not ending anytime soon. It was that marble that I polished so regularly, for I was all but certain that assiduously and assuredly Nao Kao had led me onto this flight.

THE FIRST TIME is a rush, you know. The first upgrade. The first pounding shower in the Sky Club, the almighty water pressure washing away the weariness of a transpacific trek. The first time they greet you by name. Like an addict whose tolerance for the dope grows too fast, the intrepid business traveler seeks a more powerful hit. The airlines are only too happy to oblige. The domestic upgrade whose chief perk is overhead bin space, and perhaps a sandwich on a longer flight, gives way to upgrade certificates that will see the traveler from Detroit to Singapore in the finest style commercial airlines can offer.

Later she appears, the woman holding a sign bearing your name on the jet bridge. With her, you are whisked into another level of the traveling elite. You slip out the secret door, clattering down the metal steps to the tarmac, sliding gracefully into the heated, leather seats of a gleaming Porsche. You are literally and figuratively under the wing of the airline now as you ride past the catering trucks and maintenance crews, a journey few travelers even know is possible.

There are other doors, the hushed tones of the first-class lounges, the chef-curated menus to nourish you between flights or during the long delays. From made-to-order dinner in the JFK Sky Club to the heaping baskets of goodies in the galley, it is possible to nosh your way nonstop from the moment you pass through security until the flight attendant announces that the time has come to stow your tray table and return your seat to its upright and locked position – and your suite door to its open position.

Gratis. All of it – and like a dealer giving the first hit for free, the airline knows its business. Addiction.

The tracks on your arm – that is, your soul – grow more vast and in the search for a vein that has not yet collapsed, you must travel further and faster, frequenter and frequenter, collecting heart-shaped spoons and Tumi bags; telltale photos of God's hour, the sun peeking just beyond the tip of the wing; and stories, always the stories, of the flights gone awry, the meals we regret, the adventures hard won. At some point we decide: the small dramas the airlines bestow with such alacrity are merely the price to be paid for gazing upon the wonders of the planet.

I like to think I chose this life, but it's equally possible that it chose me. The mystics might put it down to what the stars foretold, but so many early adventures all but ensured it. I thought back to that heady middle school summer, the joyful weeks I spent on the jagged edge of France while my parents tended to their academic responsibilities – the research, the workshops, the paper presentations galore. While they razzled and dazzled the finest minds, I spent evenings around tables piled with the day's catch, the sounds of laughter ricocheting through the gardens, the dull crash of Atlantic rollers just audible during the rare pauses of our animated words.

I thought about all of this as I looked out the window near the lavatory. One of my headphones popped out as I bent over, and I marveled at how noisy the aircraft cabin was. I tried to imagine what it must be like to step onto a plane for the first time as an adult, to experience the roar of the engines not as the soundtrack to a lifetime of memories but for the first time while traveling to a wedding or a funeral or a long-anticipated week at the beach. Flight was an integral part of my life and my earliest memories are pockmarked with airplanes, but I tried to imagine how it would feel to see the world from above for the first time and know it was an experience worth remembering.

Few clouds marred the view and below us the Alaskan range was blindingly bright, the shadow of the plane dancing across the mountaintops and valleys. I thought again about a colleague's belief that people could be sorted into two categories. There are those who are of *a* place, she posited, who are born somewhere, and inhabit it so fully that it becomes part of their essence, and there are those who are of any place, who live a little here and a little there, equally at home in the tropics or tundra, megacities or mountains. Maybe, I had countered, it is only a matter of stasis. We are born to a place and, living there long enough, are simply unable to escape the way it seeps into our marrow and becomes as much a part of us as our blood or our bones. Inertia is a powerful force. An excuse, as much as a truism.

I grabbed a few squares of Ghirardelli, giving wide berth to the bananas. Bananas disappear quickly in coach, where the (mostly) novices packed in three- and four-across see them as the healthy snack option.

"Never order the eggs," a flight attendant told me once, "and remember that the bananas are frozen."

Along with "time to spare, fly through O'Hare," it was the best travel advice I have received in my years of crisscrossing the skies.

I took another look at the basket and snagged a couple more Ghirardelli squares for good measure. In an hour or two, the dark chocolate with sea salt would be gone. Salt improves the flavor of almost any food, but never more than in the din of an airplane cabin. The body craves the savory – and salty – when sailing through the skies.

∞ ∞ ∞ ∞ ∞

FOR THE PAST several months, as we traded texts, I had been ribbing Nao Kao about the books he read – or didn't. Once or twice I made suggestions that fell flat, but undeterred, I still thought he should read more than the management and leadership titles that are the purview of MBA students. An acknowledgement that he used to love literature and had not realized how much he missed it was the closest he came to conceding the point.

"What's your favorite Hemingway" surprised me then as much as anything he might have texted me at 11:00 p.m.

"Moveable Feast," I replied without thinking.

No matter how far professionally I had drifted toward Asia, I was still a Francophile at heart. Of course, the book in which the expatriate world of 1920s Paris, peopled by authors smoking and drinking and filling reams of paper with the books that were to become a staple of American literature, was my pick.

"Best Fitzgerald?"

"Cruise of the Rolling Junk"

"I don't know it."

"Ah, but it's Fitzgerald at his finest. Travelers in the bloom of youth bound for points unknown, happiness hanging from trees, rings to tilt for, garlands, bright and shiny and reminiscent of the sweetness of life, to be won. Oh, but to be able to write like Fitzgerald, " I enthused.

"I'll look for it."

"It's hard to find. You won't find it for your Kindle, either. I'll send it sometime."

"Don't be ridiculous."

"Nao Kao, when have I ever not been ridiculous?"

One of his preferred laughing stickers floated onto my screen.

"Remember when we went canoeing?" I asked.

"I remember everything, Liss. But that was probably the most ridiculous."

I went back to my work, thinking about how the little details Nao Kao revealed conversation-by-conversation proved his comment was no idle boast – from the grade I'd earned in a particular class, to the exact hue of a favorite sweater, to the specs of the camera he'd cajoled me into purchasing one weekend at Best Buy, Nao Kao forgot nothing. Some might consider the ability to lodge so many memories a gift, but to my thinking it was at least as much a curse.

My phone buzzed.

"What's your favorite line from literature? Or any book?" He must have been feeling pensive.

"There's this little memoir I love about a hardscrabble childhood in war-torn Africa," I had no sooner typed the words than I wished to recall them. Nao Kao did not need the author of *Cocktail Hour Under the Tree of Forgetfulness* to remind him that the beauty and the sorrow of life is that we never know which moments of heartbreak or ecstasy will be the most defining of our life.

"Scratch that. The opening lines in *Cutting for Stone* are probably my favorite. The idea that none of us asks to be born into this life, and that those of us who find purpose other than wretchedness, destitution, and an early date with death should consider ourselves lucky beyond measure."

"Too dark. Are you always so morose?"

Funny that you should ask, I wanted to say. My therapist, Stacy, asked me the same question recently, and I was forced to acknowledge that for all my bright and chipper exterior, my streak of darkness appears to be congenital. Memories of *Adventures with Nao Kao* were not the only treasure I had uncovered these past few months.

In the depths of my childhood closet, which I had been kindly requested for the hundredth time to set to rights only to finally do so, I uncovered reams and reams of writings dating to the days when both my orthography and penmanship left much to be desired. From the earliest writing sample, on the back of which my mother had dutifully recorded the date, in the middle of second grade, on through the musings of Christmas Eves more recent that I cared to admit, dark narratives tumbled forth.

In the earliest little story, I killed off the heroine – she was eight, like me – and on Christmas Eve, no less. It was fast-acting leukemia that got her – diagnosed around dawn, she was dead before dinner.

41

I pinned the ending of another story to the cork board in my office, simply because I liked the melancholy and morosity it evoked, even a decade after I penned it.

> *A patio in Gastown was the last place he expected to see her, but there was no mistaking Clem. Her blue suit was well-cut; the seafoam green scarf wound in neat loops around her neck was clearly silk. Where a dozen silver bracelets had once glinted around her wrist, a heavy diamond bracelet lay.*

> *As the memories broke over him like waves tumbling against the shore, her old laugh filled the air. In that moment, the street noise – the homeless man incessantly seeking a quarter, the whistle of the steam clock, the din of trains and boats and seaplanes – disappeared and he was twenty-two again, striding unsteadily toward the girl he believed he would marry.*

From deadly diseases to car accidents to star-crossed lovers, my stories had it all. Except for a happy end.

Was I always so morose?

"You know it," I replied to Nao Kao. "What's your favorite quote?"

My phone rang with fires to put out. Late night in Laos was midmorning for me.

It would be hours before I returned to the conversation, long after Nao Kao had gone to sleep, before I would see his reply.

"You don't remember? The line from *Love Story,* la."

Now that he asked, of course I remembered. What I hadn't decided was whether a belief in never needing to say you're sorry to one you loved was a romantic ideal or a selfish one, or maybe, like so many things that were neither black nor white, it was both. Either way, Nao Kao always did love Erich Segal. In grad school, he convinced me to read *Love Story,* and I still wasn't sure I had completely forgiven him for the tears I had shed.

It struck me then as well as now as an odd choice for this man to favor. In fairness, he might simply have had access to fewer books in a place where each volume was a treasured survivor of war or worse, even into the 1990s. Then again, his sentimental streak could merely be wider and longer than that of any other man, possibly of any other human, I had known. Clearly anything he'd read more recently had failed to make the same impression.

I could not claim then to be surprised that *Acts of Faith,* the title he had so meticulously inscribed on the scrap of paper I had packed away so many years earlier, the one that fluttered unsuspecting past my eyes on the afternoon I unearthed my memories, had a similar effect. For if *Acts of Faith* examines the ways in which children disappoint their parents (myriad, large and small), and parents their children (the same), it is, above all, devoted to the heartbreak of forbidden love. By the time I reached the end, I had the eerie feeling that maybe there was more to this recommendation than Nao Kao's penchant for a tearjerker. My tears weren't confined to the heartrending story between the covers.

I was slightly embarrassed to think how many times since that paper fluttered down I had asked myself what Nao Kao knew that he did not know he knew. Or what he knew that I, at least, did not know he knew.

I stuck a little heart on the text bubble and readied myself for another meeting over Zoom.

∞ ∞ ∞ ∞ ∞

IN ITS HALF-AWAKE state, my mind wandered, dipping and diving like a plane passing through turbulence. I am a Michigander, seven generations in the making on my father's side. Like any good Michigander, I have a thing for Lord Huron. Cruising along, high across the northern latitudes, a pair of earbuds delivering the music straight into my mind, I reflected on the lyrics. Perhaps it was more than the connection to the Mitten that spoke to me, for the good Lord Huron, I realized with a start, was waxing nostalgic about a girl who had ghosted him, for whom he had traversed the desert and the sea, the mountains and the trees trying to find her again. And if Lord Huron didn't have the answer to what he was s'posed to do, haunted by the ghost of you, I sure didn't. I thought back to how those five little words Nao Kao had offered me almost immediately reached into my bones. *Thanks for finding me, Liss.*

I cannot – would not – claim to be in Nao Kao's every thought the way Lord Huron's lost girl consumed his, but the rest of it I knew intuitively to be true. We might easily have inspired verse and chorus. Nothing else could account for the panic that seized me when I returned to the university and went about demanding a new uniqname and convincing human resources to scrub any trace of my middle name, refusing to rest in my crusade until I was satisfied that Melissa Claire Miller Larkin was reduced to Melissa Larkin, an anonymous administrator, untethered from her past. In hindsight I laugh to think how I fretted that Melissa Miller might be traceable. Facebook alone shows hundreds of profiles under that name today, and God knows the search algorithms at the turn of twenty-first century were not what they have become. Don't use more than eight words. Don't cite Wikipedia. And for heaven's sake don't talk to strangers online. We had only just barely survived Y2K.

"I can still picture you sitting in class," Nao Kao wrote to me once. "I am surprised, sometimes, by the suddenness and the clarity of memory."

"Do you still wear your pendant?" he asked me another time, and it took me a moment to realize he was speaking of the little dog that had rested in the dimple at the base of my throat for so many moons. Lost, years ago now, and fittingly on a long-haul flight. The fastener gave up the ghost while I slept, and the pendant disappeared without a trace.

"A man doesn't remember details like that unless he cares uncommonly," my therapist said when I finally leveled with her about where my mind was. To say she was surprised is to understate the matter. The rest of the world was out searching for toilet paper and Clorox wipes. I was searching for answers to a jigsaw puzzle with no start and no end – a mess of middle pieces, each devoid of color or pattern, the assembly of which was entirely on me.

Occasionally, I tried to get Nao Kao to bring a memory into focus for me, to see if a few more words would allow me to retrieve it from the mists of time. Periodically he would indulge me, offering up scraps I'd long since consigned to wherever memories lodge when the brain no longer wishes to retain them. So it was with the memory of Nao Kao having removed his wedding ring.

I had forgotten until he reminded me recently, and now it bothered me. He said I had roughed him up about it sometime after we went to the wave field for the first time, though he would not remind me exactly when that was. I might have told him plainly that I could not recall even many mundane details, but to do so felt like rubbing salt into a wound.

"You mean I gave you the third degree?" I asked bemusedly.

"Or the thirtieth," came his reply, the little gray bubble popping up on my phone.

Whatever details his mind still held, and I had no doubt they were all there, he doggedly kept them to himself and would say nothing further about why he removed it – or when. If I concentrated hard enough, I could almost capture an image of myself racing up and down the moguls of the wave field, windmilling my arms in a poor impression of the skiers who soared down mountains rather than dashing across a blistered green field. I think I may have packed us a picnic – sandwiches and strawberries and chocolate chip cookies – but my mind could not be trusted not to merge, reflect, and refract so many shards from the past into even more broken pieces.

Even now, after a conversation of hundreds of hours stretching across months and into years, I still had not admitted to Nao Kao the extent to which the holes in my memory made Swiss cheese of our time together.

∞ ∞ ∞ ∞ ∞

I TOLD HIM on the night of the famous debate. I hadn't intended to do it then. I was not entirely certain I would tell him at all. But he had poked me about the debate, suggesting I watch and provide him with updates since I was "stronger." Unexpectedly, the word triggered something inside me that had lain buried for so many years and instantly put paid to my own, long-running, internal debate. If ever I was going to come clean with Nao Kao, this was the moment.

The rest of the world might have been consumed by the likes of "Proud Boys, stand back and stand by," and "Keep yapping, man," but I was in my own world, telling a man nine thousand miles away the meaning of the breadcrumbs I had been leaving along the trail for the past few months.

∞ ∞ ∞ ∞ ∞

IT MUST HAVE been sometime in the early summer of 2001 that Nao Kao started staying at my apartment. Most students scattered at the end of winter semester, but he and I plodded through our coursework and soaked in the relief of early summer, our conversations lengthening with the days. He didn't stay over too often, just on nights he missed the last bus back to North Campus and his apartment in the aptly named Northwoods.

Nao Kao would stretch out on the tatty, brown couch, a hazard of a furnished apartment that had seen god knows what over the years.

45

He would cover himself with a jacket if the evening was cool, or not even that if it was warm. It was only later that I considered that when you spend your early years in a refugee camp, a pillow and a blanket are far down life's list of necessities. In class, I studied Maslow's hierarchy of needs; with Nao Kao, I learned it.

It was totally kosher, him in the living room, me ensconced in my bedroom, though in hindsight I realized his wife might have disagreed. What she did not know would not hurt, though, and anyway, Harry and Sally were wrong. Nao Kao and I were the exception that proved the rule. Platonic friendship was utterly possible.

∞ ∞ ∞ ∞ ∞

NAO KAO –
I was sorting through materials from our master's program and thought I'd see if you were on LinkedIn. You look to be doing well. I hope so.
        – Liss

Friday night seemed the best time to send a hesitant (on my part) – possibly even unwelcomed (on his part) – message. Only a nerd like me would check LinkedIn on the weekend. It was after eleven when I convinced myself that the world would not blow up if I hit send.

∞ ∞ ∞ ∞ ∞

IN HINDSIGHT, THE summer of 2001 probably wasn't as blissful as I remember. In my mind, it's a great, shining stretch of halcyon days, though more likely it's merely knowing that it was the end of our own *Trente Glorieuses* that made those months seem infused by a golden aura. Summer I classes slid into Summer II, broken by the fireworks for the Fourth of July, one of the few occasions I recall gathering with classmates other than Nao Kao. My mind's eye has retained a picture of me nursing a Mike's hard lemonade and leaning against a rickety porch banister at a big house on Division, one of those places where ten or twelve kids lived each year, the unlikely combination of *Cecilia* and *Slim Shady* providing the soundtrack against which the young and carefree contested round after round of beer pong. How or why I ever came to be on the porch escapes me, and I can only assume Nao Kao had a hand – probably *the* hand – in convincing me to shed my anti-social ways and join him on the most American of nights.

The peak of summer in Ann Arbor is the Art Fairs, when the streets are closed to traffic, the artists display their wares under blue and white and beige peaked tents, when the scents of elephant ears and corn dogs compete for olfactory space alongside the fare of the high-end places on Washington and Main and points in between.

As if decreed by higher powers, the July Art Fairs inevitably span the hottest days of the summer, days when the heat is broken only by rumbles of late-afternoon thunder that send vendors and shoppers alike skittering for cover. To look at Nao Kao, though, you might have thought the mercury rose no higher than the day the first robins heralded the coming of spring, clad as he was in the jeans and long-sleeves I'd long since come to think of as his uniform, sandals his only concession to the warmth.

We wandered with the masses, popping into tents filled with black and white photographs, with pottery, handstitched jackets, carefully carved benches, canvases whose edges bled with color.

"I can't believe people buy this stuff," Nao Kao eventually uttered in disbelief.

"Why not? It's nice stuff."

"But do you see the prices? A lamp for $800. A hammock for $300. A light switch cover for $45. $45! For a light switch cover!"

"So? It's expensive stuff. That's why we're only window shopping. But there are a lot of rich people here."

"Really, Liss? That is what you think. It's expensive stuff, just let the rich people buy it?" Nao Kao was raising his voice in the middle of North University in a way I had not heard before and certainly was not expecting.

"Um, yes? Except that makes you angry. So, no?"

"It does not matter, is that what you think?"

"I'm not sure what to think right now, Nao Kao. I thought we were just checking out the Art Fairs, seeing what was here. Certainly, I didn't come down here figuring I'd buy anything to furnish my apartment!"

Now I was raising my voice and people were beginning to turn in our direction. I steered us off North U and past the Chemistry Building. If we were going to cause a scene, no need to do it in the middle of the fair.

"Ah, but you did!" He pointed an accusing finger at the bag in my hand, the little wall clock I had picked up with the pink and blue lily pads.

"Nao Kao! What is making you so angry?"

"How much was that little clock?"

"I don't know. Fifty bucks? But it's a clock, not a light switch cover! Again, why are you so angry?" Now I was definitely shouting and, not surprisingly, we were attracting stares from passersby who were crossing to the other side of the walkway, giving us wide berth.

"Stop, Liss. Stop and listen. After everything I have told you about Laos, everything you know, you still have to ask me this question?"

I opened my mouth, once, twice, like a fish gulping at water.

"Do you know what the per capita GDP in all of Laos was last year?" Nao Kao's voice was lower, its timbre sad more than angry now.

I shook my head.

"$325. Let that sink in." Nao Kao almost spat his disgust. "I have checked out at Meijer behind people spending more than that on a few weeks' worth of groceries," he added more quietly.

"I'm sorry —"

"Sorry? Sorry? No, Liss, I do not want sorry. I want you to listen. You have studied economics, yes?"

"You know it."

Nao Kao smiled slightly, despite himself.

"Now I will tell you the meaning of what you studied, the aspects of economics I think you could not learn in class, here where a hammock sells for as much as many people in my country earn in an entire year."

Nao Kao paused, searching, I realized, for whatever he felt would be most comprehensible to my obviously small mind, since I had proved myself singularly incapable of grasping the big picture.

"Last year in Laos, inflation was over one hundred and twenty-five percent. We are a country on the brink of insolvency."

My eyes widened. Nao Kao had my complete attention; my green eyes riveted to his dark ones.

"But even these facts I think cannot convey to you the magnitude of the situation."

I began to protest, but Nao Kao stopped me firmly, his hand raised at shoulder height, its palm facing me in the near-universal gesture of telling another to cease and desist.

"I want to explain this so that you can understand not in an economist's terms, Liss, but in the terms of daily life. Please."

I nodded slowly, slightly ashamed at the worldliness that masked my ignorance.

"You know, the first time I saw a full pack of cigarettes, it was a complete surprise. In Bangkok. I was eighteen, maybe nineteen years old, and I had never seen cigarettes sold by the package. Why not, you ask? Because almost no one in Laos can afford an entire package of cigarettes!

"If someone wants a smoke – and you know more than half of the population smokes, right? We can thank Joe Camel and the Marlboro Man for that – but when someone wants to smoke, they buy *a* cigarette. One. *A single one.* It costs less than one U.S. penny. That is how poor the people of Laos are.

"I love the U.S., Liss. So many years I dreamed of studying in this country. But I have learned so many things here, things I could not even dream, and I am not speaking of the academic education I am receiving. Before I understood America only through the movies, the news, or in a textbook. To be here now in person is a great gift, one I will not forget. But I do not want to forget where I come from either. Or what I will return to."

A penny for a cigarette. I let that idea spin through my mind, as though launched on a downward race through a coin vortex, its circles becoming tighter and faster before landing with a plink at the bottom. As this new knowledge sunk in, I considered not only what my little clock represented, but also the five-dollar waffle cones or pitchers of beer, half of which I usually spilled anyway, or the takeout left to molder in my fridge. I remembered my shock the first time I flew into São Paulo, the plane swooping low and casting shadows over the corrugated metal roofs of the shacks below. And Brazil was far, far wealthier than Laos. I couldn't help but wonder at the difference between our worlds, Nao Kao's and mine.

"I'm sorry, Nao Kao, I –"

"No need for sorry. But I think I will go back to my apartment."

We parted ways at the bus stop, Nao Kao still agitated as he boarded the bus that would carry him back to the calm of North Campus, to the plentiful trees and quietude that seemed to settle him. I walked back to my apartment, with the weight of the clock dangling from my conscience as well as my wrist, noticing the leaves turning over in advance of the storm. The first fat drops landed as I reached my building considering how cavalier I must have seemed all those times I goaded him about tickets to the Ark or breakfast at Angelo's. Even encouraging him to order a double instead of a single at the Washtenaw Dairy suddenly felt callous.

I had failed to infer so much.

∞　∞　∞　∞　∞

DESPITE THE HUNDREDS of hours we had spent conversing for the past year, I had little idea of what to expect in Vientiane.

You don't become a Million Miler, the one sitting in 2A compliments of Delta's generosity, by staying home. For the better part of two decades, I had planted trees and donated carbon credits in the name of offsetting whatever harm I inflicted on the planet with my round-the-world ways. When I started down this road, launching myself into the orbit of world-weary road warriors, I might have guessed that the vagaries of bad weather, broken seatbelts, overweight aircraft, and absent flight crews were to become a way of life. I could not have guessed the extent to which travel and its rituals would sear themselves into my soul.

Travel and its rituals: escape. I would not realize the connection until it was too late. When the college asked on Thursday who could be in Prague by Monday, they knew the answer before they asked the question.

Was anyone available for a weekend roundtrip to Osaka to escort a wayward student home? What about an unexpected run across the equator to check-in with a university partner in Santiago who had gone a little quiet? Anyone for travel that will involve forty hours in the air and thirty-six hours on the ground?

Anyone? Anyone? The answer, invariably, was Liss. From filling in at the last minute on a workshop panel in Portland to multi-country, monthlong slogs to visit a parade of partners, Liss was available, forever and always.

Such dedication did not pass unnoticed. The publications stacked up, the presentations, too. Advisory board member, grant reviewer, accreditation consultant – my CV no longer listed them all. A rolling stone collects no moss; Liss Larkin never said no.

In the early years of our marriage, the years when I still tried, I would call as the wheels hit the runway, letting Jake know I had arrived over the din of the landing announcements. We talked whenever we could, which is to say whenever *I* could, me sharing an anecdote of cultures colliding, some piece of this life that was ours, but mostly only mine.

As I traveled more, the time between calls lengthened and soon, maybe too soon, the calls became texts, then one text, "hi, honey, I'm here." By that time, "here" could have been anywhere to Jake; he knew only that here was not "there." Knew and was grateful, I should say. As for myself, I had made my bed.

The first time I forgot to let Jake know I had arrived in some far-off land he texted me. The second time, it seemed we both forgot. The gulf continued to widen, then yawned all the way open; *no news is good news* shorthand for everything else we no longer shared. "When are you leaving again?" he would ask on the occasions my presence at home lasted more than a week. Eventually we did not communicate at all when I traveled – and we were both just fine with that.

Indifference can look mighty similar to liberation.

I thought back to the stories I had tried to share: the early morning laps I'd swum unwittingly alongside a freestyling rat at one of Jakarta's swankiest hotels. The second-hand humiliation I felt at a Roman lunch where a colleague declared the carbonara in Tokyo to be superior to that of the present trattoria. The stunning reds as the sun sank to the horizon beyond Manila Bay. The afternoon I had spent in Vietnam adrift in the Mekong after so much debris was sucked into our engine that the blades gave a final protesting sputter before falling silent there in the middle of the great muddy river.

"Why are you telling me this?" Jake would ask irritably, and then he'd pointedly return his attention to his guitar, assiduously bringing the sharps and the flats back into line. Oh, but that guitar was the backdrop of our relationship, Jake slumped against the soft red leather of his favorite chair, alternately tuning and strumming, strumming and tuning as he hummed along. "What do you want now?" he'd ask impatiently when I had the gall to interrupt, only to return his attention squarely to the instrument before I'd even finished my thought. If he'd ever found the nerve to tell his academic parents how much the music meant to him, to pursue it beyond the boundary of our living room, maybe we both would have been happier.

I thought now of the old stories Nao Kao could recount with me, tales of adventure I'd shared once, twenty years ago, but whose every detail he knew by heart. Ambivalence was too kind a word for how

Jake felt about hearing such stories. He might know the name, date, and location of every concert he'd ever attended, but ask him where I'd choked down a plate of tripe or been forced to bail from a still-moving taxi cab and he'd come up blanks every time.

In the face of such disregard, I began to keep more than just my traveling adventures to myself, and the chasm gaped open. Millimeter by millimeter, the tectonic plates of our own little planet were drifting apart.

What cause, these gales? I'd asked that question of myself so often through the years. Only later did I consider that it was not the presence of some mysterious force, but an absence of one, that caused such stormy seas.

Gradually I came back into the moment: me, coursing through the air, bound for parts as yet unknown. Vientiane. Luang Prabang. Laos.

∞ ∞ ∞ ∞ ∞

THE LEAST DENSELY populated country in its corner of the world, what passes for development in Laos these days is almost entirely dependent on China. As a result, many projects are not only funded by the Chinese, but completed with Chinese workers using Chinese materials purchasing Chinese goods paid for in Chinese yuan. The unwitting traveler might mistake some cities for China. If Laos was not quite so desperately poor as Cambodia, neither was that much of a measuring stick.

The most positive descriptions of Vientiane, Laos's capital city, included the words languid and laidback. Lonely Planet called the tuk-tuk drivers sleepy. Academic texts, rather than those focused on driving tourism, tended to be more straightforward. Despite considerable investment and dramatic improvements, significant room for the development of the infrastructure remained. When pressed on life in the city, Nao Kao offered little more than "it's quiet." By Asian standards, he wasn't wrong: the population topped out under a million, making Vientiane one of the least populous capitals on the continent.

The one colleague who truly understood where I was headed was also my best friend, Catherine. She'd traded the bright lights of the big city after graduate school at Columbia for a stint in the Peace Corps and then, drawn by the inexorable pull of our hometown and the prospect of working for our alma mater, returned to Ann Arbor, where she lived only a few streets away from me, just as we had grown up.

Catherine pleaded with me vainly to at least reconsider my stance on malaria medication. Despite having been my partner-in-crime on a West African adventure on which the anti-malarial had left me so ill that the disease itself might have seemed a respite, Catherine's business was international health, and she could not, in good conscience, let me travel to the red zone without one final plea.

"Even if I fill the prescription, I might not take them, you know. I don't have to." If I sounded petulant to myself – and I did – I could only guess how I sounded to her.

"Fine, you don't like the drugs, don't take them and just, you know, maybe get malaria. The upside is that you would never need the drugs again. Either because you would now be immune – or because you will be dead," she tried in a bit of reverse psychology or tough love or both. Her closing argument recalled the words a neurosurgeon flung at my truculent grandfather once in exasperation: dead men don't need brains.

Still, I was unmoved. After all, this was a woman who, despite her reputation for offering unparalleled health and safety advice, had once pushed her own envelope so far as to have given birth at Salvador Mundi Hospital in Rome.

"You know half a million people die of malaria each year," she continued.

"But over two-thirds of them are under the age of five," I countered.

"You know only enough to be dangerous, Liss. Besides, whatever else you may get up to, officially you are traveling on university business. The university won't sign off until you've visited the travel clinic at least. *I* won't sign off."

And there it was: official university business.

Oh, sure, I had my stay in Luang Prabang where I would admire the architecture of Wat Xiengthong, that low-sweeping, double-tiered roof that is so recognizable, and the worn dome of Wat Visounarath, standing sentry over Visoun village for more than five hundred years. The Kuang Si waterfalls and the Pak Ou caves figured prominently in my itinerary and I had arranged a day trip to Chomphet and penciled in some seriously needed poolside R & R at the hotel.

But first, I would spend two days in Vientiane, visiting our newest partner institution, the National University of Laos. Meetings at the university and the requisite tour, a few highlights of the city, tea and lunch and afternoon snacks, always food on these visits, so much food, and never more so than in Southeast Asia. Nao Kao the vice-rector, showing off the institution he had almost personally midwifed into being. He had been hired immediately after graduate school, his newly minted American degree a point of pride for the still-nascent university. From that initial faculty role, he had ascended the rungs rapidly, his climb that much higher and faster than mine. Official university business.

∞ ∞ ∞ ∞ ∞

"SESAME NOODLES, MISS LARKIN?" the flight attendant, Janelle, proffered a small dish of the cold soba I remembered fondly from the before times. Seven hours to Seoul?

I nodded happily.

"First flight since?" she asked, having noticed, probably, how quickly I scrambled to re-secure my mask after every sip of water or between the courses at dinner.

"First long one," I replied, thinking of the one, shorter flight I had taken on which I was able to keep my mask securely in place for the duration of the flight. For two hours from Detroit to Atlanta, I neither sipped nor peed. Fourteen hours from Detroit to Seoul precluded such practices.

"I guess it's like anything: the first one is the hardest," Janelle noted sagely.

"It's amazing to think I used to spend each week in a different time zone," I mused. "I hadn't gotten jetlag in years. And now I'm just praying I will make it through dinner without dozing off in the soup!"

She laughed and moved along with the little dishes of sustenance.

Larkin, I thought, not for the first time. What was I ever thinking? There had been plenty of time for asking that question, not only during the homebound months of the pandemic, but in all the years before that.

I met Jake Larkin in an economics class my sophomore year when we were assigned to the same study group. Earlier that year I had broken up with college boyfriend number two, Alex, whose crooked smile and mop of blond hair I could still picture. When Jake asked if I would meet him at Good Time Charlie's, I demurred on the grounds of sticky floors and benches, never telling him the truth. I had not been back to Charlie's since it had been the scene of the crime, the place

54

Alex chose to call time on our relationship, halfway through a plate of nachos.

After a string of frat boys, athletes, and too many outright players, all of whom recognized that I was both better looking and more naive than I realized myself to be, a genuinely nice guy was a revelation. It was not until later that I realized how much of the economics homework I did for the group, how many times I explained the guns and butter curves that needed no further explanation – if only one had been to class.

Like me, Jake came from an academic family. His parents were on the faculty at Northwestern, his mom at the medical school and his dad in biostatistics, and they shared with my parents the accolades of an academic life, starting with summa cum laude and Phi Beta Kappa, running through federal grants and endowed chairs. Nice, steady families, three PhDs and an MD between them.

Both of our families were bound to be a bit disappointed by our undergraduate academic choices, though the doctorate I would later earn would more than make up for my lack of direction, or more specifically, the disappointing course correction I had made, as an undergrad.

How I ever found the nerve to tell my parents that I was declining my acceptance into the business school was something I pondered well into adulthood. I was, the secretary behind the desk intoned slowly, as she adjusted her glasses to get a better look at me, this oddity before her, the *only student* who declined admission to the b-school that year. That year was deep in those heady, bubbly days of the late '90s when a BBA from Michigan could command six figures out of the starting gates. Undoubtedly, whichever waitlisted student accepted an offer in my stead felt that they received Willy Wonka's golden ticket and, presumably, made better use of their b-school credential than I would have done.

By all appearances, perhaps even to myself, I had renounced all hope of a future in international business when I checked the seldom-used box, "I decline." For years I resisted the idea of a doctoral degree, that credential of credentials waved before me by my parents. Competitive to a fault, as recently as freshman year they had tried talking me into grad school with the lure that fewer than one percent of American women held doctoral degrees. Surely, I would want to join such rarefied ranks. *Investment banking or bust,* I had declared doggedly, but when the dream was within reach, I wondered if it had not been the thrill of the chase that motivated me above all.

As I fingered the form, my pen hovering over *I decline,* a new vision was already forming: grad school and a doctoral degree, but not to teach at the university as my parents did. I wanted to run it. Jake, on the other hand, found no joy in the rhythms of academia, having switched majors three times from sociology to psychology and finally to political science. He applied only reluctantly to the School of Public Policy, and then only in a last-ditch effort to remain in the town he'd come to love. As far as academic awards, cum laude would have been high enough honor for him. I found these attitudes – the antipathy even – perplexing, if not troubling. They were red flags I should have heeded much sooner.

Later, I rediscovered a lifetime of old journals. I read in reverse, beginning with the most recent, and as the references to my doubts mounted, so did my dread of what else I might uncover. When I read of the summer we spent backpacking together through Europe after my graduation that I was *beginning to feel suffocated under the weight of constant togetherness,* the words landed like a punch to the solar plexus. Later I seemed to reconsider, and I turned the pages with the sinking feeling that my younger self doth protest too much. This was confirmed as I read further, until, there in black and white, I confronted the truth: *I am afraid I am only going back to Jake because it is easy.*

Absent from those fading pages was any mention of Nao Kao, but from across the years I could sense it, that apparition that had wordlessly guided so many of my life's decisions.

As I thumbed through that old journal, my energy ebbed until, by the time I reached the last words I ever inked as Liss Miller, I was already numb.

> *I do not love him the way he loves me. I cannot. I went back to him and I will marry him for better or for worse. The realization creeps forth that it is not the present I regret; it is in the future that I fear I will. At some point, I must stop asking whether this is the best life I could have had under any circumstance and just be happy that it is a good life. After all, we make the best choices we can at the time we make them with the information we have. These choices are based necessarily on what we know about ourselves and what we think we know about the world.*

My heart ached for the girl-woman who composed those words.

NAO KAO

"WHAT IS IT, DAD?"

"Hmmm, what's that?" I looked up from phone and away from the ghost I'd encountered.

"You look startled. As though you've seen something wonderful or terrible."

My daughter's acute perceptivity astonished me.

"Ah, it's nothing. I received surprising news from an old friend."

She finished her eggs and gathered her things. I heard her start her motorbike and leave as I pushed now-cold eggs in a circle on my plate. Surprising news from an old friend, I'd told her. That might cover almost anything, but in this case, it barely scratched the surface.

Liss Miller was alive.

Despite the years that had passed, I still thought of her sometimes, of her stories accompanied by peals of laughter, of her broad smile and mane of red curls. I could be in my office, balancing budgets or reviewing proposals and those piercing green eyes would appear in my mind. Other times, it might be an image of her bent over her notebook writing, or looking over her shoulder at me in class. It would take my breath away when that happened. I'd offer a quick prayer for her, that she was alive and well and happy, but I'd long ago given up on receiving confirmation of such.

Until this morning, on LinkedIn, of all places. A perfunctory message accompanied the connection request:

> Nao Kao –
> I was sorting through materials from our master's program and thought I'd see if you were on LinkedIn. You look to be doing well. I hope so.
> – Liss

At least she didn't ask if I remembered her.

I replied immediately. "What a pleasant surprise to receive a message from you, Liss. I'm glad to hear from you. All my best, Nao Kao"

I found my own memory box and lifted the lid. Tassel and cords. Three-ring binders of class notes and papers. Photos. Mostly of campus – the Diag under a blanket of snow; a portrait of a squirrel clasping a nut; the peonies in full bloom in the Arb, their pinks and whites and yellows profiled against a clear spring sky; the fall foliage at the Law Quad, the reds and oranges still vibrant after so many years. Twinkle lights strung across Main Street. Commencement at the stadium, the first and only time I set foot in the vaunted Big House.

At the bottom of the stack, photos from a day at the beach, Grand Haven as I remember it was called. A long pier capped by a red lighthouse, seagulls scratching at creamy sand, a man wrestling a massive blue and white kite. Memories I'd assumed I'd never share again. I thought again about the innocuous note she'd written. In all likelihood, I never would share them again.

I uploaded copies of a few photos of campus to Facebook with the caption "feeling nostalgic for Ann Arbor today," then grabbed my helmet and gloves and keys for my bike. I rode until evening, through town and along the river, the great muddy Mekong that formed Laos's border with Thailand guiding me south out of the city and toward the rice paddies where farmers were diligently harvesting their crop on an unusually clear day. The open road, with the sun beating down and the wind in my face, was a cure for most any ailment.

When I checked my LinkedIn messages that night, she'd already responded. I replied in kind, confirmation, I hoped, that my words were sincere. She was a pleasant surprise; I bore her no ill will. That night, I tossed and turned, and only knew I'd slept a wink by the fragments of dream that scattered when I awoke: snow in Ann Arbor.

Oh, Liss.

LISS

I HAD NO shortage of ideas to fill Nao Kao's summer with everything I thought necessary to experience the quintessential Ann Arbor summer in 2001, even, arguably, to experience the quintessential American summer. Although our afternoon at the Art Fairs had not been a raging success, Nao Kao – for whom "grudge" was a four-letter word and his frustrations only fleeting – was still eager to visit Top of the Park, where at least I knew overpriced home furnishings would not be on offer.

We went one evening after class, a half dozen graduate students high on the sweetness of languorous summer days, Nao Kao, me, and other assorted classmates. There atop the parking structure, we grabbed sandwiches from one of the concessions as music filled the air. The night was warm, and as dusk descended, lightning bugs came out in force, flashing their lanterns as we chattered away.

I almost did not enroll in grad school at Michigan, I had felt such a need to escape the phantoms I sensed in the shadow of every building. I told Nao Kao that once, when I learned that he, too, had seemed destined for another state, another university, another program. He expected to attend grad school at the University of Minnesota. To his surprise, shortly before he was to leave Laos, plans changed and he learned that he would study instead at the University of Michigan. He was used to life being decided by higher powers and unseen forces; nothing shook his equanimity. Nao Kao merely pulled out his map to learn where he was headed. The only thing that would have bothered him, he told me, is if he had not gotten to experience a "real" winter, and especially snow.

"Florida would have been a disappointment," he said, though I figured that news, too, would ultimately have moved through him like water through sand, with no more than a slight disturbance as it continued on its predestined course back to the sea.

"Do you ever consider how little control we really have over our lives?" he mused one time, in a thoughtful mood, but for once I was not keen to pick up the thread of this morose notion, and I changed the subject.

Surely, with enough force of will, the universe could be bent, and life coerced, into taking whatever shape we desired.

The water park was our last great adventure of the summer. Still on the brink of owning my own car, I convinced a friend from undergrad who was back in town to drive us. I rode shotgun, Nao Kao pressed in back with my bursting bag of provisions for the day and the miscellany of Michael's messy life besides.

Michael had had a crush on me since we met in junior year, and he would have been only too happy if I had ever bounced his way during one of my rough patches with Jake. It was clear from the moment Nao Kao and I hopped into his red Grand Prix that he had agreed to play chauffeur only out of a desire to obtain firsthand intelligence on the status of my relationship with Jake.

"Finished," I told him, "and none too soon. I was tired of being the only grown-up."

Michael laughed and moved his hand to my knee. I let it rest there a moment before gently but firmly placing it back atop the gear shift. In my peripheral vision I caught the quick upward flick of Nao Kao's eyebrows. Whatever ground our conversations covered, I assiduously avoided the topic of Jake, or any other guys I might be seeing for that matter. Not that there were any, serious or otherwise.

I tried to remember how many months it had been since Jake left, how many months since I had even spoken to him. I gave up and instead tried to remember the name of the guy who had asked me out two or three times before my disinterest finally dissuaded him sometime in the spring. Ray? Rich? Rob? His name definitely started with an R. I gave that up too, focusing instead on the green mile markers poking up along the highway.

Michael's hand crept back along my leg and I left it: the path of least resistance.

Nao Kao asked me once the meaning of "this phrase, friends with benefits – what exactly does this mean?"

Even today, Laos is a conservative place. As I explained what it meant, Nao Kao had almost clucked his disdain, and I watched him visibly swallow down the question of how familiar I was, exactly, with this troubling practice.

"That Michael, he likes you," Nao Kao said to me when I saw him next.

"Tell me something I don't know. Why do you think he agreed to drive to the waterpark?"

"Did you –"

"What? Let him take me to bed in exchange for services rendered? As though I'd tell you if I had!"

He looked shocked – and hurt. Generally, I treated him like a family publication. When I talked to Nao Kao, nothing stronger than an occasional *damn* crossed my lips, and certainly no biting sarcasm. It wasn't that his English wasn't up to the task, but the cynicism and sarcasm that were my natural linguistic habitat just didn't translate, culturally. As for certain other choice words: by his own admission Nao Kao had "hot ears," and though I never minded making him blush, I also never sought to make him genuinely uncomfortable. With Nao Kao, I was the child my mother always begged me to be, the one who acted as nice as she looked.

"No, Liss, la. I just wondered if you ever tried to *tell* him you weren't interested?"

"Of course not, Nao Kao! I wouldn't want him to think I was presuming he was interested!"

I could see the wheels turning as Nao Kao sought to unravel whether this was the illogic of America speaking, or merely the illogic of one stubborn and unreasonable Melissa Miller. I did not answer his silent questions – and I certainly did not tell him how close I had come to writing a check I never wanted to cash. I would not, I was certain, be seeing Michael again.

∞ ∞ ∞ ∞ ∞

ALL THROUGH THE summer I rode my bike, pedaling miles each day, as though the spinning tires could carry me away from the confining reality of life under lockdown. Late in the summer, I crashed, tumbling over my handlebars, blackening my eyes, wrenching my shoulder. I had no one to blame but myself, for I crashed in a place where the inner voice urges caution. I like the feel of cruising downhill while banking around this particular tight corner and I rarely exercise the appropriate prudence and apply the brakes. I did not see the orange construction barrels until my fate was sealed.

Picking myself up, I did have the wherewithal to pull out my phone and use the camera to confirm I was not gushing blood, not that I had a plan if I was. I was at least two miles from home, with no way back but to dance, or ride, with the one that brought me, my bright turquoise road bike, the color of the Caribbean. Never mind that the seat was sideways.

My predicament was made worse by the fact that I had been on my way to the pool and was foolishly sporting naught but a neon green swimsuit and pink flipflops. Even my shorts were stashed in the bag slung across my shoulders. What few pedestrians I encountered scurried from my path, undoubtedly alarmed by the blood dripping from my knuckles and ankles. I left a trail of shiny, garnet drops as I rode, in the style of an injured animal. Only the hounds were missing.

When I texted my little tale of woe to Nao Kao later in the week, he told me I was lucky.

"A couple of years ago, I was riding tandem on my motorbike with my daughter when we became entangled in some wires hanging by the road. This caused the bike to overturn and she became trapped under it. Much flesh on her legs was burned away."

"Oh my God, Nao Kao. Was she okay? What happened?"

"In the end, she was ok."

Knowing him, this could mean anything from requiring a simple bandage to necessitating an amputation. Imperturbable. Asking further questions would be futile.

And then he cracked a joke, for Nao Kao was an expert in the adage that if you don't laugh, you might cry.

"Too bad it was wires that got us and not a cow. At least we might have had dinner that way."

"What kind of driver are you?" I asked. My question was not mean-spirited, at least I hoped not, but I was curious – and it seemed a better diversion than continuing to exchange stories of gruesome injuries.

"Cautious. And you?"

I considered offering the same reassurance, but I had fed Nao Kao enough half-truths over time. He will know if I lie, this man, I am certain, and after what I have put him through, I mustn't do that, inconsequential as his question may be.

"Fast and aggressive," I replied, and let that sink in, however he might interpret it.

"No cows or chickens on the roads there," he responded, an observation I could not top.

"Alright, you, don't be too reckless now, ok?" Nao Kao offered by way of good-bye, the gentle familiarity of the salutation lodging softly in my mind.

So, it was that we rebuilt a friendship, one anecdote at a time. Mine, long-winded and often sarcastic, tended to rely on humor and wit and repartee, Nao Kao's responses as succinct as the occasional tale he'd offer me. "Loosen up, la," he'd reply to one or another grievance I aired. "Not my job to judge, la."

"Those people just don't like questions, la."

And the occasional "oh la la."

Thus, did our personalities re-emerge across the years.

∞ ∞ ∞ ∞ ∞

ON THAT FATEFUL second Tuesday of September in 2001, I was at work, tucked away in the recesses of the International Institute where officially I worked as a graduate assistant supporting the area studies centers. I landed the job largely on the strength of an internship in the House of Commons when I was an undergrad.

Often in the International Institute we kept a television on at low volume, the posh accents of the BBC providing the backdrop to our work. On September 11, the television was off though, until a harried student rushed in and, his voice thick with the sounds of New York and something else, something I would momentarily place as the sound of shock, and maybe more than a tinge of grief, urged us to turn it on.

We did so as the second plane slammed into the South Tower. We closed the office then and as I walked back to my apartment, I did so with the sensation that the ground underfoot might give way at any moment. Down South U and across State Street, past the Cube and across Thompson, all the way to my little place on Madison, my footfalls were the only sound I noticed in a town gone eerily quiet. The sky overhead was an unbroken blue that belied the rupture all around us. In my apartment, AOL Instant Messenger boxes flashed and pinged on my monitor, a clarion cry from every quarter. All of us, everywhere, trying to make sense of the images being broadcast from every station in the land.

Incongruously, my apartment was filled with sunlight on that bright September morning, as I sat in terror watching the acrid smoke roll through Manhattan. I placed a frantic phone call to Catherine, my oldest and dearest friend, my college roommate of four years, and the woman I missed more than the rest of my friends combined, now a grad student at Columbia. Her voice trembled knowing her boyfriend was at work across the river in New Jersey. He did not need Peter Jennings to tell him the score; he was watching the towers burn from his office windows.

As the south tower collapsed, dozens of IMs flooded into my account simultaneously. Most were a simple, six letter code for a world gone to pieces. OMG WTF. The exception was Nao Kao, who asked simply if it was okay if he stopped by.

Over the course of the past year, Nao Kao had morphed from an unknown classmate into the kind of friend I never knew I was missing. From pedagogy to philosophy, literature to adolescent larks, there was little we did not discuss. "A conversation is not one person talking and the other just listening," a grumpy date had once scolded me. I was self-conscious then of exactly how much talking I did in comparison to Nao Kao, but when I mentioned this to him, he merely shrugged and said, "I like your stories."

I imagine no one else shared with him tales of coed life in which a freshman year hallmate performed the Sunday morning walk of shame following a night in which her panties had been lost in a frat house. That Nao Kao would recall almost twenty years later that said hallmate later found them pinned to the house trophy board offered definitive proof that *I like your stories* hadn't been a hollow line.

"Did you call your family?" I asked him when he arrived.

My mother reached me first that morning, calling from her office in Tisch Hall. Rachael Zick was not easily given to panic, but that morning she was nearly frantic at not being able to reach my father, deep in the woods of one or another western state consulting on forestry matters for the federal government. He was in Oregon, I reminded her, where it was not yet 7:00 am. "I left a message for him to call from his cell phone," she said, and I knew the matter was serious. At thirty-five cents a minute (though minutes were free after 9:00 p.m.), the cell phones we all had were for *emergency use only*.

Nor had she been able to reach Theo, half a world away and, I thought but did not say, safer and more secure in China than we were in Michigan. We were not a family given to superfluous shows of affection, but she and I had said we loved one another, and spoken in reassuring tones to remind ourselves that we were still solidly here. She ended the call by asking me to call immediately if I heard from Theo or my father, and for once I did not roll my eyes. We could, none of us, ever unsee what we witnessed, the plane in, the bodies out, the towers down, the smoldering remains of it all thrusting skyward in a jagged pile, but we were alive, and on September 11, that was all we could ask.

"It is too hard to get through right now. I tried once, but the international lines were jammed. I will try again tonight. If I call late enough here the connection is usually stronger anyway."

We sat on the couch all afternoon, mindlessly flipping between the ghastly soundtracks of Peter Jennings and Tom Brokaw, the drone of the news uninterrupted by a single commercial break.

Early fall in Michigan can feel like summer and September 11 certainly did. I wore denim shorts and a strappy, blue tank with *Michigan* emblazoned in maize letters across the chest. Every time I glanced up, Nao Kao was looking, glancing, staring down my shirt. Fleetingly, I thought to ask him what his wife might think, but ultimately, I let it lie. He was, after all, only a man.

∞ ∞ ∞ ∞ ∞

I HONESTLY DIDN'T expect to hear back. So much time had passed, so much water had flowed under that bridge. Twenty years later, virtually our entire adult lives, it was difficult to imagine what we would even have to say to one another, and I knew that if he hadn't been the vice-rector at the National University of Laos, I likely never would have talked myself into hitting send. Even as vice-rector, if I had known that he was also a consultant to the Ministry of Planning and Investment, I would almost assuredly still be staring at my legal pad today. I teased him once about being a "mucky-muck," but even then, I don't think he understood how seriously his success since he returned home intimidated me, and how close I came to convincing myself not to send the message.

It was not just one student looking to study in an offbeat location though. In one of those twists of fate, just a few weeks after my conversation with her, I was charged with the development of CLMV programming.

"Not too much V, though, Liss," my boss added, "we've got plenty on Vietnam already. And see if you can find a few alumni to work with. Local perspective always helps."

Removing Vietnam from the equation left Cambodia, Laos, and Myanmar, as unpromising a trifecta as I could think of in the circumstances. When I had searched out a list of alumni contacts in the region, I received the names of a few expats, whom I was promptly told not to contact. Local, in this case, was more a state of mind than a mailing address.

Presumably once upon a time, someone at the University of Michigan had a record of Nao Kao Inthavong. If nothing else, the university liked to boast of having one of the largest numbers of living alumni in the world. But whatever file might have once existed had long since been thoroughly expunged. If I kept quiet, no one would be any the wiser.

The consummate professional in me could not let it lie, though, this connection to one of the great and the good in Laos. Never mind that I had not spoken of him, let alone to him, in almost two decades. Or that I had every reason to expect that I would be one of the last people on earth he would want to hear from.

I began an informal poll of trusted friends. Maybe they would have advised differently if I had shared all the details then, rather than the vague explanations I offered for my hesitancy. Under the circumstances I presented, the consensus was unanimous. My professional integrity demanded that I ask Nao Kao to be part of anything CLMV-focused. He was the perfect candidate, whatever our personal circumstances had once been.

And yet, given the circumstances as I knew they were, it felt nearly impossible to reappear out of the mists, beating the drum of favors-for-alma-mater. Something would have to give. I swallowed my pride.

∞　∞　∞　∞　∞

AT SOME POINT during the evening on September 11, Nao Kao left to join the vigil on the Diag. There were fifteen thousand stunned students gathered that night, eyes wide, many with tears falling. It was a crowd into which I could not cast myself. When I asked the next day whether he had reached his family afterwards, he answered in the affirmative. Unfortunately, he added, the news on her end was not good either. One of their girls was deep in the throes of malaria.

That Nao Kao's daughter was battling malaria in a world where sterilized needles were considered cutting edge medicine is one of the details I have never forgotten. That the woman back home caring for her, my age, barely beyond adolescence, a wife and mother and survivor of wars and refugee camps, tended to all of this while her almost equally young husband secured their future on the other side of the world, was the other. For I have no doubt, had her history contained less pathos, this newlywed woman – the nice, normal girl – left with two infants while her husband pursued an American education, I might have felt less compunction about what happened next.

Nao Kao was ambitious, adventurous, intelligent, and kind. I might have wondered – no, I did wonder, and more than once – what the smartest and most interesting person I had ever known was doing hanging around with the likes of me. We would while away the hours talking about everything from the spread of AIDS in Asia to *Roe vs. Wade* to which accents were the most challenging to understand. (Texas, Nao Kao decreed, one hundred times out of one hundred.)

From our early forays into politics and the Vietnam War, Nao Kao broadened my knowledge of Southeast Asia, and especially the Thai-Vietnamese-Cambodian tensions that underscored so many issues in that region. In turn, I did my best to explain the growing divide between what was increasingly being referred to as Red and Blue America. He did his to explain the difference between the Lao and the Hmong and why he felt the Hmong in America struggled to never quite attain the same levels of prosperity and high educational status that defined so many other Asian immigrant populations in the U.S.

The day after the towers fell, a day when the major networks still broadcast without commercial interruption, when the planes punctured the buildings at least once an hour on tv, when the skies over Michigan were blessedly blue and clear – and free of all contrails – Nao Kao suggested we try canoeing.

Years of swimming had given me surprising upper body strength, and I could dig into the water as hard as anyone. As a result, my strokes were strong, yet I lacked a steady rhythm. I hacked at the water more than I plied it. I was, in fact, an exceedingly inept canoeist. Nao Kao, seated in the back of the canoe, struggled to steer a straight course for us.

"Stop, Liss, stop. Just sit. Stop paddling."

"Don't be ridiculous. Of course, you can't do this by yourself. It takes two people to paddle a canoe."

I was annoyed with Nao Kao, but I was more irritated with the guy at the livery who made me take the front position in the boat, even though, at 5'8", I was tall for a girl, and easily had a couple of inches – and undoubtedly a dozen pounds – on Nao Kao. Sexist canoe guy!

I dug in harder and felt the canoe begin to veer uneasily into the soft mud of the bank. I pushed hard against the muck and shot us into the middle.

"STOP. Give me your paddle." It was a tone I had not heard from him before, the tone of a man used to calling the shots – and having them obeyed. Domineering, as it were.

I turned on him, eyes flashing, and rose to do just that at the same moment he leaned forward to grab the oar from me. The boat lurched, rocking from left to right, and again we both shifted our weight at the wrong moment. The canoe flipped just as I thought it might stay upright.

Somehow Nao Kao had managed to keep his beloved camera out of the water. Bracing himself against the overturned hull and treading water to keep the camera dry, I heard him swear for the first time. The Huron River is not so deep or so swift, but one of our oars had sunk hopelessly beyond my view and I gave it up for lost. I swam after the one that was still afloat, then righted the canoe. I dragged myself in. It was not pretty, but it also was not the first time I had faced this predicament. Now was probably not the time to share that piece of information with Nao Kao. I landed with a squish in the hull. Nao Kao gingerly handed over his camera as I thought about the previous times I'd flipped canoes, about the time I'd fallen into a pond when I was certain I could reach the beach ball that had bobbed into the water, the paddle boat that I'd steered directly under a "water feature." By comparison, Nao Kao had nothing to complain about.

"Put your hands on the side," I instructed him, feeling the boat wobble slightly as he did.

"Other options?"

He was clearly looking to avoid flopping into the canoe like a dead fish, which is probably what I had most closely resembled.

"You can use that big limb for leverage." I pointed to a partially submerged tree trunk bobbing in the current. "Hang on and I can sort of shove the canoe in that direction."

Navigating the canoe in any determined direction was easier said than done in the circumstances.

"This is entirely your fault."

"So, swim to the edge and slither out, then step back in," I suggested.

"What? Like I am a monitor lizard? I will be filthy!" Nao Kao was aghast.

His temper was not helped by the fact that his reference to a monitor lizard brought an immediate smile on my part, as I remembered those long, lazy animals sunning themselves on the banks of Bangkok's klongs.

"It's not like you're completely clean here in the river! What? You're not going to go home and take a shower?"

"I may be wet, but I am not covered in mud, which I will be if I 'slither out' there at the edge."

"Ok, well what better ideas do you have?"

"This is entirely your fault."

"Yes, you've said that already."

Nao Kao glared, which made me laugh. At least he hadn't lost his glasses. Our current predicament was amusing, but he was practically blind without his glasses and I was sure getting a new pair would have been an ordeal. Plus, he would have refused to let me buy them, even though this was, and he had just felt the need to clarify – twice – entirely my fault. *Or at least mostly,* I thought, remembering his tone when he told me to stop paddling.

Contemplating his options, Nao Kao was at a distinct disadvantage in that he was wearing his usual uniform of blue jeans and sandals. The sandals had washed away (possibly an advantage for regaining his position in the canoe, but it would be a long walk once we were back on dry land) and the wet denim constrained him heavily. I scooped one of the sandals from the water as it floated by, then waited as Nao Kao managed to lurch back into the canoe. It bucked precariously, before settling nicely into the water. Gingerly, I proffered our single oar as a peace offering.

Barely twenty-four hours since death and destruction rained in Manhattan, I was soaked but happy, unaccountably so, given the circumstances. I felt his eyes penetrating into me from behind and turned to meet his gaze. I knew the look, despite myself. Like a cat that had got all the cream, Nao Kao was drinking me in. In the brief instant where our eyes met, he had undressed me so completely that the clothes I was wearing might have floated downstream with our paddle for all the coverage they provided. Instantly, the mood shifted. That he turned his attention so quickly and intensely from the immediacy of the moment – me or him or us in that narrow little boat – confirmed what I knew in my gut. I chose to ignore it all the same.

"He will have to declare war," Nao Kao stated abruptly, followed by a litany of reasons that George W. Bush would not hesitate to go after the Taliban. Nor, Nao Kao predicted, anyone else he suspected of aiding them.

"I will tell you about war," began a man whose life had been so marked by it. If I thought I had heard all of Nao Kao's musings on war, I was wrong.

"It does not stay where they put it. The bombs are not confined to a neat little square, nor the destruction, nor the deaths. In my country, we are still feeling the war twenty-five years after it ended. The Vietnam War. It was not fought only in Vietnam. It was all of Indochina."

As if I could have forgotten. As penance for soaking him, I held my peace.

"People in the United States, they hear *Vietnam* and they think about helicopters over Saigon. American soldiers suffering the effects of Agent Orange. They do not consider napalm in the mountains of Laos, all the people there or in Cambodia or even in Vietnam who have suffered because men in America decided to pour poison on jungles half a world away. If old men make war and young men fight it, where do the babies fit in? The ones born even today with birth defects from chemicals their mothers encountered as children?

"People in the U.S., they do not think of the roads that decades later explode with a buried mine. 'Stay on the path, beware of UXO,' that is the order on every signpost in Laos. UXO. You know this? Unexploded ordnance. It is something serious where I am from. The farther from the cities, the greater the risk, of course. A farmer walking in a field, across a rice paddy – maybe he makes it across, maybe not. An animal hoof that strikes down just so? The cow might have made a nice dinner, except that the meat will be laced with shrapnel. And it will be scattered for kilometers.

"You are driving on a road, especially a small one? Hopefully, the road has been completely cleared, that the crews did their job properly, thoroughly. But off the road, just there to side, there where you might stop to fix a tire or relieve yourself – there are no McDonald's on the roads of Laos, you know. Then? Bye-bye, good luck."

He rubbed his temples, as though to sharpen – or erase – the scenes that danced through his memories, these aspects of his past to which I could listen, but could never fully understand.

"Do you know that they stack them in piles in the villages, these bombs, and that children play on these piles? That even today, Liss, decades after the war is over, we continue to count the victims: two, three, four each week. Some accidents, and some from scavenging, yes, scavenging among the bombs. But, why, you ask, what is there to scavenge among the bombs?"

Here Nao Kao laughed, not his usual, joyful laugh, but something harsh and jagged.

"Good American metal, Liss. Because the bombs that fell from the sky, payload after payload, were made of metal better and stronger than what most people in Laos had ever known. Today, you can see homes with bomb casings propping them up, as stilts, and the people in them turn bombs into spoons."

This was the first time I had heard Nao Kao's voice tinged with such bitterness, even more than when he had disdained the conspicuous consumption on display at the Art Fairs. He let his words hang between us as he picked up the paddle and returned us competently and quietly to the livery.

"Lose an oar?" the attendant asked.

Nao Kao sat mutely, looking pointedly in my direction, waiting for me to offer up the apology on our behalf. I did so meekly, but with a bright smile and a twinkle in my eyes. The attendant chuckled and waved us on.

"He would have made me pay," Nao Kao observed, his mood still dark, as we made our way to the bus stop. Not for the first time, I am sure he was correct.

"Your feet okay for walking? Does it hurt?" I asked, looking at his bare feet. He'd chucked the one sandal that remained to him disgustedly in the trash as we left the livery.

Almost immediately, bewilderment replaced bitterness in his eyes. "You think this is the first time I am walking barefoot? I didn't even own shoes until I started school. My feet will be fine." He laughed.

"Well, do you think they'll let you on the bus without sandals?"

"What? No shirt, no shoes, no service?" he asked, laughing again, then added, "You should come up to Northwoods sometime you know."

"Go on, Nao Kao, or you'll miss the bus!" I admonished, more harshly than I intended, for fleetingly, certainly unbidden, had come the unwelcome thought: I wondered if we weren't beginning to play with fire.

NAO KAO

"Is it safe to stay there?" my mom asked when I reached her on September 11.

"Ann Arbor is far from New York," I replied, "and I don't think the terrorists are interested in Angell Hall."

"If it is not safe you should think about returning home."

"Mom, it's fine. I told you: Ann Arbor is not near New York. Or Washington. It's better to stay and finish my studies."

"Better for you. Hard for Noy. She has to take care of two babies by herself. The little one sick with malaria."

Noy. My wife. The other woman who complained I did not call her often enough.

"She didn't tell me, Mom."

"Too busy. She doesn't want to worry you."

I nodded.

"Nao Kao? You still hear me?"

"Yes, Mom, sorry. How long is the baby sick? Will she be ok? Tell Noy I'll send more for medicine next month."

"You should tell her yourself, Nao Kao. The baby is very sick. It's a bad one, but Noy is a good nurse to her. She is a very good mother, Nao Kao. You should be proud of her."

"Calls are expensive. I can pay for phone calls or pay for medicine." *Or ice cream and canoe rides with Liss,* my conscience reminded me.

"Ok, but next week you call her, not me. And think about what I said, if it is safe to stay and study."

"Yes, mom. Good night."

"It's almost afternoon here, my son. Sleep well and study hard."

Malaria. Medicine. Babies. Two babies. I inhaled deeply, calculating what it would cost this time. I could buy more rice, more peanut butter, less chicken next month. A few dollars saved on groceries in Ann Arbor could buy a lot of medicine in Laos.

I thought about messaging Liss, but looked at the time and knew she'd be fast asleep. She had enough worries tonight; it was her country under attack this time, not mine. Better to let her sleep. We saw each other almost every day now. First, she was my window into campus and also America. She knew every sidewalk and bolt hole on campus,

73

the out-of-the-way places to take a walk or shoot a roll of pictures or sit quietly without an entire sorority house traipsing past.

Perhaps more importantly, she had become the laughter in my days, and an escape from the realities of needing to put food on two tables, one here and one on the other side of the world. She was my reminder that not every young person was weighed down by the need to feed a family. I pushed from my mind what would happen when she graduated and left Ann Arbor. I had three months to figure it out.

LISS

I<small>N THE END</small> I never should have doubted. He replied overnight, a weekend LinkedIn nerd like me, with a gracious note that my message was a pleasant surprise. We exchanged a few texts. He suggested we stay in touch.

When I saw how quickly Nao Kao responded and read the words he wrote, I realized I never doubted he would reply. Unexpected and unwelcome can be synonyms, but in this case, what was unexpected would never be unwelcome. For all that had happened, I would have replied as quickly.

The Chinese believe in the red thread of fate, the invisible thread that ties together those whose lives and destinies are fated to intertwine. The red thread may twist and stretch through time, but it never, ever breaks. As I considered his note, and the twists and turns our lives had taken over the past two decades, I could not help but think that maybe he and I were bound by our own thread.

∞ ∞ ∞ ∞ ∞

"S<small>O, IS THIS</small> work or pleasure?" the flight attendant, Janelle, asked.

I was stretching my legs in the galley again, taking advantage of the mid-flight quiet. Most of the crew was tucked up in their sleeping berth, with just one attendant left in charge of the lot of us. This was the easiest part of the flight, though, with most passengers asleep or at least making a pretense of trying. Janelle had a stack of old *People* magazines in her lap, and had been thumbing through another disinterestedly when I appeared looking for more water.

"Maybe a bit of both?" I replied hesitantly.

She laughed.

"A little late to decide. Where did you say you are headed?"

"Vientiane."

She looked at me quizzically.

"Laos," I clarified.

"Wow. Laos. Flight crews are good with their geography, you know – all that time looking at route maps. But I'm not sure even our captain could point to that one on the map."

I chuckled, remembering how frequently Nao Kao had lamented that sad fact.

"I have been flying to Asia for twelve years, but you might be the first passenger I've encountered going there," Janelle continued. "Does Delta even fly that route?"

I shook my head.

"Korean or Vietnam. Codeshare only."

"I guess that explains it. And you're traveling by yourself?"

"Maybe?"

"So maybe work and maybe pleasure and maybe alone and maybe with others. Got it."

I liked her spunk. They might whisper amongst themselves, but most flight attendants would be too polite to imply a passenger was slightly nuts. Especially one flying up front.

"Have you ever been there before?" she asked.

"Never. And I don't have high expectations. I'll be satisfied with air-conditioned transportation and a divided road. I'm not positive how much of either I'll get."

We were back in familiar territory.

"Oh, those tuk-tuks can do you in! If the bumps don't get you, the fumes will!" she said.

"And yet, better a tuk-tuk than the back of a moped. I have often been grateful that whatever other indignities life has in store for me, commuting to work on the back of a motorbike in the middle of the monsoon rains is not among them."

"With bald tires," she noted, appreciatively, then added, "Amen."

My mind wandered to the first time Nao Kao told me about his beloved motorbike. The entire family arranged behind him, his wife balancing their babies just so as he wove along the pitted road. The roads were the least of it though, as one must always remain alert for errant chickens, herds of cows, wandering children, and cargo that had sprung free from motorbikes up ahead – and such cargo might consist of anything from plate glass to livestock. Repeatedly he had promised me a ride on the fabled bike, a ride I wasn't sure either of us believed would come to pass even as he offered, even as I agreed.

"Worst city for traffic?" the flight attendant asked, bringing me back to the present.

"Jakarta."

She nodded sagely. "I almost missed a flight there once. Multiple sources assured me that travel time from the hotel to the airport was an hour. I left five-and-a-half hours before my flight, thinking I should arrive at the airport at least three hours before departure."

I had visions of the bottlenecked roads I had encountered in Jakarta, the futility of the lines painted on the concrete as cars jammed six or seven across on a road painted with three lanes, scooters shooting between, the shoulders jammed with anything with an engine, and a few conveyances without.

"Four-and-a-half hours later we arrived at the airport," Janelle said. "My God, I almost had a heart attack."

"A nightmare," I laughed. I'd had a similar experience there and wondered who these hotel concierges were who insisted on the one-hour-to-CGK nonsense. I told her about the bribe I'd handed out of the window of a bus in exchange for completing an unimpeded right turn at a major intersection.

"But, hey, at least I didn't encounter any horses on the highway in Jakarta. That was the cause of a jam I sat through in Manila once," I added. How I had missed the exchange of travel stories.

She laughed.

"Oh, but I've missed it," Janelle said, echoing my thoughts. "And now the best. Favorite city?"

"Tokyo is the greatest city on earth," I declared confidently, almost daring her to argue, which she did. I knew I liked her.

"That'd be Singapore for my money. Those botanical gardens? The ones in the domes?" She let out a low whistle.

"Gardens by the Bay is great. And the Jewel at Changi is almost as amazing. But Tokyo still gets my vote. Ueno in the early morning, the buzz of the cicadas filling the air. Or Zojoji in the shadow of the Tokyo Tower. Talk about old meets new. Ginza on a Saturday night or the Shibuya crossing. Asakusa on a festival Saturday! The giant crepes in Harajuku! Yanaka and Sendagi!" I enthused.

How long since I had last experienced any of Tokyo's pleasures? If I'd once found six months between visits too long, the amount of time since my last trip didn't bear considering.

"Sounds like I should visit with you! You a travel agent? A tour guide?"

I laughed, thinking she was closer to the mark than many who worked in international education would care to acknowledge.

"Study abroad," I said, the shorthand for my profession easier at forty thousand feet than the academic explanation. "If a city is worth visiting – if there is a chance in a thousand that a student will want to study there – I've probably been. And Japan is my personal favorite."

Nao Kao and I had many differences. The greatest vacations of my life have involved deep water and colorful corals. Nao Kao tried snorkeling once and swore he would never do it again. His ideal weekend escape would be camping under the spray of the Milky Way, tent optional, communing with nature to the greatest extent possible. A hotel without room service was roughing it for me. But on Japan, clean, polite, orderly, beautiful Japan – Japan, with its dainty blossoms and ancient temples, the trains that ran like clockwork, and the taxi drivers with their white gloves – yes, on Japan we both agreed. It simply took the cake.

"So, Miss Maybe Work Maybe Pleasure, what is it that takes you to a city most people don't even know exists?" Janelle asked, our rapport firmly established.

Provided you are not in violation of a federal law, a conversation with a flight attendant is like visiting Las Vegas. What happens here, high above the earth, stays here. Certainly, when it comes to divulging the details of stories that are otherwise better left forgotten. Perhaps in an effort to piece together the story for myself, to clarify or justify or convince myself that this was even happening, that I yet clung to some scrap of sanity, I told her how I came to be on this flight.

I started with the professional stuff, a deeper dive into a flight record heavy with forays to the far flung and foreign. If she cared to look, she would see. Years ago, I had joined the club of those who hit all six inhabited continents in a calendar year, and half of them more than once.

And then I told her the rest. I stood in the galley and condensed a drama of twenty years to twenty minutes. As I talked, Janelle's eyebrows crept up her forehead and her eyes widened beyond all expectation. I think she was actually holding her breath.

Finally, she let out a low whistle. "Flight attendants hear a lot of tales, Miss Larkin," the disbelief in her voice was palpable.

"Liss, please. Everyone calls me Liss," I interrupted her.

"Liss, girl, let me tell you this. Flight attendants hear a lot of tales. But this one tops them all. To think that man would even speak to you! You must have got under his skin good."

I shrugged. On some level, the level of say, the steady stream of texts that pinged and popped across my devices, the unselfconscious selfies, the invitations to spend an hour enjoying coffee together half a world away, I must have done so. Not that it figured to matter once he knew what I had done this time.

"I hear a lot of tales," she repeated. "And all I can say is truth is stranger than fiction, of that I'm certain. Don't let anyone tell you otherwise."

She offered me another bottle of water and I returned to my seat, snuggling back in to the nest of pillows and blankets I had made for myself. If I pinched myself hard enough maybe I would awake at home in my own bed, as I had almost every night since the pandemic first stretched its fingers around the world. Surely that would be for the best.

∞ ∞ ∞ ∞ ∞

FOR ALL THAT some perceive as brashness on my part, I have never been bold. Without a legitimate, professional reason for reaching across time and space, I never would have sent Nao Kao so much as that initial message on LinkedIn, threads of any color, invisible or otherwise, notwithstanding. Without that message, there would not have been the ceaseless string of texts and emails that have colored my days since that fateful decision, nor the constant churn of questions or memories in my mind.

Maybe I should have simply asked for a favor. In retrospect, I probably could have. If our roles had been reversed, I realize now, I would not have minded, would not have found it rude. Undoubtedly, it would have been easier. Less fun, but easier. I am sensitive to the trope of the ugly American though, and bursting out with the request seemed more than a little gauche. There was also the fact that the favor would involve working directly with me, a prospect I understood only too clearly that Nao Kao might not relish. I needed to gauge whether I was actually a pleasant surprise, or whether he was simply too polite to indicate otherwise.

To do this right, I needed to tread carefully. Two lines on LinkedIn are one thing. Sharing the texture of your life with someone with whom you once shared so much, but with whom you haven't spoken in nearly two decades is another matter entirely. To say nothing of the fact that I needed to address the elephant in the room, to acknowledge that some kind of explanation was in order. And then I offered to vanish back into the ether.

What I lack in boldness, I more than make up for in curiosity. When Nao Kao replied to my email, he wrote of his career, his colleagues, his children, his extended family, and even his pets. Only by reading between the lines could I recognize the omission. About my suggestion to disappear, Nao Kao said not a word. It was time to harness the power of the internet to see what I could learn.

∞ ∞ ∞ ∞ ∞

"YOU'VE NEVER BEEN to the Big House?" I asked Nao Kao in August, before the start of fall semester.

"No, Liss, of course not. I barely arrived in this country before football season started last year. American football. I think it was November before I understood the importance of football as a way to understand the university, to understand the U.S., even. And then to go sit in the cold on a Saturday afternoon? I thought maybe this year, earlier in the season."

"You're right, sadly, about the importance of football to understanding this country. But you're wrong about something else," I told him.

"What's that?"

"Sitting in the cold. Students stand."

"Stand?"

"Yes, for the whole game. The student section always stands. That's where the tickets will be, right?"

"I assume so, la. But will you come?"

"No."

"No?"

"No."

"Because?"

"Because football is ruining college. All of athletics is. But football most of all."

"*American* football," Nao Kao clarified, a glint in his eye. "Because football as it is played in every other country would be an improvement."

"I'll have you know that Alex, the guy who dumped me at Good Time Charlie's and then stuck me with the bill for the beer and nachos, was a soccer player. So, I'm no fan of football, American style or international style! At least not on this campus!"

Nao Kao laughed.

"There is only ever one way to win an argument with you, la."

He walked over to my bookshelf and scanned the titles.

"This one, isn't it?" He held aloft Murray Sperber's *Beer and Circus* like a trophy. Sperber, he knew, was one of my heroes at the moment, and if I were inclined toward the traditional academic career full of books and scholarly articles, I might have followed the course he charted, with so many works peppered with the ways big time college athletics was undermining the core functions of the university. This was one topic among many of which I never grew tired, as Nao Kao knew better than anyone.

"If I read it, and tell you all of the ways that you and he are correct, then will you come to a football game?"

I laughed.

"Deal."

"As I said, there is only one way to win an argument with you. To read a book. Then you are satisfied!" Nao Kao said. He wasn't wrong.

Nao Kao made quick work of Sperber, was sufficiently outraged by the harm athletics wrought, and brandished a pair of tickets to a non-conference game on September 15. On that day, though, the stadiums across America would be silent, their emptiness an homage to the terror of the preceding week.

So it was that on Friday, Nao Kao popped over late in the day to brainstorm backup plans.

"One thing I know, canoeing is out."

"And no more pictures. I'm not in the mood." I paused.

"Greenfield Village?" I suggested, half-heartedly.

"Remind me again what this is."

"Kind of an outdoor museum," I started. "You know – Thomas Edison's workshop, the Wright Brothers' home, that kind of thing. It's in Dearborn."

Normally Nao Kao loved history, but today he wrinkled his nose.

"Not in the mood?"

"Too much history right now," he said, and I remembered the way he had once described history in Laos as being very close. September 11 wasn't just close. It was still enveloping us.

"Well, there's always Stucchi's."

"Liss, really. I am being serious, la."

"Me too. You don't have any ideas and you didn't like mine. And ice cream is always good. At least when the weather is warm, which it won't be for long. This isn't Laos."

He rolled his eyes, but could not suppress a slight smile.

"Besides, what haven't you done yet on campus? The natural history museum?"

He took off his glasses to rub his eyes, the back of his knuckles massaging the sockets, first left, then right.

"Ahh, the famous dinosaur bones."

I moved to the kitchen and began pulling down plates.

He shrugged.

"No matter, we can decide later. Or I can just start working on a paper. I have one due next week already."

This elicited a bit of side eye from my usually unrufflable friend.

"It's your last semester and you're going to spend it all in the library?"

I ignored him. We both knew the answer to that question.

"Well, do you want to watch *Au Revoir les Enfants* with me?" I asked as I portioned out the cartons of orange chicken and lo mein. Nao Kao still preferred the foods that bore some mark of familiarity, even if I was certain the sauce on the orange chicken existed nowhere outside of North America, but I was not going to complain. I preferred Chinese food, even mediocre, imitation "Chinese" food to that other ubiquitous college town fare, pizza.

"Remind me again why you are taking this class?"

"Because I wanted to take the comparative education course that is only offered every other year. And my assistantship covers all my tuition, so I decided to take a French class as long as I'm here. It's an independent study," I reminded him.

"What is this movie? *Goodbye, children?*" Nao Kao didn't speak much French, but having grown up in a former French colony, *au revoir* was still a common enough phrase that he recognized it right off.

"Holocaust movie. French children hiding from Nazis at a boarding school run by priests."

"It's a true story," I added, as though this would be a selling point.

"No happy ends, I'm guessing."

"Are there ever, Nao Kao?" I asked, thinking of the horrors of the past week, the planes, the flames, the plunging bodies.

He was silent, but stayed for the movie. I didn't even try to hide the tears that were so predictable, nor the sniffles or half-choked sobs that accompanied them.

"You should leave. Last bus and all that," I sounded pathetic, but really, who watched a movie about Nazis hunting little children in the days after September 11?

"Too late. It's gone past just now. I will stay here."

I turned on my computer and began to type to the sounds of Nao Kao settling to sleep on the couch, the music I had downloaded from Napster offering a late-night soundtrack interrupted by the occasional ping of an instant message.

∞ ∞ ∞ ∞ ∞

GOD BLESS SOCIAL MEDIA. And those who still make their posts public. Scrolling backward through time, I saw that mere hours after I received Nao Kao's email, he had posted a trove of campus photos, spring, summer, winter, and fall. The last was a group shot of our cohort – or my cohort, plus Nao Kao and perhaps others who had also taken education courses throughout the year. He is standing just behind me, his hand resting casually on my shoulder. I am wearing a sweatshirt and jeans, while the girl next to me is dressed in a flimsy blue and white sundress. That didn't exactly narrow the window of when it might have been taken. I tried to recall the names of the other students in the picture, or even the professor, but drew only blanks.

The holes in my memory aside, the connection to campus was too obvious to miss. I finally did what I originally intended to do.

"Nao Kao, would you, whether you personally or your team at NUOL, want to partner with UM on some Southeast Asia programming?" I texted him.

"That sounds promising. What do you have in mind?" he replied, almost immediately.

"Honestly, I'm not sure. We could discuss it to determine what makes the most sense. We need to offer our students more that focuses on the region, especially the CLMV countries, but we don't have a firm idea."

"Sure. It would be an honor for NUOL to affiliate with UM, and for me to give back to the school that gave me so much."

"Wonderful! I was hoping you'd say yes. We'd love your expertise and input on developing the programming – courses, study abroad programs, faculty exchanges, whatever makes the most sense."

"I'll think about it and send you a message. Thank you."

"Hey, no problem. It's always nice to do business with friends."

The conversation was so much easier than I expected; I couldn't imagine whatever had led me to put it off. I crossed "Ask Nao Kao about CLMV stuff" off my to-do list and moved my finger to the next item. My phone buzzed.

"Friends, huh? That's the best you can do?"

I stared at my phone, blinking hard. I wasn't seeing things.

"I don't know," I pecked out the letters slowly, my heart hammering at the unspoken implication that hung between the lines. "What else do you have?"

Then, "Got a meeting – gotta run," I added before he could reply. It wasn't the first time my courage failed me.

After that, it was no difficult task to coax him into attending the virtual alumni reunion a week later. Business and pleasure. The invitation from the alumni office that I forwarded him before he was even officially back on their radar or in their database asked attendees to wear maize and blue.

"I don't even have a shirt anymore," he apologized.

"Just wear something navy. You'll be fine."

"You always were pragmatic," Nao Kao replied.

My thumbs hesitated, frozen, over the screen, the thought already fully formed. Oh, Nao Kao. If only you knew.

I was nominally a responsible party for the reunion; certainly, the people who were truly in charge made sure to recognize and thank me for my work with them as the reunion began.

"So, you're kind of important," Nao Kao texted me, as though gauging whether I had lived up to any of the potential I had displayed when I used to spend so many hours in the library, my nose deep in a textbook. Had the game, he was weighing, been worth the candle?

"I am not even a dean," I protested. For if I had done well enough, there was no mistaking whose career trajectory shot off at the steeper angle.

"But you could be," he replied.

"Only if I were allowed to rule by Fiat," I responded, and was rewarded with a string of laughing emojis.

"Didn't you have your hair up a minute ago?" he asked a few minutes later.

I leaned into my screen, visually sorting through the sea of Zoom boxes. Each was the size of a domino on my laptop, and I was reasonably sure he had connected on his phone, where each attendee's face would be thumbnail size. I imagined him peering intently at his phone screen, eyes practically crossed, biting his lip in concentration, as he assessed the ways in which the woman in her little square stacked up to the girl in his memory.

My phone buzzed again and a half-dozen pictures popped up. I was struck by how similar he looked, how his face had not changed. Also, that he was bundled up like it was winter in one picture, when in reality I knew it must be one hundred degrees.

"Why are you laughing?" he texted me.

"Because I am looking at the pictures you sent and know you cannot possibly be anywhere that would necessitate a scarf."

"Send me some of you," he replied.

The only photos stored on my phone were travel shots. Me with big game in Africa. Me with big tuna in Tokyo. Me atop a big wall in China. I chose a few anyway; this was my life.

"Are you ever home?" he asked.

"I am now," I replied.

"What's your favorite city?" he asked before quickly adding, "Let me guess, it's Singapore. So clean! So orderly! Am I right?"

"Tokyo," I replied, laughing to myself, "but you get points for methodology."

"I am glad you like Asia," he responded. "Too many Americans do not."

I responded with the sushi emoji and pair of chopsticks.

"You always were good with chopsticks," Nao Kao wrote. "I remember you could eat M&Ms with them."

I tried to shake the cobwebs loose, to pry some such memory from the crevices of my mind, but nothing would come and I drifted into other chats. "The speaker said 'pivot' – Zoom Bingo for me," a colleague wrote, and we laughed in our living rooms and bedrooms and home offices at the absurdity of this brave new world, together but yet alone.

"I've got another call, Liss," Nao Kao's name buzzed on my phone. "Let's catch up more soon."

The next time we exchanged messages he asked what I was wearing before signing off. I sent him a selfie so he could judge for himself.

∞ ∞ ∞ ∞ ∞

I POPPED ON my video monitor and played with the route maps, badly missing the in-flight magazine with its plethora of maps and, more importantly, the crossword puzzle. One more casualty of the pandemic. I noticed how much sparser the maps were than the last time I completed this exercise.

For years, Delta's Asia flights connected through Narita, a definite perk on the day-long journey to Singapore or Bangkok or Manila. Sadly, as more than one flight attendant had recounted to me, Delta's difficulties with the Japanese government mounted until they'd been forced to shift their Asia operations to Incheon, and a deeper partnership with Korean Airlines. Now, woe betide anyone hoping to fly Delta to Narita, even on a visit to Japan. A shame, for as far as the airport lay from the city, I preferred it to Haneda by degrees of magnitude.

I thought about the first time I had flown across the Pacific, Detroit to Narita to Bangkok, how utterly foreign it all was, from the wall of heat that hit me in the small hours of a December night when the heavy glass doors slid open past customs to the sounds of the city and the sticky sweet fruits. I was in middle school when my dad accepted a visiting professorship at Chulalongkorn University in Bangkok. My memories of our months in the city had gone soft around the edges, but my most vivid memory still remained sharp.

We were trapped in particularly awful traffic crawling for hours through the city one Saturday, me with mangosteen juice pooling in my lap. Even now I was shocked that my mother, whose lifelong quest amounted to, *when in Rome, do as the Romans do* (also known as: avoid being perceived as the Ugly American, no matter the cost), allowed me to peel open the luscious, pulpy fruit in the backseat of that car. I had wiped my fingers on the pleather seat and been horrified by the vivid purple stain I left on the sticky material. Smearing at it with the back of my hand only caused it to spread.

All of the best establishments posted signs warning "No durian — No mangosteen" and if I understood from the first time I had encountered durian that no proprietor wanted to risk so much as a whiff of that pungent fruit on the property, I had not understood the interdiction against mangosteen until now. As more of the deeply hued juice ran down my leg I realized: I would shortly look like the victim of an attempted murder.

In front of us two scooters crashed, a load of live chickens spilling from the back of the larger one, our driver repeatedly blasting the horn as though the act didn't merely add to the cacophony. If anything, our horn only excited the chickens, who flapped their wings madly and raced in circles. From the edge of the road a lithe young woman appeared and lifted her skirt in our direction. As the only automobile in a sea of scooters, we were an obvious mark.

There was nothing under the skirt except what she was born with.

If I was intrigued, my sixteen-year-old brother was entranced, his eyes going wide as in a slow-motion film. The origins of the word "streetwalker" were now eminently clear to both of us. Our mother, wedged between us, her legs slick with sweat from the hours our bodies had been pressed together, a bit of the mangosteen juice beginning to creep onto her thighs, too, was horrified. Nothing in Rachael Zick's prim and proper upbringing as a belle of one of the better families of New Orleans had prepared her for this moment. Her arms flew out to either side as she futilely sought to cover our eyes, as though we might unsee this woman and her goods. Years later she told me that this, her first brush with prostitution in the developing world, prostitution that bore no hallmarks of the gloss of *Pretty Woman,* had imprinted itself as strongly into her worldly mind as it had into the impressionable minds of her children.

When I first told Nao Kao the story, it was not the events themselves that surprised him so much as our reaction to them.

"All over the world you traveled, but none of you ever saw a prostitute before?" he asked incredulously.

"Yes. Or no. I mean, I had seen – and I'm sure my parents, too – plenty of women who were undoubtedly prostitutes. Late at night or early in the morning, in Paris near the Bois de Boulogne or along the Embarcadero in San Francisco. Stumbling through London's squares at sunrise. That kind of thing. But none of us had ever seen a woman so desperate to turn a trick that she was willing to display her wares – *all* her wares – in the middle of a traffic jam on a Saturday afternoon!"

"But your car was stuck and there were three men inside – if she could entice even one of them for fifteen minutes, I'm sure it would have put rice in her belly." He spoke without judgment, only a resigned understanding of the realities of life lived on knife's edge.

The act of putting food on the table was no metaphor here, and Nao Kao understood that as well as anyone. He had arrived in Bangkok to study at Chula just a couple of years later; the National University of Laos would not accept its first class until the year after he began college. Though he could have transferred to the new, national institution to finish his studies, a degree from one of the region's leading schools would open far more doors for him than one from a brand new and entirely unknown university. Obviously, his gamble had paid off.

In my half-awake, half-asleep state, I catalogued my travels in Asia, the cities and countries I was always urging students to prioritize for their time abroad. I remembered my last trip to Asia. On that trip, I had swung through China, from Hong Kong, where I'd strolled along the Avenue of Stars to see the junks in the harbor and the Star Ferry plying the waters, to Beijing with its endless ring roads and portraits of Mao and finally to Shanghai, a glitzy, gritty, glammy city that manages to be equal parts high tech and highly inefficient. I love Shanghai, that megapolis that's risen so rapidly alongside the Huangpu River, futuristic skyscrapers jammed next to alleys that once were opium dens. Especially in Asia, I like to wake up early and walk in the morning, to feel the sticky warmth in my lungs before the day's heat fully bears down on me, to smell the meats roasting, to immerse myself in the routines of a city awakening from its relative quietude, the sounds of millions rising in tandem with the sun. Honking, sweeping, hollering: it is not yet a din, but give it time.

As we bumped along the highway in the sky, the seat belt warning dinging, the captain asking the fight crew to take their seats, Janelle scurrying to do just that, in my mind's eye I could see Shanghai. It is a city where laundry still hangs from trees next to hotels whose marble lobbies gleam and the scents of incense and cigarette smoke mingle with dumplings and noodles and sweet, sticky sauces. The food is to die for, but it is the water that could literally kill you. Of course, it is the pollution most people think of, and some days it can be thick enough to leave a layer on your tongue, certainly thick enough to create sunsets that set the sky ablaze. Above all, though, when I picture Shanghai, I picture the millions and millions of people living and laughing and loving and also shouting, frequently shouting, cheek by jowl.

My mind drifted to the pajamas, too, as I remembered how Delta used to provide soft, gray pjs on the flight to Shanghai. I wondered whether they would again or whether this, too, would be another business decision, the way they no longer flew the inter-Asia connections, the way that today, it is almost exclusively Korean Air or bust for any traveler in Asia who is lashed to the mast of the Sky Team. Never mind that I count Korean among my least favorite airlines on earth, it was their aircraft that would carry me the next six hours from Seoul to Vientiane. Once I would have considered that but a hop, skip, and a jump away. Now it felt like a year. I could not say, though, whether that was because I was so woefully out of practice or because of the mounting trepidation that churned inside of me. If it is true God hates a coward, I may be in trouble when my time on earth is at an end.

At last the meditative aspect of flying did its work. I drifted off dreaming of gray cotton jammies that clung to me like clouds to trees on a ridgeline.

∞ ∞ ∞ ∞ ∞

WHAT DO WE know that we don't know we know? Of course, it's not always what we don't know. Sometimes we're simply too stupid or too stubborn to acknowledge it. There is comfort and safety in the denseness of a dumb mind that abandons us with terrifying speed once we are forced to recognize that we were not dense, but wallowing in denial. The line between these states – dense at one end of the taut rope and denial pulling valiantly against it – is more ephemeral that I care to admit.

After years of sleeping soundly, I had suddenly begun to have nightmares. For weeks on end, I awoke in a cold sweat, the sensation of drowning – or more frequently suffocating – fresh in my mind, my pajamas and sheets soaked through with the evidence of my terror. It only seems fitting that it was while I was gazing out another airplane window, enjoying my front row seat to God's hour, that magical moment when the sun cracks the horizon and turns the sky all razzle-dazzle, that my own conscience cracked open.

Almost since the day we had said "I do," the idea of divorce had rattled through my mind. Scratch that. Since the day we said I do, the literal wedding day, the idea had lodged itself in my mind. Admittedly, though I prefer not to, I almost did not say "I do," so strong was the voice begging me not to go through with it.

I thought back to the keynote I delivered on literacy and blogging one glittery night in Charleston. I was there to share the origins of my project with an assembled audience of bibliophiles who had earned this stay at the Charleston Place for their efforts promoting literacy in schools around the country.

"What was the impetus behind your journal?" the moderator asked.

"Agatha Christie is great, really," I began nervously, as though I might offend the great, dead dame, "but let me tell you: all the whodunnits start to run together after a while. Even Ms. Christie only had so much originality. So, my husband suggested a blog. I think he hoped it meant I wouldn't ask him anymore if he knew whether I'd already read *Murder on the Blue Train* or if I was thinking of *Murder on the Orient Express*. And, more to the point, once I finished reading my book of the moment, he *dearly* hoped he would no longer be the primary audience for my extemporaneous reviews. Maybe others were interested in what I thought of *The Murder on the Links*, but he was not!"

Laughter, slightly uncomfortable, tittering laughter, I later realized, reverberated through the courtyard, dancing between the twinkle lights, sluicing through the fountain.

If I flitted through life as sparkly orange, a trail of glitter dancing in my wake, Jake was gunmetal gray, stolid and, frankly, a little dull. Despite the ambivalence he displayed toward his own studies in college, he taught high school English – and his students adored him. His classrooms were lively, and when the mood struck, his teaching could veer toward performance. He'd write little ditties sometimes, quasi-songs to help students remember the sonnets of Shakespeare or the trials and tribulations of Homer and his men and on the occasions when he shared them with me, I'd allow myself to wander down the rabbit hole of what-ifs that started and ended with what if Jake had had the courage or the ambition to pursue what he'd once been so passionate about? Whether Jake had truly left behind whatever passion he'd once possessed for the rhythms of the spoken word, or merely concealed it from me, I knew his ear for language was finely tuned and keen. Of course, I asked him to help me edit my speech. That it earned a laugh was all the better as far as he was concerned.

I realize now that the audience may have been laughing with me, but at a certain point, one I could not pinpoint, Jake had begun to laugh at me. Eventually, nothing I said was quite right to his ear, and nothing I did was quite right, period. He rolled his eyes at my trials and triumphs and I retreated further inward and out of this life with a man who was happiest when I kept my own counsel – or better yet, when I was on another continent.

I counted my other lives as I drifted off to sleep. Alternate lives I might have lived as Mrs. Ex- This or Ex- That. I had names for these other lives, like books of the Bible – Matthew, Mark, Luke, and John – or bands – Peter, Paul, and Mary. And I counted them, the way other, saner folks might count sheep. The way Bing Crosby counted his blessings.

Though it percolated for years, once I knew to the depths of my soul that I needed out, it was impossible to think of anything else, to unknow the injury upon my spirit, the death by a thousand paper cuts that I was slowly dying. Once I had realized this, each moment threatened to subsume me in a tide of regret and grief.

What cause, these gales? The winds of the storm lashed my face, my mind, my soul.

And so, as the plane swung low over Dakar, the wide plains of West Africa clearly visible out of the window, the United Nations plane on the runway – the only other one at the entire airport that day – slipping into view, the situation became critical. The realization of what those nightmares meant unmoored me as nothing had. Nothing, that is, since Nao Kao.

∞ ∞ ∞ ∞ ∞

I FELT THE bed sag next to me, rousing me from deep sleep. It took me a moment to get my bearings.

"Nao Kao! What are you doing in here? Go back to the couch!" I squinted at the time. It wasn't quite one in the morning.

Instinctively I sat up and tugged the covers up to my chin. Nao Kao had seen me in a bathing suit. He had seen me soaked through in the river. In both cases, he had gotten a better eyeful than my oversized YMCA camp t-shirt and I Heart NY boxer shorts offered. Still, this felt different. This was my bedroom. It was the middle of the night. And in a single fluid movement, he was under the covers.

"Liss, please."

91

"Nao Kao! No!" His hands moved under my shirt and across my stomach.

"Stop it, Nao Kao. Stop. You're married. Married! What are you doing?" I clutched awkwardly at the covers as he groped at me with greater determination. As my eyes adjusted to the dark, I realized with rising alarm that the pile next to the bed consisted of his clothes. *All* of his clothes. Peeking out from the jeans I could just make out underwear, not boxer shorts, but tighty whities. Despite the circumstances I could not help thinking that there was a first time for everything.

"Liss, please. I want you. I need you. Please." His voice had gone all husky, less silk and more gravel, his accent more pronounced. His hand slid up my torso, cupping my breast.

"Oh, Liss." He opened his mouth against mine and began to kiss me. I pulled back, away from him.

"Nao Kao. Nao Kao! Stop! Think!"

Think, Liss. Think. I needed the advice as much as he did. For weeks I had sensed that we were on a collision course with this moment, the tension between us building until it could have been sliced with the proverbial knife. Yet, I had convinced myself it wouldn't ultimately happen that way. Nao Kao and I were nothing more than good friends. He was married. He was *safe*. Or at least that had been the plan. I hated it when life did not conform to my plans, and never more than now.

"I am thinking. About this. About you. About what I want to do with you. Please."

Never before had I known my desires to be in such open warfare with who – or what – I believed myself to be. Or not. An adulteress, for example. I might be a flirt, but I was certainly not, definitely not, an adulteress. I twisted my shoulders sideways, seeking to buy myself time and space.

As my hips rotated in tandem with my shoulders, I felt Nao Kao's fingers slide into my shorts, tugging them down over my hips, a movement that raised goosebumps from my toes to my temples.

"Nao Kao. STOP."

For the first time he seemed to hear me. Without his glasses I hardly recognized him and even through my t-shirt, I could feel his heart racing, his chest warm against me. I started to trace a line down the center of it. Stopped. My mind spun. This was not okay. None of it.

Unless it was. Which it could not be. This was adultery. A crime as old as time.

"Nao Kao,"

"Shhhh. La." Gently he placed his finger across my lips. "Please."

I felt him slide my shorts the rest of the way down my legs, past my ankles and toes, could almost see them puddled at the foot of the bed. An image of him on the soccer field came unbidden. I had never gone to watch the IM games in which he played, but I imagined now he must be very good.

"Nao Kao, do you even have a condom?"

It wasn't purely a stall tactic on my part. Just as Nancy Reagan's War on Drugs had hammered into my head the image of a frying egg as "this is your brain on drugs" in the 1980s, so had the safe sex campaigns of the 90s drilled into my head. No condom, no way.

"No."

He didn't even have the decency to sound sheepish.

In the dark he must have sensed rather than seen my alarm. He propped himself onto his elbows and began telling me how many tests he had undergone to secure his visa. He was, beyond a shadow of a doubt in his mind and in the view of the American government, free and clear of any and all STDs when he stepped foot in the country. In the year since, he had lived a monk's life. He recounted all of this factually, yet urgently and with more than a hint of a plea in his voice. My brain whirred.

He began to stroke my hair, ever so softly, brushing it from my face as I drew a jagged breath. Under the covers his hand found mine and he laced our fingers together.

"Please, Liss."

"No condom, no...." my voice trailed off as I felt his weight shift. Although I was thin, I was certain I outweighed Nao Kao, but there was surprising strength in that sinewy body of his. He began to move against me. This couldn't be happening. Nao Kao was my friend. Only my friend, but also my friend, not some random date. Surely, I was to have a say – *the* say – in what was about to happen.

I pressed hard into his hip bone, stilling him, buying myself more time to work through this predicament. If he weren't married....but no, it didn't work that way. The band of gold delineated a bright line, whether he was wearing it or not, and we were so far over the line I struggled to make it out in the distance.

93

He kissed my throat. *This. was. not. happening. He. was. married. Married! Married!* If I repeated that often enough, perhaps I could literally will this decision away.

"You take those pills, right? The ones in your bathroom."

My mind flashed back to when I dropped a glass and cut my finger a couple of weeks ago, sending Nao Kao scurrying into my bathroom to rummage through the vanity for a band-aid. Evidently that wasn't the only thing he found. I imagined him contemplating this since that day.

"But your wife —"

"Shhh. Liss. Enough. I want you. Please."

Maybe it didn't matter. After all, if he hadn't been married, I had no doubt we would have done this months before. It might have been the friends with benefits route that simultaneously intrigued and appalled him, perhaps, or even a proper relationship. Either way, the end result would have been the same; still, my rationalizations stung — any way I sliced this, every fiber of my being knew what I was about to do was wrong.

Almost involuntarily, I felt my mouth open, felt myself begin to kiss him back, felt his warm fingers trail along my heaving ribs, further and further south. I had crossed my own personal Rubicon. I relaxed and let him pull my shirt over my head. Our bodies merged one into the other and for a brief, shining moment I allowed myself to forget how utterly wrong this was.

Afterward, he curled next to me, his arm slung gently across my middle, his fingers absently fondling my breast, then tracing a path along the inside of my arm until his fingers reached mine and he curled them together. I waited until I was sure he was asleep before I let any tears fall; I might never tell another soul what I had done, but I knew definitively now exactly what I was capable of.

The birds were not yet chirping when I drowsed awake to the soft sounds of Nao Kao's voice, whether a prayer, perhaps, to the gods for understanding, or merely a lament for what was not and never could be, or a brief moment of thankfulness, I do not know.

"You're beautiful, Liss."

His voice was so quiet it barely registered, but I stirred enough that now he felt me move and squeezed my hand in his. When I opened my eyes, I realized he had moved to the other side of me, so that we were almost nose-to-nose. Confusion registered on my face.

"I wanted to look at you. I like to watch you sleep."

He pressed his index finger into the place where a deep dimple appeared when I smiled. If that was the award he awaited, he would not receive it this morning.

"It's dark. You can't see me," I replied, half-angry and half-teasing. I wondered if he noticed the same sharp edge that I felt in my voice.

"It's here," he said, tapping the side of his head. "I don't need my eyes to know." He moved his hands along my body, moved his face toward mine to kiss me.

I turned away.

"Nao Kao, I think you should go." My tone was firmer now, my voice set, my decision made.

"Come on, Liss. It's not even light."

"I want you to go. Now. I need to think."

"Are we still on for the museum later?"

"Just *go*."

The door latched quietly behind him and I rolled into a ball and sobbed. I had been half in love with him for months. I had never felt so shitty.

NAO KAO

"WHAT ARE YOU DOING?" Liss asked, and it was a reasonable question.

"Only what I've wanted to do for months," I might have replied, had tried, in my way, to reply, but I couldn't help but feel the trueness of my sentiments did not reach Liss as I wanted them to.

I'd never meant for things to turn out this way. I'd never meant to date another woman while I was here, to meet someone with whom I could converse until we ran out of words. When we made snow angels, I told my family; by the time we wandered through the Art Fairs, I studiously avoided any mention of "my American friend." Whatever amusement members of my family might derive from my misadventures earlier this week on the Huron River, I knew I would never speak of it.

Maybe, if not for September 11, it might not have happened. But life is short, and if I hadn't appreciated that before, over the course of a life begun in the shadow of war, the long arm of hunger and disease never too far from reach, I certainly appreciated it as we sat transfixed by the horror in New York. Even here in the relative safety of the American Midwest, ensconced in an ivy tower, you never know when your time will come.

I considered kissing her on September 11, pulling her to me as we sat on her couch, Peter Jennings narrating the previously unfathomable. That day held too much sadness, and rightly so. It needed the sadness.

Lying on the couch, replaying that devastating Holocaust movie in my mind, I couldn't help but contrast the heaviness of the past week with the life and lightness of the woman clicking away on the other side of the wall.

If not now, when? I asked myself, and knocked lightly as soon as I noticed the rapid-fire typing had ceased. To my amazement, she was already under the covers.

You're married, she had protested, the truth crystallizing in that moment. I'd been tempted once to joke with her about being on date, held back by the fear that the sentiment would appall her and that she would cut me out of her friendship circle completely and ruthlessly. Liss took marriage seriously. She planned her life so carefully: she would never understand how I had more or less stumbled into marriage.

"I want you," I had replied, and the trueness of the statement caught the words in my throat as I spoke them. Those three words were inadequate to my meaning: you, physically, in this moment, yes, but also, you, all of you in all ways. Always. I am not good at expressing my feelings in the best of circumstances, and in the warmth of Liss's embrace, my words failed me. It would have been easier if I had a plan, not merely a desire.

PART II: LOVERS

~

LISS

W HERE IS THE line between friends with benefits and an affair of the heart? That is a question I have had more time to ponder than most, and since I haven't answered it yet, I don't expect to, not in this lifetime at least.

I did not expect to hear from Nao Kao after I sent him from my apartment at first light that Saturday morning. I certainly did not expect to find an email from him by the time I powered on my computer after strong tea and a hot, tear-soaked shower.

If I had lowered myself in my own esteem when I finally relented to his pleas, that certainly was not the case for him, for whom the previous evening had been something he had wanted for so long and had finally found the nerve to pursue. He would be at the museum at 2:00 p.m., if I still felt like going. "Or you can come to my apartment. ;)"

I smiled in spite of myself. How easily one slips into another skin. How easily one becomes – how easily *I* became – the other woman.

∞ ∞ ∞ ∞ ∞

I BOUGHT MY first car just a few weeks before September 11. A bright blue Civic, its gloss like the sheen of a poison dart frog, with a manual transmission. My dad convinced me that despite the fact that I would not need it for a few months, August was the time to buy. He also observed that parking a new car in an open lot that often served as a shortcut for those in varying states of inebriation at 2:00 a.m. would not be my wisest move. Having attended a New Year's party in the building next door, where the riotously drunk hostess toasted the coming year by hurling dinnerware discus-style from her balcony, I realized my dad was not wrong. So, I kept the car at my parents' place, just a couple of miles from campus on a leafy side street where it was far less likely to come to harm. I imagined once that things would have unfolded differently if not for that decision. On such small decisions do larger events often hinge, but in this case, it's unlikely. Although the pressure points may have been different, the facts would have remained immutable.

Nao Kao had not yet seen the big lake, and did not – could not – entirely believe that standing at the edge of Lake Michigan was akin to standing on the shore of the ocean. September was the tail end of the season for going to the beach, but the air still held the warmth of late summer for at least a couple of hours in the afternoon. If we were going to go, the time was now.

"I want you to wear a bikini," he had said baldly when we hatched the plan a few days earlier. Neither of us had class on Wednesday, which also looked to be the warmest day of the week.

"A bikini?" I questioned, alarmed. "I've only owned Speedos for years. I've only *worn* Speedos for years!"

"So, buy one. I want to be able to do this." He kissed my collar bone gently from my right shoulder to my sternum and then up the left side.

How I transitioned from reluctant participant in middle-of-the-night transgressions to a willing participant in a sordid affair defies easy explanation. The obvious answers abound. I liked Nao Kao, my best friend and easiest conversation partner of the past year. My respect and affection for him only grew when I realized this was no torrid one-night stand. I was young and single, with all that entailed; for all my terror of maternal tantrums, I enjoyed the prospect of scandalizing my mother. Above them all, though, hovered the greater truth, the veracity of which left me questioning my entire character. I was energized by the quiet thrill of shattering the good girl mold that had so guided, one might even argue constrained, my life, until the moment I'd allowed myself to be with Nao Kao in every sense of the word. And now, in another first, I was contemplating skimpy swimwear.

Finding a bikini in Michigan in autumn was about as likely as finding a down jacket in Havana in July, but I would try to fulfill Nao Kao's wish. I spent the night before our trip scouring Briarwood Mall where I turned up what was likely the last bathing suit in the state on a JCPenney's clearance rack. If a lavender and navy haltered tankini was not exactly the itsy bitsy teenie weenie polka dot bikini of Nao Kao's dreams, at least it wasn't a Speedo.

"Where are you off to so early today?" my mom asked when I showed up for my car. My timing was poor. In another ten minutes she would have been safely on her way to work.

"Beach," I mumbled, willing a sink hole to open under me, new car notwithstanding. Insurance would cover the cost of a replacement.

"The beach? You mean Lake Michigan? And by yourself?" Then ominously, "But who will help you with your sunscreen?"

If her family did not have such a strong history of skin cancer – if my grandfather had not succumbed just a few months prior to a particularly aggressive melanoma – I might have snorted with derision. Or ignored her. Or both. Instead, I attempted a dodge.

"A friend?"

Rachael Zick was not born yesterday. Steely and determined, she had elbowed her way into a field dominated, as all of academia used to be and much of it still is, by an old boys' club. She turned that intensity on me now, leveling her gaze, remembering too quickly the friend who had tagged along on a couple of occasions when I had come to do laundry, but whom she had not seen for many weeks. I was keeping Nao Kao at a safe distance.

My parents liked him. They had invited him to dinner once or twice, after New Year's, when he so impressed my mom with his command of the finer points of Laotian history and French colonialism in general. With them he seemed to relax, and would chat contentedly in a way he rarely did in class – or with me.

Only by sitting quietly after the plates had been cleared did I learn when one of his daughters had begun to crawl or walk, or that they had started to babble and coo at him when he called home, this stranger in a faraway land who existed for them only in a photograph. (This past year I asked him why he seemed so much more relaxed with my parents. "You always made me a little nervous," he admitted. "Sometimes you still do." Not surprisingly, he would reveal nothing further.)

My mom's eyes flashed as she settled on the only possible explanation.

"Melissa Claire Miller. He is a married man! A married man, Liss! Do you know what they call women like you? Do you, Liss?"

As if I needed the reminder.

I drove away with her words ringing in my ears. If I had not felt it before, I could feel it now, the scarlet A firmly tattooed on my heart.

∞ ∞ ∞ ∞ ∞

THE INTERCOM INTERRUPTED my reverie.

"Is there a doctor on board? Please identify yourself to the cabin crew."

I was not a doctor, not the kind to help in this kind of emergency, at least, although I am good in crises of the non-medical variety. From missed flights or lost students, to passports left in trains and hotels safes – or simply vanished out of backpacks or pockets or the backseat of a cab – to students who discover belatedly that they have booked airfare for the wrong dates or the wrong cities or even the wrong countries – to vans with blown out tires high up in the Andes, I have handled all of these, I am told, with aplomb.

Earthquakes around the Ring of Fire are run of the mill emergencies. Political protests in Haiti that render impassible the only road to the airport require a bit more ingenuity. If you are the victim of a wild dog attack somewhere outside of Goa, I am available to tell you that the rabies vaccine is your friend – though I will also likely suggest that you should have proceeded directly to the hospital, rather than making me your first call.

Yes, the concrete problems of the world, the kind with actual solutions – appointments at embassies to replace lost passports or intravenous drips to replace lost fluids – problems to be solved, crises to be diverted, normalcy to be restored, at this I am masterful. It is the problems without clear solutions at which I flounder.

The student who learns via text from an aunt that a parent has passed away in Tennessee, while the student is studying in Turkey, that is much harder for me. So, too, the student who drank too much in too many bars and awoke with too many regrets: yes, these are the kinds of problems that leave me feeling at sea.

My own life has followed a similar pattern. The troubles I could name and resolve, I have done so admirably, and with clear eyes and competence. It is the crises that are not so concrete, the ones that build slowly or burn untended too long that have proved my undoing.

∞ ∞ ∞ ∞ ∞

ONE OF THE glories of summer in Michigan is the long days, sixteen hours of daylight at the peak of the season. If the sun doesn't crest as early as it does over Cadillac Mountain, it rises early enough, and gradually as we got to know one another again, Nao Kao and I learned the rhythm of one another's routines, or our routines as they existed, at least for me, in the middle of a raging pandemic.

I would go for an early morning run greeting the sun as night became day, or, even more gloriously, a swim, and then I would chat with Nao Kao for an hour or so. A similar window occurred in the evening, and I would sit in my breakfast nook, watching the rabbits and deer in the waning light, occasionally snapping a picture for him of the nature he so missed in the urban heart of Vientiane.

At first, our conversations were discrete, with a clear beginning and a firm end. At some point they began to wend through the week in a single thread, touching on everything from our time together to the classes we were teaching to *Seinfeld* memes and what it meant to be a good parent. Parenthood, or more accurately in my case, the lack of it, was the one regret I could not pin on Jake. He had been ambivalent but willing to have a family whenever the topic arose. But parenthood was incompatible with a lifestyle in which the next airplane was never more than five days away. Whether the lifestyle itself was a reaction to Jake might have been a closer question, but nothing would see me consider the change in lifestyle that parenting would require.

When I grew too nostalgic even for him, this man who feasted on Segal and Wilde, and cited Dickens's Oliver as his favorite character in literature for his innocence and bravery, Nao Kao would remind me of the horrors of parenthood even in a place where children still respected their elders.

His twins were grown, students, both of them, at the National University of Laos, a fact about which he was unquestionably proud. His youngest daughter, born a year after he had returned home, American diploma in hand, was completing her last year of high school, and determined to strike her own path.

"She wants to go abroad," he explained.

"Seems fair. You did. Twice," I reminded him.

"Yes," I could sense the hesitation.

"What does your wife think?" From the family photos he posted semi-regularly, I was positive – *positive* – that Nao Kao was still married, yet he consistently refused to acknowledge as much, refused to even acknowledge that I was asking the question. *A nice girl. Normal.* How I wished I knew anything of her beyond those two bland adjectives. When an opening presented itself, I tried.

"This one is different. Her sisters are happy here, but the youngest one, she is restless. You know what that's like."

It was not an accusation, I was certain, though it gave me a pang that one of my defining traits was something Nao Kao clearly wished was different about his own daughter's character. I felt a pang for the girl, too. A restless nature made for an interesting life, but not always an easy one. Nor was it lost on me that he had expertly dodged the question I'd actually asked.

"Her future is not here."

"I see. So, any plans for the weekend?"

Big feelings frightened me. If he hadn't understood this before, he had clearly learned the lesson by the third or fourth time I steered us to softer ground. Often, I realized after the fact that he had tried to shake the yoke of reticence and share something larger or deeper with me, only for it either to go over my head or send me searching for the likes of weekend plans. "I always knew it was my fault," he'd responded after I managed to explain where it all went wrong. It must have been seven months before the weight of those seven words finally hit me, the acknowledgment of how much I meant in his life.

I shared my triumphs and anxieties, the minutiae of a life lived, for the first time, quietly at home. In Nao Kao's life were beer and pizza and weekend hikes, temples, and wedding-upon-wedding. After all, the median age in Laos is under twenty-five; couples are always tying the knot. Pictures and videos of all things Japanese would ping for attention, and not a few articles, either. Whatever, it seemed, that caught his attention, and that in turn he thought might catch mine, zipped from his phone onto mine, one text bubble and buzz at a time.

Nao Kao's motorcycle, a serious upgrade over the scooter he had left behind when he came to Ann Arbor, was his most prized possession. He loved it far beyond his car, which he drove out of practicality when strictly necessary. He asked me if I had ridden a motorcycle yet – aside from the mopeds when you were in France, he added – and again I was struck dumb by the strength of his memory, the details he had retained from my long-ago stories. "No," I replied, "not counting those old French mopeds, I have still never so much as sat astride one."

Once he took his motorcycle – and me – on a virtual tour of the UNESCO World Heritage Site at Luang Prabang, riding north to where the Nam Khan and Mekong Rivers collide, stopping along the way for chicken and rice or to photograph some particularly picturesque vista of mountain or jungle that he thought I would appreciate. In Luang Prabang, he plucked me from his pocket, so to speak, and set his phone to record. In this way, he toured me through the magnificent temple complexes at Wat Xieng Thong, the dramatic peaks outlined in white rising brilliantly against a blue sky, and the red, stacked roofs of Wat Mai whetting my appetite to see the country firsthand.

"Come," he intoned, at the very end, lest his meaning be lost in the currents between dense and denial.

If I asked him a question that he did not want to answer, he ignored it, a maddening habit I pointed out more than once, along with the fact that it seemed a point of pride for him never to refer to his girls by name. Occasionally, when there was something he wanted from me, some obtuse or existential question about which he wanted my opinion, I would open my archive of unanswered queries and ask again, alongside a comment that the question was not rhetorical – and that my responding to him was contingent upon him extending me the same courtesy. I hoped it was no more obnoxious than it was endearing. As Stacy reminded me, "if he didn't want to talk to you, he wouldn't." We all have our quirks.

One of his older girls was engaged and I teased him, though again harassed might be more accurate, about how soon he would be the father of the bride – and the joys of grandparenting that might not be much further behind.

"I hope they will wait," he said simply, and whether he meant to marry or to procreate, I did not press. The next time I led the conversation down that path, I was met by a wall of silence.

More places he did not want to delve with me – or maybe even without me. For months I tried to get a straight answer to what I was certain I knew from my internet sleuthing. Happily, or not, I could not say, but I was certain he was still married. Yet try as I might, I could not extract an admission of this simple fact. I remembered his penchant for Shaggy: the possibility that Nao Kao was a total player was never far from my mind.

Occasionally, my level of annoyance would rise enough that I would disappear for a few days. Perhaps his absences followed a similar pattern. Largely what stood out, though, was how natural our conversations felt, how the gap of time – what was, essentially, our entire adult lives – simply fell away, how talking to him now was as comfortable and uninhibited as it had been all those years before as we sat over cartons of tepid takeout and laughed about life.

The silence of the years disappeared at speed. Refraction, that bending of the light that is responsible for rainbows, seemed to me to be at work here, too, knitting our lives into a braided arc, erasing the empty space since we'd last known each other, filling voids with dazzling color.

"How much do you want to know?" I asked when he expressed concern that I was seeing a specialist for the third time.

"I will want to know a lot," he replied, the verb tenses an acknowledgment of the lateness of the hour; the word choice an acknowledgement, however tacit, that what lies between us, in addition to thousands of miles, is no normal friendship.

Always, always, I was surprised by what he remembered. From the clothes I had worn to the furniture in the living room, it seemed no detail escaped Nao Kao's attention. Once I began to tell him the story of when I had come face-to-face with a wild boar in Rio. It was trotting down the street as my family headed toward lunch.

"Yes, I remember," he said, "and then the van you were in got stuck between the building and the café you were going to and when you opened the door, you landed in the laps of the diners."

"Brazil is also where you met the boy," he added, before I could even praise the prowess of his memory.

"The one with the wandering hands. You spent New Year's Eve with him at the party on the beach."

With those dozen words, I was remembering myself on that champagne-soaked Atlantic beach, spent fireworks raining through palm fronds, Claudio's fingers working their way under the flimsy little straps of my tight, white New Year's dress, his mouth on mine.

Game, set, match, Nao Kao.

∞ ∞ ∞ ∞ ∞

IF HE JUDGED the decisions I made, whether they pertained to him or Jake, or even the deal with the devil I had once made that kept me working for a boss who ogled and pawed at me for far longer than I should have, he kept the judgments to himself. He offered mild praise for my professional successes, and directed the occasional probing question my way as we debated one philosophical question or another. I valued his insights, and appreciated that they were mine for the asking, whether in regards to handling an intransigent faculty member or navigating home repairs.

Often, he encouraged me to meditate, something many others had tried and failed before him. I would rather read, I insisted, and eventually he gave up. We are who we are. Once he and I might have sought to mold or influence one another, but the passage of time mellowed even that instinct. We discussed our life's philosophies, but we did not debate them.

In an echo of the past, mostly he listened, maybe with half an ear, maybe with both ears, but always it seemed, willingly.

The only time Nao Kao gave me the impression that my actions might have been beyond the pale was when I recollected the disastrous end to my marriage.

"If that is how you ended a marriage…" I could not catch the rest of the message before he quickly unsent it.

"Nao Kao, what did you say?" I asked, annoyed.

He changed the subject.

"Nao Kao! Tell me. What did you say?"

I did not like the signals my intuition was sending.

After what seemed an inordinately long delay, the telltale typing dots appeared.

"Let it go, Liss. It was a long time ago."

Shit.

Even if I couldn't remember everything, I remembered enough. I remembered the salient facts: a wife, two kids, and a visa type that compelled return to and service of a country few here could even find on a map. And that was only half of it. *Un vrai casse tête. Ou pire, un crève coeur.* A massive headache. Or worse, a broken heart. Or maybe both. Yes, definitely both; I was in the unenviable position of not needing to choose between headache and heartbreak. I could have both.

All the same, I chose door number three.

"I DREAMED ABOUT you last night," I told Nao Kao in the fall, as the leaves began to turn, as we in America began to come to terms with the extent to which 2020 was destined to be our collective annus horribilis.

"What was I doing?"

"You were mad at me. So mad. Shouting at me about drinking the water. We must have been in Laos because we were at lunch and I wanted a bottle – factory sealed and branded, preferably Danone – and you accused me of being dramatic and making a fuss."

"And?"

"You tossed your napkin onto the table, balled up your fists, jammed them in your pockets, and stalked away."

The laughing reaction popped up.

"Water is fine here. You can drink."

"Not likely. I'm sure it is fine for you, but Delhi Belly is for real, so I'm just saying, if I ever come to Vientiane, don't make me drink the water."

"Don't be ridiculous."

"Ha! That's what you said in the dream."

"So, what's the campus like these days? Quiet?"

"You have no idea. These should be the best months of the year. The band, high-stepping through the practice field in the bright afternoon, the drumline pounding out their rhythms."

"Go on."

"I am missing it all. The smell of burgers on the grill wafting from the cafeterias. The student orgs handing out ice cream cups alongside pamphlets and flyers. The great white event tents that should go up by midweek in preparation for the pre-game tailgates. This year, the music of student life has given way to the music of nature, to crickets and birds and the wind softly rustling the leaves. The library is all but empty, the fountains are drained, and the footpaths are deserted. So many signs, Nao Kao: keep your distance, wear your mask, complete your health screening. They are plastered everywhere.

"Only the shell of fall remains, the unbroken blue of the sky, the crisp mornings giving way to the sunbaked warmth of the afternoon, the green of the leaves yielding gradually to the yellows and oranges and reds, reminders that some rhythms, at least, remain untouched."

"Thank you," he said, "You made me feel just now like I was there again. Even after all these years, I miss it sometimes. It is still my second home."

∞ ∞ ∞ ∞ ∞

"GOOD MORNING, FOLKS. This is your captain speaking. We hope you have had a relaxing flight and enjoyed the hospitality of our Delta crew. It looks like we will have a bit of chop heading into Incheon today, so I have asked the flight attendants to begin the final meal service a bit early and prepare the cabin for landing before we begin our final approach. Thanks for bearing with us and being with us. Enjoy the rest of your flight."

The smells of breakfast filled the cabin, and the lead flight attendant was still translating into Korean when my friend Janelle appeared with my granola and poured me an extra glass of tomato juice. Like the sea-salted chocolates, it is another of those foods we are biologically programmed to crave in the high-decibel din of the airplane cabin. From her basket of warm bread, she offered me a second croissant. I accepted, happily.

I was still greedily eating in, quite literally, the experience of finally being back in the sky when Janelle appeared again.

"I've added it to my list, Miss Larkin. Liss. Vientiane and Luang Prabang, both. So whatever else happens, whatever you accomplish on this trip or don't, I thought you would like to know that at least I'm sold on traveling there."

It took me a minute to realize she was referring to my work, to the hearts and minds operation that is international education that I had shared with her, my belief in the value of global citizenship as an end in and of itself.

So many invisible threads bind the world together. Because of the little nudge I received to go to Michigan for grad school and because the paper pushers sent Nao Kao there instead of Minnesota, our lives had intersected. Because of that, I was on this flight; whenever she traveled to Laos, and whomever she met and touched along the way, Janelle would add her own invisible threads to the web. We think we control our lives and our destinies, but there's a mighty fine line between free will and the work of the universe; in those moments when control appears in our grasp, it's easy to forget that we are merely the momentary inhabitants of not only the planet, but the stars and all the great heavens, which are governed by forces unknown and unknowable to us. All of the matter that has ever existed or will exist is already here. We are but star dust.

I looked away so she would not see the tears that pricked my eyes.

∞ ∞ ∞ ∞ ∞

MOST OF THE country may have been in a daze in the fall of 2001, the jagged remains of the World Trade Center still literally stabbing skyward, but Nao Kao and I created our own world for one blissful moment in time. We explored one another hungrily from the afternoon we met at the museum through the falling of the leaves, like Adam and Eve and the forbidden apple – consequences be damned, the fruit was just too delicious. It had been a long time for both of us and, while I can't say what Nao Kao thought, I can say he, at least, was good.

"Have you ever been to East Lansing, to Michigan State?" he asked one afternoon as we lay in bed.

"Of course, I've been to East Lansing! Why do you ask?" Though they had made their academic careers at the University of Michigan, my parents met as graduate students on the banks of the Red Cedar, and my childhood and adolescence had been polka dotted with afternoons on that sprawling, park-like campus.

"There is a workshop at the College of Education I might like to attend."

I traced along his happy trail, tickling lightly to make him laugh.

"It's difficult to get to East Lansing from here."

That was true. No train, no bus, nothing but personal transportation conveyed students, many of whom had grown up together, between the rival schools.

"Mm-hmm." I turned to look at him. Kissed him lightly, teasing. Enough of this beating around the bush. If he wanted a ride, he would have to ask.

"Who else is going? Which class is this for?" I finally asked.

I was certain our illicit relationship shone all over our faces, and I was grateful that in this final semester before I would collect my diploma and leave Ann Arbor, we were not taking any of the same courses.

"The workshop examines the question of higher education as a public good or a private good, but it's not for a specific class."

I was intrigued despite myself, as he probably knew I would be.

"I thought it might be interesting," he continued, "and I've heard the campus is beautiful, especially this time of year."

"Oh, it is. Ann Arbor is the better town, but there's no comparison between the campuses – MSU wins that category every time."

"Yes, I would like to see another campus."

"It would certainly enhance your American experience."

"Yes, that is what I am thinking."

I sighed. Predictably, I had tired of this game before he did.

"How are you getting to East Lansing, Nao Kao? What is your plan?"

"I thought we could go together, la." He laughed nervously, perhaps sensing my frustration.

I turned back over and looked him squarely in the eyes. "Only if you ask me properly. Repeat after me: Liss, will you come to the workshop at Michigan State with me so that I will have a ride there?"

He laughed genuinely, but repeated my request verbatim, even adding the word *please*, which I had, as usual, forgotten.

So, it was that we came to find ourselves in East Lansing one gorgeous fall Saturday when the trees poured forth their colors, every shade of red and orange and yellow known to nature. Their rainbow put me in an uncommonly good mood when the workshop ended and we spilled out of the Erickson Hall kiva and into the bright sunshine. The light danced on the water, seeding the river with prickles of diamonds from one end of campus to the other. Squirrels – the bold and well-fed breed that inhabit college campuses from east to west – skittered across the sidewalk.

"Time to explore," I announced happily. "I might be a Wolverine, but I know a good campus when I see one and, honestly, this one is the best."

"Please tell me you do not want to rent the canoe." Nao Kao eyed the livery across the river from the College of Education, the aluminum hulls bobbing along the banks.

"No, no, enough about the canoes. This campus is great because of the gardens. And the ice cream store."

"The ice cream store?"

"Yes, they have their own dairy here. Not just the ice cream store – they actually have an entire herd of cows!"

"You're serious?"

"We can drive out to the farms if you don't believe me. Maybe we can even see the cow that has a window in its stomach to show the different chambers. A cow's stomach has four, you know?"

Nao Kao blanched.

"I'm kidding. Well not about the cow with the window in it. That really does exist. But going to the farms. C'mon, let's go for a walk."

The sky was brilliant blue as we meandered through campus.

"I'm going to give you a proper tour," I announced after lunch in the International Center. "I want to show you the bell tower and the library and all of the gardens. Especially the gardens. We can walk along the river."

From one end of campus to the other we roamed, Nao Kao occasionally reaching for my hand or slinging his arm over my shoulders in a way I would not have entertained in Ann Arbor, where spies, I was convinced, lurked around every bend, family friends and colleagues of my parents who might further incriminate me.

The trail inside the Sanford Natural Area was dappled with leaves, the sunlight filtering in through canopies of color giving it an ethereal quality. Around a bend we happened upon a doe browsing in the undergrowth. Nao Kao squeezed my hand hard, stopping me so that we would not startle it.

"This place is like a heaven," he whispered, bringing his arm around my waist. I could only nod my assent.

After the deer scampered away, I realized I had been holding my breath.

At the Dairy Store I ordered us doubles, *my treat*, I announced magnanimously, and handed Nao Kao a waffle cone heaped with mounds of chocolate chip cookie dough and strawberry ice cream, more than one person could, or should, reasonably eat, but of which he made quick work.

"Why did you ask for bread there?" he asked, eyeing the plastic bag I clutched with a few stale slices of bread inside.

"So that we can feed the ducks."

I steered us to the spot where the Red Cedar tumbles over a few tiny rapids, where a lone kayaker was taking advantage of the recent rains that had swollen the water from its summer trickle to practice his moves in the middle of the little river. I opened the bag and began tearing the bread into small pieces, handing them to Nao Kao to toss into the water. Ducks and geese flapped furiously for the scraps, their honks and quacks joining the happy chorus of fall around us. I laid back to watch the clouds floating across the sky.

"Thanks for coming," Nao Kao said quietly, settling next to me, our supply of duck carbs exhausted. He tousled my hair, brushing my cheek with the back of his fingers.

"Do you want to go to the planetarium?" I asked suddenly, nearly smacking my head into his as I sat up remembering the Saturday night shows I'd attended as a kid.

"I've never been to a planetarium. What's it like?" he asked, and I described the high dome and the simulated sky.

The last stop on our tour was Spartan Village.

"My parents lived here when they were graduate students at MSU, and my dad's parents before them," I told Nao Kao, oddly proud of something over which I could claim no credit. "Actually, I lived here, too, for the first few weeks of my life. Until they moved to Ann Arbor."

"I thought your mom was from New Orleans?"

My mom. Rachael Zick. The last person I wanted to think about right now. Especially with him, the man at the heart of the mother-daughter rift. I groaned inwardly. Why had I brought us here?

"Yes, she is. But one of her professors at Tulane encouraged her to apply to the graduate program at Michigan State. It's where she had earned her PhD. So that's what my mom did."

"Did you say your grandparents lived here, too?" Nao Kao asked, changing the subject. Perhaps he had picked up on the tension in my voice.

"Yes, my dad's parents. Actually, my great-grandfather also studied here. I broke a long chain of green and white by attending U of M!"

"I hope in several generations, there will be such a chain for my grandchildren's children," Nao Kao said thoughtfully. He squeezed my shoulder, drawing me to him.

"Thanks again for coming, Liss. For making this tour. For everything." For once I allowed him a quiet moment of contemplation, my hand resting gently atop his, my fingers curled around his index finger.

We ate dinner at Hobie's, broccoli and cheddar soup out of Styrofoam cups, while deciphering the signatures that covered the walls. I handed Nao Kao a Sharpie and encouraged him to add his name to the tangle of those who had come before.

"Only if you write yours, too," he said, hesitant, I think, about the impropriety, although clearly this was the thing to do. *Liss Miller*, I scrawled, in big bold letters, then, feeling naughty, added a heart and *Go Blue*.

"Always the mischievous one, aren't you?" Nao Kao asked, shaking his head, but his eyes were smiling.

"Guilty as charged. I am a terrible influence," I deadpanned, and, to prove my point, kissed him hard on the mouth as I handed him the marker.

Later, in the darkness of the planetarium, I let him return the kiss as an imitation Milky Way sparkled overhead.

∞ ∞ ∞ ∞ ∞

I LIFTED MY window shade and took in the cloud formations below. Once, I knew the difference between cumulous and cirrus clouds, but like so much else that I had forgotten, now I had to settle for simply knowing that once I knew. In the course of the thousand generations that separate me from that first human, Lucy, so few of us have been allowed to assume this seat in the heavens. Today's sky was no riot of reds, oranges, pinks, or purples, but still the privilege was not lost on me. Flying remains the best and most magical elixir I know.

I thought again about the absurdity of what I was doing. My first international flight in two years and it was not bound for London or Tokyo or even Dubai, but a city that few outside of *Jeopardy!* circles could pronounce or locate. A site visit to the university and then a few days of vacation in Luang Prabang. Business and pleasure. Like everything else connected to Nao Kao. Working with him to develop a collaborative online international course on the competing interests of the United States and China in Southeast Asia, we are eminently professional. Reputations are lost far faster than they are made and neither of us, I am certain, wished to endanger theirs. Methodically, we worked through the process of integrating the course he was teaching in Vientiane with the course I was teaching in Ann Arbor.

More than once as we worked, he accused me of being too serious, too regimented, too concerned about the small details that he knew would work themselves out. *Loosen up, la.* I was the tightly wound one, he the calming presence, old patterns repeating themselves after so many years. I could practically picture him removing his glasses and rubbing his eyes, his knuckle massaging the pressure points, yet managing to laugh despite himself.

Thus was our dynamic and, as more than one colleague noted, most people just don't have that much fun when they are debating the merits of the Sino-Laos Railway or the damming of the Mekong River and the resulting cratering of the downstream fish catches, to say nothing of the makeup of the Mekong River Commission. Such topics were, I knew, more esoteric than that which many undergraduate courses covered, yet the students immersed themselves in these joint lectures as I'd rarely experienced. Whatever our relationship, if the energy we brought to the classroom served to engage students more completely, to help them see Asia in a new light, to find the topic interesting and fun, I was all in.

Students often struggle with whether to travel to Europe or Asia if they know they can only study abroad once. One hundred times out of one hundred, I push them toward Asia. I am not, as a student once accused me of being, anti-Europe. Watching the morning mists rise off the Danube from the heights of the Buda Castle, or wandering Rome at Golden Hour, or the sight of Paris's cobblestones glistening in the rain – all of these are singular pleasures in life. As the pandemic closed in, my world shrinking in inverse proportion to the havoc the virus wrought, I frequently took solace in the memory of a stroll past the *bouquinistes* who line the Quai Voltaire, or of a breakfast of buttery croissants and strong, black coffee in Florence in sight of the River Arno. I reveled in the memory of early morning swims in the Aegean against a backdrop of Greek ruins, and of St. Petersburg's White Nights, the golden spire of the Saints Peter and Paul Cathedral gleaming through the early hours. What these experiences have in common, all of them, is the past.

Asia, on the other hand, is where we are headed. Oh, there is history aplenty, and stretching back thousands of years rather than hundreds, but history there is more fluid, as anyone who has visited an ancient temple adorned with what appears to be a giant disco ball in Vietnam can attest. History adapts, but does not constrict the way it can, say, in Paris, which has known building height restrictions since the seventeenth century.

In Singapore, I ran out of shampoo and when I called the front desk for more, it arrived by way of robot. I needed toiletries; I met the future. Likewise, for the multilingual robot called Pepper who has sized me up and helped me with my shopping in Tokyo's vaunted mecca for the sport, Ginza. Don't even get me started on the subway in Seoul or the laser light show along Shanghai's Bund. Europe is lovely. But if you want to see what is in front of us rather than behind us, we denizens of this rocky, watery orb called Earth, you have to go to Asia.

Much the way I had once felt he made me a better student, now I felt as we played to our strengths and bantered about the end of agricultural collectives and the funding of irrigation loans that Nao Kao made me a better professor. Whether he was in front of me or behind me, remained to be seen. To know that, I, too, had to go to Asia.

∞ ∞ ∞ ∞ ∞

"I JUST DON'T want to be an imposition."

"Liss, please consider something," as ever, my therapist, Stacy, was a source of sanity all through this pandemic life. I loved how she made me stop and take a step back from whatever issue I brought her.

"I want you to consider how easy it would be for him to – using your word – 'disappear' if that were what he wanted to do. If he wasn't interested in talking to you, he wouldn't. Period."

"But why text me at midnight to say 'Happy New Year' and then be all cagey and weird when I reply? It's like you're always telling me about being able to recognize when a guy is just not that into you. I mean, he probably had, what, twenty chats going, but here I am thinking he has something to say beyond 'hey, it's a new year over here.' And then he thinks I'm clueless. I don't need more people in my life who think I'm clueless."

"Don't think I'm going to let the fact that you believe the world thinks you are clueless slip by. We'll come back to that, but –"

She paused. More than once this therapist of mine had acknowledged the challenge of helping me make heads or tails of a man whom I had not seen in nearly two decades and whose background and culture were so far removed from anything she usually encountered. Still, it was her observations that helped me truly see the extent to which I had not only been hurt, but inflicted hurt as well.

"Liss, I don't know this man. But that won't stop me from saying, and with as much conviction as I have ever said anything, that you are the most jarring thing that has ever happened to him. And not once, but twice. Imagine you are him, in the middle of a happy weekend morning, and receive a friend request with your picture. What does that do to a man? To his heart?"

"It wasn't a friend request. It was LinkedIn."

Stacy glared at me.

"Do you want to know what I think about New Year's?"

"That's what I'm paying you for."

She laughed.

"He drunk dialed you."

"He – he, what?"

"Drunk dialed. You've never done that?"

I stared at her through the screen.

"No, Liss, of course you haven't. But most of the world has at one time or another. Plus, New Year's is sentimental as it is – *should auld acquaintance be forgot*. Surely you know that."

"I guess."

"You're a fascinating study, Liss. You don't get it, do you?"

I wasn't even going to try to defend myself. Stacy tried another approach.

"Maybe he didn't drunk dial you. Maybe he was intending to carry on a full-fledged conversation in the middle of the night. But then he got interrupted by someone."

"Like his wife."

"For example."

"But we're 9,000 miles apart. I think we are almost literally as far apart as it is possible to be on the planet. And we're just old friends."

"I imagine that the fact that you actually *did* have an affair before would not exactly reassure her. And he told you not once but twice that he was imagining being with you under the open sky, gazing at all the stars in the heavens. *With you*," she added again for emphasis.

"You're exaggerating. He told me he was imagining being with some friends under the open sky. He didn't specify whether I was one of the friends."

"And you didn't ask."

She had me there. Not only had I not asked, but I had changed the subject entirely, immediately asking him about work. If a more obvious "don't hit on me" move existed, I had not mastered it. In truth, I wasn't opposed to him hitting on me. But when that text popped up, well, to paraphrase Clark W. Griswold, I could not, would not, have been more surprised if I had woken up with my head sewn to the carpet. In my state of surprise, I panicked and froze and fled to high – read: safe – ground. Work.

"Well I'm asking. Would you?"

"Would I what?" I picked at the hem of my skirt, worrying the black thread between my thumb and my index finger.

"Would you go? There?"

"To Laos? Sure. I've never been. I could add it to my list."

It was during exactly one such conversation that Stacy had told me God hates a coward. Actually, she gave me the full quote, "God hates a coward. I don't actually believe this is true. But it's something to aim for," words of wisdom for which we can thank Laura Ingalls Wilder. Obviously, I still wasn't aiming in the right direction.

Stacy sighed.

"To see him, Liss. To sleep under the stars. Or—"

I cut her off.

"It's not a decision I'll ever be asked to make, so it doesn't even bear thinking about." I conveniently omitted the virtual tour of Luang Prabang he'd shown me, the imperative "come" with which he'd ended it. I was choosing to believe he'd spoken in jest.

Because I knew the answer was yes. If he asked in a way I could not brush off, I knew I'd be on the first flight. Whatever that may say about me and my moral failings, the answer was yes. Being able to admit this to myself, but never out loud, surely made me a coward, though I tried to assuage my ego by reminding it that I would never, ever make the first move. Not now and not in the future. My spirits buoyed as I silently improved my morals through this little calculus. My inner compass might not point true north some days, but it's not so broken that it doesn't know arctic from austral.

"But what if he asked?" I bristled at how Stacy seemed to have read my thoughts.

"But he never will. As sure as the sun rises in the east and sets in the west, cross my heart and hope to die," I added dramatically, the promise of little girls' secrets ringing in my ears.

"You do realize that this utter lack of clear communication is what led to everything in first place, don't you?"

I gave her my best thousand-yard stare.

"One final question, Liss. When you were married, did all of your friends know Jake's name?"

I nodded, puzzled by the turn her line of questioning had taken.

"But you still don't know his wife's name, am I right? And if I remember correctly, you had to wait for months before he would even confirm he was married?"

Now I followed.

"Why do you think that could be?"

She wasn't a therapist for nothing.

∞ ∞ ∞ ∞ ∞

"YOU SAID THAT you'd tell me." Nao Kao's words in their little gray bubble centered me.

"If I'm going to tell you the story, you have to promise me that you will be able to compartmentalize."

"Okay…."

"I mean it. Are you able to compartmentalize?"

"Yes"

"How well?"

"How well? Liss, what kind of a question is that? What does that mean? I can compartmentalize."

"I need to make sure, to be absolutely certain."

"I can do it. Tell me the story."

"I need to be able to work with you, Nao Kao."

"Yes, of course. It's fine. Please, tell me."

"If you are angry with me, even though I won't be able to do anything to change that, I still want you just to tell me. To acknowledge that so that at least I know."

"I won't be mad."

"You don't know that, Nao Kao. So just promise me, if you are mad, that you will tell me, and not pretend that everything is fine and you're not angry."

"Alright"

"Alright, what?"

"Liss! I will tell you if I am angry. And I promise to compartmentalize. Now will you please tell me whatever you want to tell me?"

"I've told you before that if we ever met in person again I would tell you the end of the story."

I hesitated again.

"Which was honestly just a dodge on my part because, realistically, I just…. well, what are the odds that would ever actually happen?" I continued.

"Stranger things have happened. But go on."

"See, I wasn't even sure if I should tell you. Actually, I'm still not. I mean, I never, ever planned to. But then I never planned to talk to you again, and definitely not for hours every week for months on end. So, then it feels like I should tell you, even though it's possible that you'll be angry and then you won't want to talk to me anyway, and then it's like, what was the point? Plus, it might be awkward to work together."

"Liss, enough, please. Just tell me."

∞ ∞ ∞ ∞ ∞

MY MIND RICOCHETED from Grand Haven to East Lansing and back to Grand Haven again as the plane was cleared for landing and the flight attendants made their final pass, returning jackets to owners, ensuring suite doors were secured open, proffering the basket of chocolate mints. Janelle paused her efficient movements to wish me luck, "whatever that means." Her eyes were smiling and I could almost see her laughing behind her mask.

"I hope to see you on another flight. I'd love to hear what happens." She winked and continued on her rounds of the cabin.

Grand Haven was the first slice of the past that I broached with Nao Kao, and I did so gingerly. Our conversations to that point had been almost entirely professional. Sure, he had begun to flirt with me lightly and occasionally, as though testing the waters. Considering what Grand Haven represented in my mind, at least, that it was the closest I could come to defining the line between friends with benefits and an affair of the heart, it seemed like dangerous territory.

Or, perhaps in one of those tricks of the mind, I had remembered the day and everything about it incorrectly, and it hadn't even dented the surface of his memory. When I asked if he remembered our day at the beach, though, he replied immediately.

"Oh, yes, vividly." Up popped one of those annoying, oversize stickers that would come to taunt me. This one had hearts for eyes. Asians like stickers. I know sixty-year-old men with sticker collections to rival any teenaged girl here.

"Just the other day I was going through the pictures I took when we were there," he added. I did not tell him that I already knew he had been through at least some pictures from his time in Michigan – or that he posted them only hours after he received my message.

"The waves were so big that day. Just crashing against the pier. You were worried about your camera getting wet," I teased.

"I was! I still can't believe I took so many pictures there."

"Why not? You took pictures everywhere. And look, even now, your personal business is photography."

I waited for the typing bubbles to reappear.

Like almost everyone I knew in Asia, Nao Kao was an entrepreneur who worked far beyond the capacity of most people I knew here. As best I could tell, he was the vice-rector of the leading university in Laos, a government consultant, and a professional photographer. I would not have been at all surprised to learn, would have bet money, that those three jobs, any one of which could have constituted fulltime employment on its own, was only a partial list of his commitments. He was Exhibit A in the data point that Asians work, on average, almost fifty percent more hours in a week than Americans. And we wonder why China is eating our lunch.

"But I could have better spent the time with you that day."

I blinked once, twice, three times as I processed that little line of text on my phone. That this man whom I had not seen in close to two decades, to whom a few weeks earlier I was no more than the whisper of a memory, regretted spending time on a beloved hobby during a day at the beach, and after everything else that had happened, took my breath away.

Even now my cheeks burned thinking about it.

∞ ∞ ∞ ∞ ∞

MY JUNIOR YEAR of college, "Everybody's Free to Wear Sunscreen" was the anthem that animated spring semester. The song, which elevated what might have been an obscure *Chicago Tribune* column to the fleeting heights of pop culture, punches above its weight. The real troubles in life, graduates learn, are the things they have never considered, the ones that will blindside them on an otherwise mundane afternoon. Moreover, in twenty years, these young grads, their unlined young faces so unbearably young, will happen upon old photos and contemplate in wonder how much possibility life held, and how marvelous they had once looked. Mixed in with the cautions, advice to be neither reckless with other's hearts, nor to tolerate those who are reckless with one's own.

Check, check, zing. At least the lyrics spare me the indignity of asking what to do when you are reckless with your own heart.

As for the recommendation to hold fast to old love letters, I had failed to heed that, too. A wiser woman would have printed Nao Kao's missives and saved them. They must have been lovely.

∞ ∞ ∞ ∞ ∞

As our conversation plunged along week by week, and as we became increasingly comfortable with both the present and past versions of ourselves, I mined territory with Nao Kao that I never could have anticipated. Our dynamic was the same, *we* were the same – yet wiser and more self-assured. When I stood back to consider the entire situation, I was struck repeatedly by how surreal it truly was. My mind refined the fact of Nao Kao's presence as waves work over glass, smoothing the jagged edges, rendering the clear opaque, wearing it all down to a nugget the size of a watch face whose presence in the sands of my life was undeniable, but whose origins were an utter mystery.

"I just remembered the most inappropriate thing; do you want to know what it is?" I would text him on occasion. Nao Kao always wanted to know. In this way, I reminded him that he was the only guy I had ever known, certainly the only one I had ever been to bed with, who did not prefer boxers to briefs. More than once I contemplated asking him if he had revised that opinion in the years since, but whatever lines we had crossed, well, that question screamed of driving the wrong way into oncoming traffic.

It was by teasing him about inappropriate memories that I also informed him how I had caught him looking – no, staring – down my shirt on more than one occasion, charges to which now, as a grown man well into his middle age, he could only plead "guilty as charged."

Yet there were times when I think Nao Kao, too, was caught in an internal tug-of-war, when he would go a little quiet, and I wondered how much was for my benefit and how much was for his. Still, the only time he seemed truly hesitant to travel down memory lane was when I mentioned the time at my apartment that he invited himself into my bed.

"Let's talk about anything but that," he replied, and so we did. After all, no matter my intentions when I sent my first, innocent little note on LinkedIn, I had ultimately come barging back into this man's life with all the subtlety of Hurricane Andrew. And if I still had places I was not yet prepared to probe, it seemed only fair that he did as well.

NAO KAO

Every time I considered telling her anything about my wife, I remembered Liss's old horror.

Stop it, Nao Kao. You're married. What are you doing?

What I am doing is enjoying Liss. She asked me once "what do we know that we don't know we know?" "Plenty," I replied, but when it came to omitting any mention of my wife, and later to dodging even her most direct questions, I could not plead guilty to knowing what I didn't know I knew. I plead guilty to knowing – or fearing – how Liss would respond. I merely guided the conversation in other directions.

After the initial shock, when her name appeared again in my inbox, and then the first time she texted me, I was delighted to stroll down memory lane. Aside from attending a conference with me in Seattle once, my wife has never visited the U.S. She does not speak English. She often mistakes Michigan for Minnesota, the ease of which I understand, these two foreign-sounding places, each covered in snow somewhere in the vast American interior. I understand, too, how our memories of that time differ. What was for me a time of transformation and adventure was for her a time of hopscotching from one hardship to another, with our daughter's touch-and-go bout with malaria the defining challenge of her days.

With Liss, I could reminisce freely, and indulge in nostalgia for a time and place that existed only in my memory – and hers. Beyond the ability to probe memories I had lost any hope of sharing, Liss brought levity to my days in the same ways that had drawn me to her originally. Yes, I could always depend on stimulating conversation, whether pertaining to politics or literature, but it was the mixture of exuberance and irreverence that kept me returning to the well. She deferred to me never, and poked me often.

"Wisdom comes with winters," she texted in the depths of January, adding, "I think you're in trouble."

Then, the self-deprecation. "Of course, I have just set a pan of cookies on fire, which I've extinguished to great effect with my little red fire extinguisher. So, the snow doesn't seem to be doing much for me, either. Bonus: my entire house smells like burning."

She would write me of visits to the acupuncturist gone awry, and seek my opinion on matters of professional development. She was middle-aged, yes, and divorced, and knew that life was not always kind, yet she managed to offer the same sense of escape now as when we were young and on the cusp of everything. Liss was thirty-one flavors compared to the vanilla that surrounded me.

After so many years of silence, I will not risk her retreating again.

LISS

GOOD TO HIS word, Nao Kao slathered me with sunscreen when we arrived at the beach, equal parts disgusted by the glop he squeezed out of the tube and pleased to have a legitimate reason for running his hands over me so openly there on the beach.

"You have to make sure you get it everywhere," I explained carefully, as one might to a child. "And rub it in evenly, so that I don't have streaks of it smeared on me. Or burn where there wasn't enough."

Methodically, his fingers worked the lotion into my skin.

"Shhh, la. This is not rocket science. I think I can figure out how to put the lotion on your back."

"I just want to make sure you do it right."

I heard him laugh and knew if I could see him that he would be shaking his head gently.

He started at the base of my neck, where his breath was warm against my nape as he leaned close to tease apart the knot of the halter, then smoothed the lotion into me. His thumb and fingertips worked in a circular motion covering the exposed skin at the top of my back before he gently brought the straps back together, one lavender and one navy, and wove them again into a little knot. I eased myself up onto my elbows so that he could lift my top more easily to coat the few inches of skin that peeked between the halves of the bathing suit. His fingers slid under my waistband, lingering for a moment well beyond the reach of the sun's rays. I shivered.

"I can't believe you like this stuff," he said, as worked his way back up, massaging more of the sunscreen into the small of my back.

"And the smell. You do this every time you are in the sun?" he asked, incredulously. His hands moved back down and onto the tops of my thighs. I turned over so that he could finish the stripe around my stomach. Speedos were much more practical for the pale people of the world.

"Sunscreen is the smell of summer at the beach," I teased him. And then, more seriously, "And anyway, 'like' has nothing to do with it. Look at me: I'm the color of Casper. Do you know how fast I would burn?"

"Never had that problem." We both laughed.

"Everyone can get skin cancer, you know. It might be less common for someone like you, but it can happen."

I turned to face him, and he pushed the hair away from my eyes. The motion reminded me to pull it back, to make sure my part was completely covered.

I bent my head forward for him to tell me if any of my scalp was exposed. He kissed the top of my head.

"So, do you want some?"

He looked at my slyly.

"If I say yes, you'll do it?"

"No, I'm going to get up and go ask the guy over there with the giant blue and white kite if he will rub it onto your back instead. Come on, Nao Kao. What kind of a question is that? What do you think?"

"I think you are ridiculous," he said.

"La," I answered, pulling him toward me.

"I think I need more there, in the middle," he said when I had gotten around to putting the sunscreen on his back.

"No, I'm pretty sure you're good, you're all covered."

"Maybe I just like the feel of your hands on my skin then." I realized I had missed his meaning the first time and smiled. I squeezed a bit more lotion from the tube and redoubled my efforts.

Later, he fiddled with his camera, taking a few pictures of the seagulls bobbing and diving over the beach. One stopped to peck at something in the sand.

"They don't stay still," he complained, "I won't waste any more film on birds."

He trained his camera on the kids playing in the waves in front of us.

"Let's walk out to the lighthouse," I suggested. The little red lighthouse at the end of the pier, over which waves washed hour after hour, and year after year, was the dominant feature of the broad, sandy beach. No trip to Grand Haven was complete without ambling down the pier to that squat red tower and contemplating the fathoms of fresh water spreading south to Chicago and west to Milwaukee.

"Or we could sit here."

"No, come on, it'll be fine," I said, thinking he was worried about leaving our things while we walked up the beach. Nao Kao sighed, but gamely let me take him by the hand and lead him down the pier to where the waves crashed and broke at the base of the lighthouse.

No sooner were we back than I asked, "Do you want ice cream? Let's go get ice cream."

"Didn't you bring a picnic?"

I nodded. "What, we can't eat ice cream before we eat lunch? It's not like I'm suggesting sundaes for breakfast. Not that there's anything wrong with that."

Nao Kao laughed.

"Liss, just sit here with me. Let's enjoy this. Please." He kissed me gently, his fingers trailing along my collar bone, from shoulder to sternum, as when he had asked me to wear a bikini.

"Am I allowed to read a book?" I asked, maybe a little more sullenly than I intended.

"I've brought one as well."

He fished his out of his backpack and settled in behind me, arranging his legs to either side of me. I leaned back against his chest, feeling the warmth of him against me. I snuggled in further. This made it almost impossible for him to see his book, which he set in the sand. He used his arms instead to brace us both on the beach, happy, I think, that at last I was still – and next to him.

He lifted a few fingers of sand and let it pass between his fingers.

"Time is like this, you know," he said quietly, half to me, and half to himself. "It slides so effortlessly, like sand through an hourglass. Blink, and you've missed it." I placed my hand over his and stilled his tawny fingers.

Late in the afternoon we walked the length of the broad beach, the golden sand warmed by the day's rays, even now in September. We etched our names into the sand and stood back to wait for the waves to erase them. A piece of driftwood caught his attention and he took more pictures, using the last of his film.

"Thank you for inviting me," he said, his tone suddenly solemn.

"Can you swim?" I asked suddenly. The lake was too cold, even for me, and the building waves suggested the warnings of undertow and rip current were not entirely for show.

"I can paddle around a bit," he replied. "But not swim properly, like you."

Nao Kao knew of my affinity for swimming, of the hours I had spent in the pool all through adolescence, and of the letdown I had felt in just missing the cut for the finals at the state meet my senior year of high school, the one goal, I told him, I had set for myself and failed to achieve. Torn between running cross country or swimming, I had chosen the latter on the basis of it not being the preferred hobby of my mother. Rachael Zick ran a good dozen miles daily, more when she was actively training for a marathon. By swimming, I freed myself of comparison to her – and fortunately I had been a mighty fine sprinter and an even better breaststroker. The lack of a state title still smarted.

"I saw the Gulf of Thailand a few times," he continued, "and also the Singapore Strait. But I have never seen the real ocean. Maybe someday." He sounded a bit wistful.

"Liar," I teased, "you've seen the whole ocean."

He turned toward me with eyebrows raised.

"You flew over it! You've seen it from edge to edge!"

"Incorrigible, Liss. That is what you are." He laughed.

"Do you ever think about how big the world is – and how small we are?" I asked. "Just look at this lake. Standing here, it's as vast as the ocean. But really it's just a mere drop of the planet."

"Infinitesimal," he agreed. "You want to see it all, don't you? You like to grab onto life with both arms and wrestle with it."

"There's nothing wrong with that."

"But maybe you make it harder for yourself than you need to. There's no failure in not experiencing everything between the tip of Mount Everest and the Dead Sea."

"You left out the moon and the Mariana Trench."

He smiled, but his mood was serious. He grabbed my hands and turned us so that we were face-to-face. When he leaned toward me to kiss my forehead, I saw his Adam's apple bob as he swallowed hard. He stood back again and looked at me.

"Always with the repartee. But to see it all, to do everything, you must only race from sunrise to sunset. You will miss the moment. Sometimes it is better to stop and appreciate what you have, rather than worry about what is next. Besides what will you have left for the next lifetime if you have seen and done it all before?"

I smiled weakly, the words for the moment escaping, washed away like the sands of time.

We made our way back to where we had left our blanket on the beach.

"See, I told you it was okay to leave it here," I gloated again.

"I'm glad that I was wrong. Now let's sit."

"We should go soon," I said. "It's a long drive. And the sun sets earlier these days."

"Just lie with me here for a little longer. I want to remember this. This is a day when I have wished I could freeze time, to stay in this moment forever. With you."

He turned my face toward him and reached over to pull the tie from my hair.

"I think it's late enough you will not sunburn your head now. I want to look at you like this."

He ruffled my hair loose. Red waves cascaded across my face. I closed my eyes.

"Look at me, too, Liss. Please. I want to remember this."

He draped his arm across me, leaned in, and kissed me deeply.

"Not here, Nao Kao, there are still people all around!" He sighed, defeatedly, shaking his head, his eyes still locked squarely on mine.

I let him lie a few more minutes with his arm across my back, our faces turned together just inches apart, before I told him the day was officially done.

He groaned. Despite his protests, I made him rise from the blanket and help me shake the sand from it as best we could, folding it neatly into a square. Hand-in-hand we walked away from the water. I saw him glance over his shoulder as we reached the parking lot, one last look for posterity.

The memory faded from my mind as, heavily, the plane landed with a jolt. We bumped a bit along the tarmac, the brakes screaming against our momentum.

Watching my fellow passengers collect their belongings and prepare to leave the aircraft I was struck yet again by the overt, if entirely unconscious, displays of cultural difference. Everyone who travels is aware of the American tourist stereotypes: tennis shoes, baseball caps, backpacks, slouched shoulders, sagging pants, and an expansive gait that have all been caricaturized far and wide. But the differences are so much deeper than what we wear or how we carry ourselves. I noticed the Asian passengers waiting patiently around me, the men mostly in sport coats and loafers, the women tidy and trim, their makeup in place, hair combed neatly, attired in clothes I would pull from my closet only to go to work.

By contrast, to a person, the Americans wore athleisure wear. They shifted their weight obviously from side-to-side trying to see ahead down the aisle to the cause of the delay, tugging at the handles of the bulging bags they had carried on. The seats they – we – had occupied were easy to pick out; the pillows and blankets a-jumble, chocolate wrappers and empty water bottles competing for space alongside discarded magazines and the other detritus of a long flight. I watched the Korean woman across the aisle from me carefully returning her pillows to the plastic bag they had come in, checking each crevice for an escaped belonging. Discreetly she wadded a wrapper into the palm of her hand next to her passport.

I love to teach the elements of culture to students, to share with them the quirks of personal space and time (hint: "tomorrow" does not always mean tomorrow), the hierarchical nature of society, the practical implications of collectivism and individualism. All of these dimensions are important, but the one I always encourage students to pay the greatest attention to is high-context versus low-context.

High-context cultures are indirect, nuanced, and rely heavily on non-verbal cues. Low-context cultures, and the people who embrace them, are explicitly, expressly clear. Low-context communication is frequent, and off-the-cuff. High-context is deliberate and carefully considered, the message typically wrapped in layers, like an onion skin. If a Japanese person ever tells you something will be difficult, they do not mean it can be accomplished with sufficient effort. The project is dead on arrival.

High-context is a man wearing a shirt one woman gave him to dinner with another woman.

∞ ∞ ∞ ∞ ∞

IF THE BOOKS I suggested for Nao Kao these past few months landed with a bit of a thud, the ones he recommended to me were on the mark. Beginner's luck – or perhaps he simply did know better what made me tick. Either way is possible, but say what you will about Myers-Briggs, he pegged all four of my indicators in a single go one morning. I'm not sure he even thought about it.

He asked me to guess his, and I demurred, but when he asked a second time, well, I never was good at denying him. Ultimately, I think I got two correct, the same odds as if I had been flipping a coin. But if my lack of insight stung, he had the good grace to thank me instead for playing his game.

In any case, I have long held that books, like people, come into our lives when we need them, and that was certainly the case with Alan Watts. By the time Nao Kao suggested I read the works of the sage philosopher, we in America, in most of the world outside the tightly controlled countries of mainland Southeast Asia, had lived through months of pandemic and could only guess whether the light at the end of the tunnel heralded sunshine or an oncoming train.

Nao Kao resisted recommending anything at first, telling me that if I read books because he suggested them, I would be influenced simply by knowing he had liked the book. Nonsense, I argued, and either he got tired of the argument or decided to put his hypothesis to the test, because I woke up one morning to a list of titles he thought I might enjoy. Watts dominated, and spoke to me in ways that would prove to be a mid-pandemic balm.

As I read, I was shocked by Watts's foresight – the fact of him writing in 1951, that the emerging technologies simply enabled one to pursue the future ever faster, while the planets, he remarked, were still circling the sun, and whether they got anywhere in the process or traveled faster in order to arrive yielded the same answer as it had decades before.

Like Jerry Maguire and Dorothy, Watts had me from his own hello: our lives are naught but a mere spark of life sandwiched between the darkness of eternities that come before and after we draw precious breath. Echoes of that favorite line of mine from *Cutting for Stone*, that we arrive in this life unbidden, ricocheted through my synapses.

It was in response to Watts's musings that I shared with Nao Kao my own life's philosophy, lifted so heavily from that *Chicago Tribune* column-cum-graduation anthem: one could worry, if so inclined, but the act of worrying had the same effect on future events as trying to solve a math problem by chewing gum. The things we really needed to worry about were not the things that were likely to cross our minds, worried or otherwise.

"I think global pandemic qualifies for most of us," I wrote to Nao Kao when I sent him a lengthy treatise on my thoughts.

"I like what you wrote about this book better than the book itself," he replied. "If you read the others, you should send your thoughts on those, too."

His own thoughts he kept to himself.

MY PANDEMIC CLEANING binges had not merely unearthed old textbooks and term papers. The motherlode was the box of old journals. When I came to the little bound book whose dates should have covered the most consequential events of my lifetime, what I found instead was a binding shorn of its pages. From Labor Day until Thanksgiving 2001, only a few jagged scraps remained; I could not even determine how many pages had been so viciously torn from their home.

Perplexingly, I had left one final entry intact, hastily jotted, if the penmanship was any indication, on the Monday after Thanksgiving.

I must learn not to carry the weight of the world on my shoulders. I must teach myself not only to forgive, but to forget.

When I shared those two dozen words with her, Stacy was elated. This was the answer to the nagging question of the blank spaces in my memories of Nao Kao, of that she had no doubt.

"One of the things I admire about you is that you take what you want. You set your mind to something and you do it, no matter the consequence. When you set a goal, no matter how improbable, you achieve it," my therapist told me.

"I am not sure I follow what this has to do with why I can't remember anything."

"Liss, do you ever stop to listen to what you are saying? You set your mind to forgetting. You wrote it down. You left those words, that instruction to yourself, when you left nothing else."

"But that's part of the problem. I can't remember why I didn't leave anything else. Is it because I wanted to forget? Or is it because I may as well have slapped a sticker on the front that said, 'Hester Prynne was here' if I'd left it and anyone found it?"

She laughed. Even when my sentiments were serious, my delivery got her.

"It doesn't matter. The point is that you set your mind to forgetting. Maybe if you wrote that you wanted to forget for twenty years and then remember, you would have done that. But you didn't. And you have forgotten so thoroughly that we are having this obtuse conversation about the mechanism for forgetting rather than why it was so important to do so in the first place."

Why it was so important to do so…

"Yes…I do always believe 'mind over matter.' And that when your back is to the wall, it's always better to go out swinging than looking –"

"And if you are going to swing, it better be for the fences," she finished for me. "For what it's worth, in all the years I have been a therapist, I have never encountered a mind like yours, a mind so thoroughly capable of shutting the fire doors, slamming them! – and locking behind them anything you set your mind to – it certainly seems in this instance you've cleared the fences."

"And just think – I don't even like baseball."

"But you do like him."

I sat silently for a moment, contemplating the way she could do this to me. I hated the way she could make me squirm.

"And I'm going to venture that he likes you."

I waited.

"Don't scowl at me, Liss. You pay me good money to hear what I think."

I laughed.

"Have you ever served jury duty, Liss?"

"God, no!" I shook my head.

"Well I have. And in the voir-dire, the prosecutor often asks prospective jurors for their definition of reasonable doubt. Reasonable doubt does not mean that there is absolutely, positively, not one iota of a chance that a juror could conceive of the defendant's guilt. The answer the prosecutor seeks, that he or she will repeat ad nauseum if necessary, is that without such contrivance of the facts, without bending and twisting them to an *un*reasonable degree, if the only doubts that remain are unreasonable ones, then the prosecutor has done their job and proven guilt beyond a reasonable doubt."

"If the glove fits, you must convict," I interjected.

"Something like that, Liss. And it seems to me that the only doubts that remain as far as whether Nao Kao, as you put it, 'likes you-likes you' are of the unreasonable variety. More simply, if it walks like a duck and talks like a duck, odds are it's a mallard and not heretofore unknown exotic water fowl."

∞ ∞ ∞ ∞ ∞

I MADE MY way through the airport, taking in the changes since I was last here. Incheon was once a shopper's paradise, but now many of the

136

designer boutiques were shuttered, the seating areas filled with reminders to allow space for those around you. Maybe it was better that way – jetlagged and weary, I'd more than once fallen into the trap of layover shopping, returning home with hundred dollar face rollers and designer bags I never would have purchased without the benefit of travel-induced brain fog.

Freed of the distraction of shiny objects, my mind spiraled inward, down the same rabbit holes it had explored now for months.

He certainly was not my first. I was a world-weary grad student by the time I met Nao Kao. He wasn't even my third or fourth, but whether the work of chemistry or some weird cosmic connection or merely the power of knowing that what we had could not last, he left me molten from stem to stern and that, well *that,* was a new experience. But it was never just the physical pleasure. Being with Nao Kao was equal parts terrifying and exhilarating. The flame that burns twice as bright burns half as long, and I, at least, did not need to look at a calendar to know that the countdown was on.

Matter can be neither created nor destroyed, but merely changes form. So, too, emotion. Whatever conflict I still felt over the origins of the affair, the way Nao Kao had introduced himself so cavalierly into my bed, dissipated – only to be replaced by a growing, gnawing guilt.

The first time at his apartment, I noticed a picture frame lying face down on the dresser. I wondered whether he'd placed it that way for my benefit, to spare some small measure of further guilt lest I sense judgment in their dark eyes, or for his. Perhaps he hoped to avoid any questions I might ask – or the possibility that I'd feel the judgment emanating through the air and turn tail and run, the flight reflex triumphing over fight. I allowed myself to consider, too, that the position of the photo was no temporary measure, that it might well have been transformed for him from a warm reminder of home into a bald-faced accusation. Perhaps he felt their judgment even more acutely than I – it was he, after all, who had promised to have and to hold, not I. Nowhere was it written that I had a monopoly on compunction and remorse; for all I knew, those were the recurrent themes of both our days.

When he slipped out of the room, I sneaked a peak and confirmed what I already knew intuitively: it was a family photo, each parent holding a baby, each baby with tiny fists balled, one of them captured mid-kick. The expressions of Nao Kao and his wife were inscrutable, as was the backdrop. I wondered fleetingly which daughter was now fighting malaria as I returned the frame to its facedown position just before Nao Kao reappeared. The next time I visited, the picture had been removed entirely, tucked away, perhaps in a desk drawer or on a closet shelf. Whatever his reasons, at least the most obvious reminder of what we were doing remained out of sight.

Nao Kao had the unnerving habit of watching me intently, always. I never stayed the night, and for reasons I could not put my finger on, but the existence of which probably should have told me everything I needed to know, we no longer met at my apartment. As a result, when I was with him, in the bright light of day, my nakedness was more exposed than I have ever been. I would ask to turn a light off and he would plead to leave it on. In fact, as soon as the faintest shadow appeared, he wanted to turn more lights on, not off. "I like to look at you," he said simply and unabashedly when I complained.

Once he left to grab a towel, and then, his lean body glistening with sweat, asked if I wouldn't just hop in the shower with him.

It is the only thing I refused him, at least until the very end. It was hard enough to feel that every flaw, every little dimple in my flesh, was on display as we lay in bed, lights ablaze. A shower was simply a bridge too far.

Often, I would close my eyes, imagining that if I couldn't see, maybe he couldn't either. On the occasions when he noticed, he would ask me to open my eyes and to look into his.

"I want to see you," he said, and I reminded him that was what his eyes were for, not mine.

"Not only your body, you, all of you. Eyes are the window into the soul. I want to see yours."

He would place his finger under my chin and tip my head until our eyes were level. "Now I can see you," he would whisper quietly, the sound of a man content with the moment.

Perhaps it was because I felt my soul withering that I was so keen to hide it.

Increasingly I was parrying arguments from my mother, whom I thought of increasingly not as My Mom but as The Formidable Rachael Zick, as I had heard more than one student – or faculty member – refer to her over the years. That she wasn't wrong (because honestly, Rachael Zick was never wrong) only heightened my unease. Ever the scholar, she had honed her debate and delivery skills in front of audiences far more hostile than I. She knew how to keep her arguments narrow, how to claim and hold high ground. She never wavered from that first accusation she had flung so viciously the day we went to Grand Haven.

"He is a married man: have you no shame?" she'd demanded so self-righteously.

I'd only been able to gawp that day, but now I had my answer.

"Actually, Mom, yes. But I am not so sure about Nao Kao." Not that I had the nerve to utter it.

Late into the night he would message me after I left, checking that I was home, asking what I was working on, occasionally confirming his understanding of some arcane journal article. At some point Nao Kao decided I should teach him French, and I began with the basics before he corrected me. He was not interested in learning the language of the classroom or the boardroom or even the ballroom. Nao Kao cared not how to conjugate verbs or of the difference between the formal and informal you forms. What Nao Kao wanted to learn was only fit for the bedroom.

No matter how late into the night we exchanged messages, whatever vocabulary lessons we covered, we never spoke about what we were doing. The hallmarks of high-context, indirect communication was stamped all over both of us that fall and the closest either of us ever came to acknowledging the extent of our impropriety was the afternoon Nao Kao asked me to listen to a new song he had just heard on the radio for the first time that day. The artist's name was Shaggy and anyone of a certain age can recite the chorus by heart, the man caught red-handed in flagrante delicto with the girl next door. It was the closing lines that seared me, though, the admonishment that the guy might think he's a player, but really, he's just completely lost.

Whatever response I may have made upon hearing the song has been repossessed by the ravages of time.

Then and now I was forced to consider the possibility, though, that Nao Kao really was just a player, completely lost, all alone in a foreign country by himself, no worries about being caught. I thought it would be a one-night stand. Later I assumed it was a fling. Only much later did I consider the ephemeral nature of the line between a fling and an actual "thing." Blurry or bright, lines exist, and they matter. I cannot say what he thought, on which side of the line Nao Kao may have stood, and I cannot remember anymore what I thought, but I do know what I heard and I do know what I said – and what I didn't.

I never said I love you. Neither did he.

∞ ∞ ∞ ∞ ∞

I WAS IN too deep not to tell him now. I turned off the mockery of the debate on the television behind me, three septuagenarians fighting to talk over one another, and I closed the extra browser windows I had open. I focused my attention on the Messenger box with Nao Kao's name, dusted off the cobwebs in my mind, and pushed away the ghosts.

"Well I almost told you last week, when I was giving you such a hard time about how I just could not believe how, well, unprepared you were."

"Go on, it's okay."

"I've told you before that in hindsight, well, I'm sure it doesn't probably say the best things about me as a person, about my character, but it felt like my best option at the time. My only option."

"Everything was just so impossible, the whole situation, and I just could not see my way clear. Nor did I have anyone I could talk to. Including you."

"You can always tell me whatever you want, it's okay."

"Yes, you say that. Now and then. But this…."

I was stalling, simultaneously willing myself to go through with what I wanted to say – what I should say – and seeking to extricate myself from the conversation. God hates a coward. I plunged ahead.

∞ ∞ ∞ ∞ ∞

OF ALL THE perks Medallion status confers, the one I prize above all is the Club membership. The seats are comfortable and the food is nice, but the showers are a godsend, with water pressure that is built to blast the stress and grime of travel off a passenger's weary body, and that is no metaphor. I had last showered less than twenty-four hours earlier, but it felt like a lifetime as I let the water pelt against my face. My life made sense. Risk averse to a fault, I could reason a problem to death. Ergo, I had no business here in Seoul, no business traveling to Laos, no business exchanging more than the briefest howdy-do with Nao Kao. If I stood here long enough, perhaps the water would finally clear my head, could literally as well as metaphorically wash away my

140

doubts, lifting the haze, as a good rain does to a blanket of smog, so that I might piece it all together clearly for once. I think I actually prayed that there in the anonymity of an airport lounge shower.

I tried to remember when I first asked myself whether the ball was in play. It could have been when he asked if I still wore the watch I had sported every day in graduate school – and then described its silver links and charcoal and pink face. If not then, perhaps it was when he revealed the way he pictured me still looking over my shoulder in class, the tilt of my head just so. I must have asked the question when he shared that this, *that I*, had stayed with him for far longer than I could believe. And only a fool *wouldn't* have asked the question just from counting up the proliferation of heart-shaped stickers and emojis that dotted so many of our conversations. Whether I was dense or whether I was in denial, made no difference. The truth is that I didn't ask the question. It wasn't when I first asked myself if the ball was in play at all. Whatever my subconscious may have understood, it would have remained there, below the surface, if not for Stacy. *If it walks like a duck and talks like a duck, it's probably not heretofore unknown exotic water fowl.* Nao Kao was a duck. The ball was in play.

And then he got bored. Or at least that was my impression. As always, the truth is more complex. We don't properly communicate. I would like to put that all on him, but whenever I think that, I am taken back to how I handled everything with Jake, for years, or even the openings that Nao Kao presented and I rebuffed. *'I'm imagining sleeping under the open sky with friends and gossiping about old professors and new students.' 'So, what do you have on your docket at work this week?'* Worse yet was the package with which I had undoubtedly blindsided him just days before this flight.

As they say, it takes one to know one. Or maybe it takes one to tolerate one. In any case, whether he was bored or busy or covering his tracks at home; whether we had simply said all there was to say; or whether we had exhausted all the words that could be exchanged between old friends in the midst of global despair, and without so much as a plan to meet for lunch, or even the hope for a plan to meet, Nao Kao faded to black.

Which is why the Valentine was such a surprise.

∞ ∞ ∞ ∞ ∞

I HANDED THE shower pass back to the attendant at the desk, catching snippets of the animated conversation she was having with a passenger who was learning belatedly that he was not actually booked through to Ulaanbaatar. I might feel myself well-traveled strolling through the terminal of any domestic airport in the U.S., but Incheon was a great reminder of how vast the world was, and how much of it I had yet to explore. "I haven't been everywhere yet, but it's on my list." I had seen that declaration on more than one airport wall, and it was certainly true for me.

"Seven *thousand* dollars!" the passenger exploded. "But that's preposterous! It was supposed to be paid!" I hurried off before either of them misinterpreted my snickers.

∞ ∞ ∞ ∞ ∞

"SO REALLY, YOU would take a job anywhere in this country, anywhere at all?" Nao Kao asked for probably the thirtieth time.

"I've told you before I'm not sure why that surprises you so much. Yes, I want the best job I can find."

"But you already turned down the job at the University of Virginia."

"Because when I learned more about the job, it seemed boring."

It was a Saturday afternoon in late October, and a cold rain was falling intermittently from the leaden skies overhead. We were on Nao Kao's couch having the same conversation we had had too many times lately. Quietly, he rolled the thin, gold bracelet I always wore between his fingertips.

"And the job in Oklahoma."

"I told you: that one didn't pay enough."

"And the one at Tufts."

"Not enough vacation time."

"Liss, la. Maybe you are too picky."

All fall I had been interviewing for jobs at universities from the east coast to the west coast and points in between, adjusting to the new rhythms of travel in a post-September 11 world. The first time I had been nervous, and I still had not fully adjusted to the absence of friends and family waiting at the gate, but there was, as they say, nothing to it but to do it.

I sulked in silence.

"Staying here and enrolling in the doctoral program is definitely not an option?" Nao Kao asked quietly. He knew that was my preference, and that I'd been meeting with every faculty member I knew in an attempt to circumvent the unwritten but understood – and rigid – rules.

"Nope. No work experience, no way. For once I've run into a rule I can't seem to talk my way around. The program director has told me definitely that I can apply in two years."

Assuming I land a job and accumulate the requisite work experience.

Nao Kao poked my ribs, working to elicit a smile, even a forced, half-hearted one.

"Tell me again what happened on the trip to Philadelphia last week," he said.

I squared myself to face him and drummed my fingers against his chest, then traced a lazy pattern on his stomach under his shirt. I felt his muscles tense under my light touch.

"You already know. I don't want to talk about it again."

"I'm sorry, Liss," Nao Kao's fingers found mine and squeezed. "You'll find a job."

"That's easy for you to say. Your future is already mapped out for you," Nao Kao's face flickered with disappointment at how easily those words slipped through my lips.

"Besides, I wanted that one." I leaned forward and kissed him, our tongues meeting momentarily before I changed my mind.

"Time for me to go, Nao Kao," I said as he sighed in resignation.

The job in Philadelphia was the one I wanted above all the others. Assistant Director of International Programs. It consisted largely of extensive travel around the U.S., hitting all the fall and spring fairs to recruit students from other universities to enroll in summer language, internship, and study abroad programs. Yet, almost miraculously, there were no quotas by which one was to be judged, and the salary was surprisingly good.

From the start – when I'd arrived at the ticket counter at 5:00am on Monday morning only to discover the university had not completed the booking process for my ticket – to the finish – when a greasy, leering cabbie returned me to the Philadelphia airport in the midst of a fierce autumn storm that would soon cancel my return flight – the interview had been a disaster. For if my adventures with the airlines weren't testing enough, the universe had seen fit to install me in accommodations with a broken radiator that roasted me all through the night and ensured I spilled soup literally into the lap of my prospective boss at lunch.

One of my professors loved to remind us of the value and importance of living with ambiguity. At first, I hadn't understood her meaning. Now that I did, I wanted nothing more than for her to keep her ambiguity to herself – hers and mine. Not that there was anything ambiguous about the job in Philadelphia. Nor, I was increasingly concerned, the predicament that threatened to overshadow even my job search.

∞ ∞ ∞ ∞ ∞

"WOULD PASSENGERS ON Korean Air flight 7833 with service to Vientiane please make their way to Gate 256 for the screening process. Boarding will begin in thirty minutes. Korean Air flight 7833 to Vientiane, please make your way to Gate 256. Thank you."

I checked my watch: 10:00 p.m. I tried to remember whether the time difference between Seoul and Ann Arbor was twelve hours or thirteen, and if that made it 9:00 a.m. at home or 10:00 a.m. or even 11:00 a.m., but my brain felt like soup. The fact that it did not matter what time it was in Ann Arbor landed like a revelation. And to think I had done this twenty-plus time a year for over a decade. I floated through the lounge and down the escalator, the star of my own dream. How appropriate.

"I had a dream about you the other night," I told Nao Kao as winter faded to spring, the sun setting not only later, but further north each evening in its annual trek across my picture windows. Only at the equinoxes did it set in the dead center of those big, west-facing panes of glass.

No response. I looked at the time, calculating the new difference: we jumped an hour ahead; Laos did not. I wondered if Nao Kao had disappeared into a meeting or just from this conversation.

In for a penny, in for a pound. I forged ahead anyway.

"I was at a food court in Ikspiari, you know, in Tokyo, trying to decide what kind of noodles to order. They had all the usual choices: soba, udon, ramen. And there was something new, something I'd never heard of before, called khmer noodles."

"Why Khmer and not Lao? Or Hmong?"

"I don't know. Because it was a dream and dreams are weird?" At least I had gotten a reaction.

I thought about a dream a friend had shared with me recently in which she and I had been flying to Hong Kong only to end up on a

144

cruise ship in Amsterdam. Displeased with the turn of events, I had asked the captain to set course for another port, as the one we were headed for was "inconvenient to my connecting mode of transportation."

"Anyway. Just as I was ordering them as khmer noodles you appeared and began shouting at me that 'it's pronounced kʰmae!' You were plenty exercised about the point and made rather a scene. It was quite rude of you, really, and most un-Japanese. And then you disappeared – poof! – as suddenly as you showed up."

The laughing reaction popped onto my screen.

"Then what?" Nao Kao asked, shocking me.

"I decided I would rather eat udon."

More laughter.

"I still don't understand why I'm in a dream with Khmer," he said.

"Right. Got it. Well, I don't understand why in the only two dreams you've ever appeared in, you were shouting at me in both of them. I'm not sure why you're doing so much shouting, but if we ever do meet in person, you're going to have to promise me ahead of time that you're going to tone it down. No shouting."

"I'll try. But if you come, you will have to promise not to mix me up with those Cambodians."

I sent him a laughing sticker.

Try as I might, as an American, I found it difficult to appreciate the seriousness of the rivalries and tensions between the countries of Mainland Southeast Asia. We might blunder on our foreign policy, we might have had a president who tried to stare down Angela Merkel and the rest of the G-7, but our place in the world was never truly threatened. Other countries were unlikely to send tanks rolling down our highways or to arbitrarily redraw our borders. Our territorial waters were not in dispute. If there was a river to be dammed to the detriment of those downstream, we were the ones doing the damming, not the ones whose lives and livelihoods were threatened as the fish stocks diminished and the riverbeds ran dry. *Red Brotherhood at War* was not hyperbole.

In grad school I had tried to make a comparison between the rivalries in Southeast Asia to those between Texans and New Yorkers. It seemed fair to me; after all, there had been a Civil War here, too. I had already told Nao Kao about the time I heard a couple of cops cursing the 'damn Yankees' over coffee at a North Carolina Waffle

House, as though the cars driving south from Rocky Mount had all originated north of the Bronx.

From the amount of time Nao Kao contemplated his response before replying, I knew he thought I was off the mark.

"I suppose it is similar," he said carefully, "if Texans and New Yorkers had been rivals for centuries. Or if they fought their long and bloody war within the lifetime of most of their current populations. And with tanks and machine guns." Indirect to the last, he would force me to infer that he agreed to disagree, even on such an objective topic. What the textbooks say is true: direct people frequently feel they have to work very hard to understand indirect people, and that can be an exhausting endeavor. Amen.

That old conversation had come back to me as we worked on our current course. I sent him a passage from *Brother Enemy*, about the war between Vietnam and Cambodia in the 1980s, which concludes with a final observation from the author that, effectively, Cambodia is a child with Thailand and Vietnam as the parents, though he quickly acknowledged that Cambodians would bristle at this suggestion. I asked Nao Kao what he thought of the analogy.

Of course, they would bristle at the thought, he wrote, and I could almost feel his irritation coming through the screen. Cambodia and Laos had been yoked together by France during that country's forays into colonialism in Southeast Asia. Nao Kao might have preferred a dream featuring Lao noodles to one starring Khmer ones, but it was immediately clear whose side he would take in a larger geopolitical debate.

If the Vietnamese wanted to position themselves as the Big Brother of the former colonies of Indochina and had used their relative might to ensure a generation of schoolchildren had learned by heart a tune of their devising that praised the "brotherhood" of Vietnam, Laos, and Cambodia, Nao Kao's disdain for the Thai rang through just as clearly.

"Now the Thais," he explained once, "they always feel they are the smarter, superior race. Just because they were never colonized, even if they weren't entirely free of European influence. But then, nothing here ever is."

His words rang in my ears as the barrage of announcements filtered through the terminal around me, gate changes, mechanical troubles, and last calls for boarding for destinations from Sapporo to

Xining, Colombo to Kuala Lumpur, every last one of them imparted in English.

∞ ∞ ∞ ∞ ∞

SEPTEMBER AND OCTOBER are the glory months on college campuses, nowhere more so than in the north. They are the months the music permeates: the brassy notes of the marching band, the crowd noise and hip hop pumped into, and subsequently out of, stadiums while linebackers and running backs vie for starting positions. From the open windows of dorms the length and breadth of campus come the notes of Mozart and Bach, Katy Perry and Taylor Swift, Eminem and the Backstreet Boys, the Beatles, and Simon and Garfunkel, boy bands, hip hop, rap, and jazz, music of every genre and every age. In the later afternoon, when even the nightiest night owls have ventured forth, traffic begins to build on the main thoroughfares, windows open, the last warmth of fall breathed in, the bass thumping out.

Even in the shadow of September 11, there was a misty magic to those months. After a lifetime of autumns in Ann Arbor, the final six as a student, I knew this was the last, and I reveled in it, savoring every trip across the leaf-strewn Diag, every steaming cup of joe from Espresso Royale, every trip up the great, white steps of Angell Hall. Nao Kao never did make it to a football game, but for the rest of it we checked the boxes: an afternoon at Elbel Field watching the band refine their footwork for game day, more than one heaping ice cream cone from Stucchi's, sticky pitchers of warm beer on the patio at Dominick's, and always the *Michigan Daily* crossword.

"What is a five-letter word for piles of wood?" I would message Nao Kao late at night, when I was supposed to be working on my portfolio.

"How would I know? Why don't you look it up online?"

"That would be cheating."

"But asking me is not."

"No, phone-a-friend is totally legit."

My mind went back to the lecture halls of my undergraduate years, statistics and psychology and economics and the rows of students surreptitiously filling in the little squares, half-an-ear to the probability of withdrawing one red marble from the bag of forty-eight black and twelve red, half-an-ear to the kid next to them mumbling his guess for fifty-two across. Nao Kao reminded me almost every time I asked that he was no fan of this game, but on this, I did not give in, even if he never did acknowledge knowing the answer to a single clue.

"Have you ever been to a fraternity house?" Nao Kao asked me one afternoon.

I laughed.

"More times than I should admit."

"What's it like?"

"Disgusting."

"I mean really."

"Me too, Nao Kao. They're filthy inside. They reek, the floors are covered in decades of spilled beer and god knows what else, and – if they're having a party, which, c'mon, these are frat houses, they're always having a party – they're so loud you can't hear yourself think."

"Sounds enticing."

"Nao Kao! Don't even think about it! They're the purview of undergrads, not geriatric graduate students like us."

"Anthropological research. Just from the outside."

"What's that?"

"A study of the frat houses. A part of my American experience, no? We can make a little tour. This Saturday. You can be my guide."

"Only if you let me take you to tea at Martha Cook the next week. I want your research to be well-rounded – you have to see that it's not all *Animal House*."

Nao Kao laughed.

"Okay, you have a deal."

On Saturday, we made for the big houses that lined State Street, their front yards littered with red solo cups, a keg or two propped inconspicuously in the corner of the porches, beer pong tables taking pride of place on the lawn.

Blue and Shaggy and Eminem echoed past the mattresses lining the walls from inside, a mostly futile attempt to keep the racket contained. By the end of the night, he could sing the lyrics to *You Shook Me All Night Long* and *Brown Eyed Girl*, so many times did those particular songs ring out.

"So, the bathrooms, Nao Kao, I didn't mention those before. The toilets are ringed with black, the sinks are gray with filth, honestly, not washing your hands seems cleaner than touching any part of the sink. And soap, in my experience, didn't even factor into the equation. There was none!"

"But other than that, you had no complaints?"

"If you're asking whether there's any paper, you have to remember to grab napkins from the bar."

"Didn't think about paper. I'm a guy," he laughed. "Besides, you always have to supply your own paper in Laos."

"Did I tell you about the girl who lived next door to me freshman year?"

"I don't think so."

"She used to stumble home every Sunday morning. When she was hungover, Catherine and I would hear her rummaging in her purse for her room key. When she was drunk, sometimes she'd bang on our door instead!"

He laughed again, these tales as much part of his "research" as witnessing firsthand the finest young minds in America, as he put it, reduced to heaving in the bushes.

"She lost her underwear once."

"Say that again."

"You heard correctly. You can use your imagination as to how. A lacy, black thong."

Nao Kao inhaled sharply, his research having taken an unexpected turn.

"And?"

"And she found it hanging on the house trophy board the next week."

"That's – that's – wow! I don't even know what to say."

"How about, 'thank you, Liss, for enlightening me about an aspect of American higher education I otherwise would have missed?'"

Under the orange glow of a streetlight, Nao Kao merely pulled me to him and kissed me, the sounds of *Cecilia* reverberating from one of the Greek houses behind us as he ran his hands along the arch of my spine to my haunches, his thumbs hooked into my belt loops.

The relevance of the lyrics – the original lover leaving momentarily only to return to find another in his place – penetrated my guilty conscience.

I shivered.

At the other end of the spectrum, I took Nao Kao for tea at Martha Cook.

Oh, Martha Cook! That jewel of a dorm, pride of place across from the president's home. That tremendous hall of leaded glass and vaulted ceilings, the stone floor that gives a satisfying clack under the heels of so many girls on their way to dinner or, later, out to the bar. That cold, stone hall is such a contrast to the lush, sun-drenched rooms that open onto it, with their ornate gold and red furnishings, plush carpets, towering fireplaces, and a Steinway to make Mozart marvel.

On Fridays, that Steinway was the backdrop for afternoon tea, a ritual leftover from the days when William Cook gifted the building to the university in the hope that ladies of fine upbringing and finer tastes (also read: rich) would make suitable wives for the law students living in the law school dormitory an arm's length away. On Fridays, the dining hall staff turned out silver-plated trays of blueberry scones and lemon bars, truffle brownies and cucumber sandwiches, miniature quiches and filo-dough delicacies. The centerpiece, always, was the great, rococo silver teapot, a resident seated primly to either side, ready with a creamy porcelain cup to be placed under the spout from which tumbled steaming amber liquid, earl gray or English breakfast, lavender, mint, or lemon.

I might not have been a model resident during the years I called it home, but the weekly tea, an opportunity to lounge like cats, and gossip like them too, in the plushness of the gold room was not to be missed.

Now I brought Nao Kao, who was sufficiently awed by the leaded glass windows that lined the hall, the Steinway in the Gold Room, the fixtures and finery of the Red Room. That I had lived in this relative palace and also attended enough frat parties to offer him a detailed description of the insides of half a dozen of the big houses simply astounded him. In America, in Ann Arbor, anything was possible.

∞ ∞ ∞ ∞ ∞

TO THIS DAY, it's an open question whether Rachael Zick would have been more appalled or less appalled if she had known that maybe there was more to the affair than met the eye, at least from the perspective of one of its parties.

I would go home to do laundry and find myself ambushed while I waited for the clothes to dry. "Are you still seeing him?" she might ask euphemistically. I vacillated from avoiding the subject entirely, pretending that she was no more than the whispering wind, to banging around in anger, protesting it was none of her business, to playing coy and responding "Oh, yes, I see him and lots of other people besides. How many people would you guess you see in an average day?"

I never let on to her that slowly the guilt was eating me from the inside out. Only Catherine, who had known me since we were barely out of diapers, and with whom I had laughed, cried, loved, and fought for two decades, could sense something out of place. When I declined to elaborate she offered the only advice she could. "You always have done things your own way. What I know is that you will do what you want to do."

Whatever judgment she rendered beyond that, she kept to herself.

Telling Nao Kao was out of the question. Not only did I see no point, but he had clearly been keeping his own counsel as well, for I could not have been more surprised by the turn in our late-night texting sessions. The discussions about my post-graduate plans became more serious, his questions more pointed, and then gradually he began speaking of his desire to stay in the U.S. – and how he might do so.

It must have been November then, just around the time of that other strange plane crash when the world was so on edge. I told him not to be ridiculous. His visa clearly compelled him to return home, to serve and improve his country, for a period of at least two years. He *wanted* to serve his country. So many times he had spoken of the good he could do, of the good he wanted to do, and especially of what it meant to him to be on a path that would allow him to be able to do well for himself while doing good for his country. I reminded him of the Chinese proverb he'd shared with me, the one that said "If you are planning for a year, sow rice. If you are planning for a decade, plant trees. If you are planning for a lifetime, educate people." Laos was planning for a lifetime – his and the nation's.

And he had a family. Just because I had fallen into the trap of believing that heaven was high and the emperor was far away did not mean I was prepared to steal another woman's husband. *A nice girl. Normal,* as I could not help thinking of her. That was never part of the deal. I would graduate and it would end and I could pretend I was still a Very Good Girl. At least that was the plan.

∞ ∞ ∞ ∞ ∞

WE HAD BEEN texting for months before we had occasion to set up a call over Zoom.

If Nao Kao saw me peering through the other side of a Zoom box months earlier at the alumni "reunion," he had kept his own camera decidedly off. After the third time he commented on my appearance, I made him send a selfie, which he did: poorly lit and almost glowering. You might think he didn't know any good photographers.

While I had seen the dozen or so photos of himself he sent me, along with others – mostly older – that I found poking around online, this call was the first time I would see him in the flesh, so to speak. After listening to him lament time and again about the weight he had gained over the years, I was surprised by the resemblance on the screen to the one in my memory. If he had been wearing a ballcap to cover the receding hairline, I might have sworn the likeness was one and the same.

As for me, although I was as self-conscious as any woman of a certain age of the crow's feet that had taken hold and the lines that told of both too much laughter and too many furrowed brows, I knew I had generally aged well, and I could not help but wonder whether my likeness felt as similar to Nao Kao as his did to me.

From the way he fidgeted as I popped onto his screen, it is possible he was as nervous as I was. He smiled warmly, the same broad smile I remembered so well, and whose memory had concealed itself in the recesses of my mind for nearly twenty years. For all my sleuthing, I had rarely found evidence of that smile in the photos he posted online over the years. Then again, no one smiles as often or as brightly as we Americans do, and I am nothing if not American when the situation calls for it. I flashed my best smile, the one I have used to win friends and influence people – from faculty members to the parents who foot the bills to the donors who fill the scholarship coffers – for going on two decades.

His obsidian eyes fixed on my emerald ones, and we spoke at the same moment, an especial hazard of Zoom, both boxes flashing, each of us pausing, trying to let the other speak first. I gestured that he should do so.

"I can't believe it is really you, Liss. My God, how many years has it been? Sixteen? Eighteen?" It was the same lilting voice that I remembered, and its familiar cadence caught me off guard, as though echoing back through the fog of time. The butterflies inside me fluttered and tumbled and multiplied madly.

"Almost nineteen, if you're counting. It's good to finally see you, too, Nao Kao."

"I just can't believe –"

"I know, I know. Me, too. But, Nao Kao, you're a busy guy. And you told me the signal might cut at any moment, so we should get started."

Almost imperceptibly, his expression changed.

We blew past the hour we had scheduled and were well into the second one before we called time on the conversation. As I hit the little red Leave Meeting button, I realized I had sweated through the sundress I was wearing. I hadn't felt such nerves with a boy, even one on the other side of planet earth, since I was fifteen years old.

NAO KAO

"LET'S SCHEDULE A call to talk through course integration," Liss texted me.

"Nao Kao, we need to talk about the course. Can I send you a link?" she wrote more urgently a few days later.

And finally: "I sent you a calendar invite for this Thursday – one for morning and one for evening. Please accept the one you prefer." She always did know how to get things done.

As she popped onto my screen, I knew I'd been correct to postpone this as long as possible. Seeing her in one of one hundred small boxes at the alumni event was one matter, but life-size Liss on my monitor, her unmistakable voice piping through my headphones, was another. I would have known her anywhere.

"How many years has it been? Sixteen? Eighteen?" I began to reminisce, the pull of memory lane too strong to overcome now that I was face-to-face with her.

"Nineteen," she corrected me. "But you're busy. We should get started." Her tone was firm, but her mannerisms soft.

"Yes, ma'am. You always did drive a hard bargain," I quipped to mask my disappointment at being denied the pleasure of mutual memories. My consolation prize was a smile that reached her eyes and brought forth the dimples I remembered too well.

My stomach flipped familiarly; Liss always did make me nervous.

"Here's what I'm thinking for our course," she began evenly, and I marveled again at her nerves.

Her hands twirled and her face lit as she walked me through a plan to integrate our courses.

"…The students can work in small groups on the impacts of various policies with the final grade based on our evaluation of their presentations." She concluded, as I recalled again the thoroughness with which she both built and dismantled arguments in grad school. Her thesis was a work of art.

"Relax about the details," I interjected finally. "This is an experiment. We don't know exactly how the students will respond. We need to allow for flexibility."

Liss nodded back at me. Something in the tentative movement told me she was as nervous as I was, but had worn the disguise of nonchalance better than I could. Now it began to fall away and I sensed an opening.

"Do you remember the online portfolio?" I asked.

"Oh my God, that was awful. Why are you making me remember that?" Liss replied, laughing.

"Only how you focused on every detail."

She stuck out her tongue, which I took as a small victory. I capped my pen in a modest attempt to signal the conclusion of shop talk.

"Did you ever find a cat?" I asked.

She blinked, as though weighing whether – or how – to respond.

"You remember," she replied quietly, a look of warm surprise suffusing her features.

"Everything, yes," I added, and paused for my meaning to sink in.

"Her name was Penny. She was a lovely copper color."

"Was."

"It was a long time ago, Nao Kao. I adopted her before I left Ann Arbor and moved to Chicago. She lived fifteen years – that's a good life for a cat!"

The false brightness of her words only exacerbated the sadness that crossed her features. Something of the memory made her sad, though as she'd said, it was a good, long life for a cat.

"Do you have any pets?" she asked quickly. She would brook no more questions about herself.

I reached down and scooped up my beloved ginger cat.

"Meet Belle. Her brother is Beast, which is fitting. I'm sure he's chasing a bird as we speak."

The sounds of our laughter mingled. "Come," I wanted to say. "Come teach here with me."

I spent the hour after our call contemplating the Green Card Lottery.

LISS

I AM NOT a white-knuckled flyer. I can jounce through the atmosphere with the best of them, and it is a mark of pride that however green I may have felt on occasion, I have never actually been sick.

As with the bumps in life, it helps if you know when they are coming. Fly across the North Atlantic in winter, and you are almost guaranteed a rough ride. The jet stream will get you (almost) every time.

Nothing in my flying history compares, though, to the turbulence of the tropics. Around the belt of the equator, from Singapore to Senegal and back again, the winds from the northern and southern hemispheres collide, resulting in ferocious thunderstorms that have interfered with cabin service on more than a few flights I have known. It is on these flights that I have dreamed my most unusual and most dramatic dreams.

From the flying carpets that carried me to Hong Kong, to the dream on the way down to Dakar that sealed my fate with Jake, my most vivid, my most terrifying, and my most inspiring dreams have always come after the flight attendants have been asked to secure the cabin and take their seats.

Into Dakar, I dreamed I was riding in a city bus, hurtling down a highway, when we smashed head-first into the car in front of us. Glass shattered, passengers screamed, and I was thrown clear to the back of the bus. When I came to, I looked myself over and was no worse for the wear aside from a copious amount of blood on my hands. The universe doesn't always take out a billboard to tell you what to do. Sometimes it relies on common sense. And failing that, I am certain, it sends dreams. Or sometimes nightmares.

From the moment I awoke and confirmed my hands were blessedly free of blood, when I lifted my shade and watched the sun break open the skies over West Africa, I understood intuitively what I needed to do. The bloody bus crash was the postscript to all those drowning and suffocating dreams. It was the root of that fateful phone call, the one Catherine, and probably others – it was, after all, the shout heard 'round the resort – still reference as evidence that I am not quite as seaworthy as my reputation holds.

∞ ∞ ∞ ∞ ∞

As HALLOWEEN SLID past, I became increasingly concerned that something was wrong. For the first time, I was presented with a problem I could not think my way clear of. Nor could I think what Nao Kao was possibly thinking every time he raised the subject of staying in the U.S., which he did now with increasing urgency. I tried to brush it off, but still, he persisted. I grew frustrated. The terms of his visa could not have been clearer, the latest date of his legal departure from this country inked in red alongside the landing permission when he arrived. I considered again the investment in his education, the ways in which his country was depending on him putting his American experience to good use. How could I take that away from him? How could I take him away from Laos? To say nothing of the wife, waiting at home, going on a second year now, and the babes in arms, one, at least, still recovering from malaria and wretchedly thin. I couldn't imagine what he was thinking. Didn't Nao Kao know? Feelings did not matter. Obligations mattered. Policies and procedures mattered. Emotion could not enter the equation. After all, there were rules and there were strictures.

I reminded him only of the complication with the visa; he did not, or at least he should not, need me to remember his duty to his family.

At night when I waited for sleep to come, I would try to picture what their good-byes must have entailed, envisioned him at the airport, awkwardly embracing his wife, their babies between them, or maybe the babies were home with a grandmother, and it was just the two young parents, there at the airport, reassuring themselves that the years would pass quickly, that this was, as Nao Kao had once remarked, the best way. It was not every day you had the chance to go study at one of the world's great universities, to rub elbows and exchange ideas with leading luminaries in the field, certainly not if you were from Laos. The future would open before them in ways neither could have imagined from the inside of a refugee camp. And then she was gone and it was just him, wandering the terminal, alternately floating above the clouds or staring at the white caps below, wide awake the whole, long way.

I couldn't fathom what he was thinking.

157

"More power to you," I replied, tersely, when he told me in the clearest terms possible that he had discovered the loophole that would allow him to remain.

∞ ∞ ∞ ∞ ∞

I TURNED FORTY-THREE in the middle of the pandemic, deep into January as thousands died each day. I made myself cookies and pretended not to care. To a certain extent, I did not: friends with spring birthdays would soon be celebrating lockdown-style for a second year in a row. Pouting would have been petty; in the face of global pandemic, one homebound birthday hardly merited mention. In the midst of so much carnage – half a million dead in America and counting – I was just grateful to begin another trip around the sun.

If Nao Kao never wished me a happy birthday – and he did not – he did send his own enigmatic acknowledgement of the day. As always, it came in the middle of the night, a collage of portraits, not of him but of his beloved motorbike. He had ridden around Vientiane and over hill and dale to Luang Prabang. In each one, his bike was positioned carefully in front of various landmarks or landscapes, intricate architecture in some, the soaring layered roofs pointing skyward, the native flora, the ginger or orchids or bamboo or ferns in others. In every picture, positioned between the handlebars, was a little brown cow.

I drove to my office to enlarge the pictures on the biggest monitors I could access to confirm that I was not seeing things. I had given him that cow, though how it had survived the humidity of the tropics for twenty years, let alone a succession of small hands, was a thought to behold. It was a gag gift on Halloween, inspired when I had overheard him struggling through the static and echoes of a bad connection with a customer service representative three continents away.

What need he had for customer service eludes me still, but after being asked to repeat his name for a third time, Nao Kao resorted to the use of homonyms. "Nao" and "now, as in at this moment" were homonyms, as were "Kao" and "cow, as in cattle." At last the hapless creature at the far end of the line understood. "Oh, Mr. Inthavong," she said with astounding clarity, "your name is Nao Kao, like 'how now brown cow?'"

"Yes," Nao Kao responded, "like that." He rolled his eyes, annoyance etched on his features. "How hard was it, really?" he asked me when he finally hung up.

"You know I'm the wrong person to ask," I said, and he laughed.

"Right. You are not actually American. It's okay, I like you anyway, Liss."

I laughed genuinely to hear my sarcasm reflected back at me so accurately and flashed my best smile, two rows of startlingly white, perfectly aligned teeth just to prove I did have something of my compatriots in me.

A few days later, when I saw the little brown cow with those great glass eyes in the greeting card section at Meijer, I couldn't resist. Knowing that it had survived this long touched me as much as that he enlisted it for a photo shoot.

The next day a picture of his office door arrived, a big block M at eye-level, and the day after that a photo of his bookshelf, where the textbooks he'd pored over in Ann Arbor dominated, the little yellow 'USED' tags still affixed to the spine.

Dammit, Nao Kao, I thought, and just when I was convinced that there was nothing more than a loosely woven fabric of an old, familiar friendship between us.

∞ ∞ ∞ ∞ ∞

AND THEN THERE was the Valentine, that baffling digital greeting, an enigmatic half-card, half-gift that sent me seeking counsel. A message in a bottle would have perplexed me less.

"Um, this seems pretty straightforward to me, what's the question?"

For a week I had been ruminating on the meaning of the "Valentine" that Nao Kao sent. Digitally, of course. Two photos, each of them signed. The first was a stylized room service cart, the domed silver warmer lifted to reveal breakfast for two. The other a pair of arms extending a box of strawberries drizzled in chocolate, with "Happy Valentine's Day" overlaid. There was no mistaking the intricate script. Pictures he had taken? The signature implied that these were pictures he had taken himself, yet there was a blandness to their composition that made me think of stock photos. I couldn't help but picture him perusing stock photos the way one selected a card from the rack at the Hallmark store.

I was still working through the questions, my mind as yet half-asleep, when my phone buzzed. The coincidence of timing seemed too great. Intuitively, I was certain he had been watching Messenger like a hawk, waiting for the little green dot to tell him I was active.

"So, breakfast in bed and a box of chocolates. How is that for Valentine's Day?" The message was accompanied by a couple of laughing emojis, no hearts.

"Not too shabby. Though I wouldn't have complained about a few flowers. Aren't roses the traditional gift?"

Forty-five minutes later, when I was assembling my own breakfast, decidedly alone and decidedly not in bed, he sent me a shot of a dozen roses accompanied by a half-finished slice of lavishly mouth-watering chocolate cake, the fork poised for another bite.

"Your flowers. And my dessert tonight," he texted. "But I can share."

If he was putting it out there that he in any way considered me his Valentine, he had a funny way of doing it: I didn't hear from him for the rest of the week. Not a picture to wake up to in the morning, not a single note of hello in the evening, no links to articles of mutual interest, not even a response to the work-related email I had sent mid-week. Mercy.

"So how exactly would you describe your, uh, relationship with this guy?" Catherine asked me when I finally put the problem to her.

"What relationship? I don't think we have one. Or maybe we do, in the same sense that any two individuals or any two objects can be described to be relational to one another."

"This isn't an academic lecture, Liss. Cut the jargon and answer my question." Catherine always did know how to cut to the chase.

"Friends?"

"Is that a question or a statement?"

"A statement?"

"Then why do you sound so uncertain?"

"Well, I guess it's not the Valentine I would send to my friends." Damn, damn, damn. All I wanted was answers. Someone to tell me what *they* thought, to make sense of so many mixed signals and crossed signs for me, not more platitudes and ambiguity. God knew, I had enough of the latter from Nao Kao.

"So, again, let me ask: how would you describe your relationship with this guy?"

"I don't know, Cath, I just don't know! I guess, um, I guess, well, I don't think there is a word for what we are to each other. Or if we are even 'anything.' Or if we are, then I don't know what to call it."

Because friends *is the only possible description, except that intuitively, this felt like the sharp edge of a knife.* Intuitively, I sensed something deeper, unspoken but present just beneath the surface. And frustratingly, for the first time in my life, I, Liss Larkin, author of honors theses and master's theses and a prize-winning doctoral dissertation, of academic papers galore, I simply lacked the words for whatever was happening in my life. Too well I knew the options: either I was plain dense or deep in denial. In vain, I searched for an elusive third alternative.

"Let me ask you this, Liss. When you and Jake were married, did you talk about him with your friends? I don't mean your innermost thoughts. Just your daily lives."

"Of course!"

"That's my point," she said. "So, you and Nao Kao might be friends, but you're not normal friends. Normal friends talk about their spouses."

"Normal friends talk about their spouses," I repeated. If it walks like a duck...

"And I have to add, you sure don't make things easy," Catherine continued. "He sent you a picture of breakfast. Rather than asking something to the effect of 'what happens after breakfast,' you chastised the man for not sending flowers. You are impossible, Liss!"

"Well, I didn't want to assume!"

Also, I didn't add, at least in that moment, or in any moment of nervousness for that matter, I suffered from the condition best described by its French name, *l'esprit de l'escalier.* The spirit of the staircase. As in, the best and most appropriate answer comes to mind after leaving the dinner party, while already descending the stairs. Knowing me, if I were French, I would suffer from *l'esprit de dehors*, my witty comebacks appearing well after the night air smacked me in the face.

At least I had not fallen down the rabbit hole of telling him that his little digital Valentine, whatever it may or may not represent, was more than I had received on any other Valentine's Day. I might have implied that I was accustomed to receiving an annual bouquet, but the truth could not be further away. Either way, and whatever we were or were not to one another, I was sure Nao Kao was not interested in hearing the ins and outs of my relationship with another man.

As his silence stretched to days, though, the question of intentionality ate into my mind, and I increasingly found myself rolling the marble around, guardedly asking another friend or two what they thought. They were split between "how could he have made this any more obvious" and "Asian cultures are warmer and friendlier and men have more latitude in their relations with women than they do here." Translation: either he has feelings for you, or he is a player. I was back to square one.

I needed a guy's opinion. Preferably a middle-aged man with long and extensive experience in Asia. Fortunately, I knew just such a person. While American, this man had lived and worked his entire adult life in Asia, first in Singapore, then in Taiwan, and now in China. I could also ask him anything, anything at all. Less fortunately, he was my brother, Theo, who had, in fact, found and married a nice girl in China, just as our mother feared. Still, beggars couldn't be choosers. I took a couple of screenshots, scrubbed them of any possible identifying information, and sent them zipping across the Great Firewall. Thank you, WeChat.

Not for the first time my brother wondered what the hell was wrong with me. I tried to explain again.

"Well, I thought maybe he was just being friendly. Like he could have sent the exact same 'Valentine' to a hundred different friends, right? Is that so crazy?"

I waited for his response; at least this was still Chinese New Year and he wasn't in his office. The pauses in our conversations on the days I caught him at work could stretch through meetings or phone calls, so that often I would just give up and read whatever response he sent when I awoke the next morning.

"Yes. It is. I'm sorry, Liss, but this is way more than friendly. I don't see anything unclear about it."

"Well this is a person I frequently find ambiguous. So, I just want to make sure I understand your interpretation."

"My interpretation is that you should enjoy your date, whenever it is. And be sure to tell me about it." Laughing emojis filled the next line.

I wished I could tell him the backstory, to see if it might influence his opinion at all. His loyalties might be to me, but if Rachael Zick should catch a whiff of anything suspicious and corner him the next time she saw him, say over FaceTime some unsuspecting Sunday, we would both be toast. My brother was putty in the hands of our mother. We were both safer this way.

"I just want to make sure I have this clear in my mind. Because this is complicated."

"Jake-level complicated?" Despite the distance, Theo had had a front row seat to that debacle. I shuddered to think how many late nights I had spent pouring my heart out to him once that deed was done.

"On steroids. Final question and then I promise I will drop this. If a guy sent this to a friend, a female friend, his girlfriend would be pissed?"

"Oh, Liss."

"It's pretty clear what your, uh, friend thinks. And if he has a girlfriend and sent this anyway, that's a definite no-no. Someone will get hurt. As your brother, I only hope it isn't you."

I chalked his reaction up to another vote for "denial."

I thought again about that final picture, the one Nao Kao sent after I suggested flowers should be the order of the day, the one that included the chocolate lava cake he offered to share. Unlike the other two, which he had planned and sent overnight, that third one, I was certain, was spontaneous. On the table, next to the flowers and the cake, I glimpsed two coffee cups, the little European ones that hold the strong, dark shots of caffeine. When I zoomed in further, I could just make out the fuzzy outline of Nao Kao and his dining companion.

The woman wore a pink and white blouse. Oh my. My mind raced with possibilities. Surely, he wasn't sharing his dessert with me, however virtual. Not on Valentine's Day. Only a cad would do that, and Nao Kao was definitely not a cad. Unless he was. But, no, that was a bridge too far. This must have been an old photo from his phone's memory. Which he had been photoshopping at dinner. Which might still be caddish, but maybe less so. I wasn't even sure you *could* photoshop on your phone. But he was a professional photographer. So, he could, by rights even should, possess mad skills I did not. But no. Surely, he hadn't sent me a picture from dinner with his wife. And yet the evidence said otherwise – I was sure I recognized her from a recent profile picture. His girls all had long hair, while the wife – and I was increasingly certain he was still married – wore a stylish bob.

Next to her, Nao Kao was wearing the Michigan shirt I had sent him.

Suddenly, I could not help but wonder whether this was some high-risk game of hearts to get his adrenaline flowing. Across time and space, Shaggy returned to mock me. Maybe, just maybe, Nao Kao was no more and no less than a player, completely lost. Looking again at the pictures, I had to admit that it wasn't out of the realm of possibilities.

∞ ∞ ∞ ∞ ∞

"LISS? WHAT IS it you want to tell me? What was so impossible?"

"Oh, Nao Kao. It was all so long ago. We were so young. *I* was so young."

"Just tell me. You don't need to be so hesitant."

"I'm not being hesitant for your benefit. You have to understand: I wasn't going to tell you. I wasn't ever going to tell anyone. For years, I've managed to almost convince myself it didn't even happen."

"I see."

How I would have liked to believe he did see. That it was all falling into place for him without me needing to articulate it. I was the one who began this conversation, though, and I owed it to us both to see it through.

"You were the best friend I had in grad school, Nao Kao. And I repaid you by, well…" I didn't need to spell it out. We both knew what I had done.

"Until the day I just magically reappeared, poof! Watch me pull a rabbit out of my hat! So, you would have had every right in the world to be angry with me, but instead you've given me so much grace to exist, to share my life, to become part of yours, however peripherally, however inconsequentially."

I gave him a minute to read all of that, regretting now that I didn't just write all of this in an email. Surely that would have been more eloquent. On the other hand, maybe this was not the kind of story to be told eloquently. Maybe it was the kind of story you needed to feel as much as read or hear. In which case.

"Go on."

"Remember when I was giving you so much trouble about the time at my apartment?" I realized belatedly that I was repeating myself.

"I do."

Recently, I had ribbed Nao Kao mercilessly about his lack of foresight, how we were on a college campus where baskets overflowed with free condoms and placards urged safe sex from every counter and kiosk within a mile of the health center and probably beyond.

On the other hand, maybe it was not as pre-meditated as I had long believed. Maybe he was caught as much by surprise as I was, with consequences neither of us could have foreseen.

As I typed the words I'd held inside of me for so long, the memory I had locked away for nineteen full years – for a lifetime, one could argue – came rushing back, flooding every circuit of my brain. The tears rolled freely and the screen blurred, but I did not need to see the keys to finish typing what I needed to say.

"I was pregnant, Nao Kao."

PART III: GHOSTS

~

LISS

WE BUMPED OUR way south, this Korean Air flight bound for parts as yet unknown to me, the crew, as always, insisting on seatbacks fully upright while they delivered trays of chicken or fish or soggy pasta. That it is virtually impossible to get an upgrade on a Korean flight when flying on a Delta ticket is only half of my complaint with the partnership.

The insult to the injury is the ironclad rule that every passenger must be awakened from their slumber during the meal service, which, whether to or from Jakarta or Ho Chi Minh City or Kuala Lumpur or, further evidence for my rant, Vientiane, is invariably in the small hours of the night. I looked at my watch: a few minutes past midnight. I marveled at the multitudes who never hesitated to fork down airplane fare in the wee small hours.

I thought back to my trip to Senegal, how clarity of action had come when and where I least expected it. After weeks of nightmares capped by the bloodied hands of my turbulence-fueled dream, it was not that I had any doubts. I understood not only that it was time to make a course correction in my life, but that it was also time to stop fighting against the intuition that had told me since I said *I do* that this was not the life for me.

A handful of times in my life – literally, I could count them on one hand – my intuition has spoken to me such that even decades later I can recall every detail of where I was and what I was doing when I heard it. In every instance it has been uncannily correct. What do we know that we don't know we know? A better question might be why we do not always heed the knowing.

Deep roots are not reached by frost.

If I needed any further affirmation that I had reached the end of the line with Jake, if the bus crash of a dream hadn't hammered the point home, the final proof came in the form of the Senegalese women who formed the backbone of their villages, these small, dusty outcroppings with a circle of huts and, if they were lucky, a nearby water source.

Students often ask me why the world's villagers are so eager to up sticks for megacities where they crowd into shanties with foul water and fouler alleys, where the best they might hope for is sweatshop labor that pays barely enough to earn their daily bread. Until you have witnessed lives still governed by the rhythms of the sun, it is a reasonable question.

The women meeting us today had walked, most of them, some five or seven sodden miles, in the daily deluge that defines the wet season in this part of the world. They had done this for the opportunity to share with us the ways in which the basic literacy and arithmetic skills they learned through the works of a particular NGO had allowed them to gain, in the words of that same NGO, "a measure of autonomy over their own lives."

A measure of autonomy over their own lives.

I rolled that phrase around, trying to remember how long it had been since I had claimed my own autonomy, since I had been able to breathe and be authentically, as me, Liss Miller, the girl with the big dreams.

Subconsciously, I knew the answer. The subconscious always knows.

I mulled the question as the van slipped and splashed through the deep mud of the single track out of the village. I was grateful for the work – and the money – of another NGO that was building bridges in the region, literally, if not always figuratively. A bridge may seem a small thing, until you consider what it is to not have one. Then people drown. *As I am drowning now*, I thought as our driver skillfully maneuvered us around a fallen tree and into the high grass and deep ruts of the adjacent ground, gunning the engine so that we passengers would not need to pile out and push. It was no idle concern.

Past the baobab trees being lashed with rain, past the mango sellers huddling under twisted pink and yellow umbrellas, their precious fruit covered with cling film as though to protect it from the torrential, pelting rains, I pondered. As we approached the city, my mind worked on the problem past billboards offering a free goat with every purchase of a new cell phone; past the line of broken-down semis, many on their third or fourth or fifth national tour of duty, having begun life, perhaps, in the U.S. or Europe before being traded down again and again until they, too, reached the bottom of the global pyramid.

For miles, these trucks lined the pitted road that led to Mali, less wealthy, less secure, than Senegal. They intermingled with carts pulled by mules, adolescents hauling loads on bicycles, and occasionally the highly recognizable white Toyotas favored by the NGOs. When a big rig gave out, which they frequently did, the driver would coax it back to life on the side of the road, tinkering with the engine or patching the tires or siphoning a little more precious fuel from a jerry can into the tank.

As it does in some people, like the finger-pointers at the check-in counter or the mid-flight air ragers, too often travel brought out the worst in us when Jake and I traveled together, or at least the worst in our relationship. From the hiking trails of Banff where our shouts echoed through the mountains as we fought over who lost the trail guide; to the argument over the tide tables in Normandy; to Golden Hour in Florence where we each stalked off to separate *gelaterias* after disagreeing over the history of the Ponte Vecchio; to the "Happiest Place on Earth," where I spent the day at Epcot while Jake explored the Magic Kingdom, we had known our share of bust-ups as we explored the planet. Even when we were together, we couldn't help but remain apart.

Only weeks before I left for Senegal, at Shark's Cove on the North Shore of Oahu, we had reached an apex, of sorts. It came at the end of a snorkeling trip gone awry.

"Can you believe all of the aholehole, Jake? There must have been a hundred of them!" I enthused, as we clambered back on shore.

He glowered at me.

"If we get there early enough, the water will be 'smooth as glass,'" he mimed a flat surface and raised the pitch of his voice to impersonate me.

"Oh, come on. I already said I guessed I was wrong. And that you didn't *have* to come in."

The sun had barely burst above the horizon when we'd pulled off onto the strip of sand that doubled as a parking lot, but even then, two points were apparent. The cove teemed with fish and the water was rough. Knowing Jake's preference for turf over surf in the best of conditions, I'd offered that he could wait on the shore. He declined.

Buffeted by the currents, Jake's shins were bloody by the time we'd had our fill of the underwater world, but despite the waves, the visibility had been excellent.

"Jake? I know your leg hurts, but did you see them all? The parrot fish, the humuhumunukunukuapuaa, there was even a honu off in the distance!" Even I could hear the artificial brightness in my voice that sought to plaster over the blood running from a good four-inch gash in Jake's shin. Already I was formulating a first-aid plan for the man whose single allergy was to medical adhesive. *His allergy, but my responsibility to ensure we always had gauze and compression bandages aplenty,* I stewed, silently but resentfully.

"You think I didn't see the fish, Liss?" Jake seethed. "Of course, I saw the fish. Every damn one. The eels, too. And the reef shark, which I tried to point out to you, but God knows you weren't paying enough attention to notice."

"What? I missed a shark! Ugh! I can't believe it!"

"Yeah, the shark. You missed the shark. *That's* what I'm pissed about. That you didn't get to see the shark. Because you've never seen one before."

I chose to ignore the sarcasm.

"Well, not –"

"Fuck, Liss! Do you ever even listen to me? To anyone other than yourself?"

Slowly, deliberately, I dried myself, counting to ten, then twenty, then thirty, deciding how to respond. The grains of sand sparkled against my skin. No matter how I rubbed, they were adhered to my thighs, to my shins, to the tops of my feet. Out of the corner of my eye I noticed Jake watching my deliberations.

"Liss! Do you ever think about anyone but yourself? Listen to anyone but yourself? Or even yourself? Do you ever even notice anyone else?"

"I notice that you're being a complete ass right now and I don't have the first clue why." My voice was steady and low, which I had discovered over the years was far more intimidating – and therefore effective – than when I yelled.

He snatched the keys to the rental car out of the dry bag and chucked them into the parking area. They pinged against the car and fell into the gravel.

"It's your vacation, have at it."

"What the fuck, Jake? This is *my* vacation? This is *our* vacation. You are the one who wanted to come here!"

"No. I wanted to come somewhere that was not work – your work. To be with you. But you may as well not even be here. You certainly seem to think I may as well not be here. You haven't listened to a single thing I've said all week. I'm lucky I didn't drown out there in the waves for as much as you would have noticed – or cared. So please, just leave." He was speaking slowly, annunciating every syllable, seeking to impart as much meaning into each little word as possible. I was so sick of this shit.

"What? And leave you here on the beach? How are you getting back to Waikiki? This is stupid."

"There's a bus, Liss. Either you take it or I will."

I fished the keys out of the dirt and opened the trunk, trying to weigh how serious he was, whether I should just climb in and drive off, leaving him on the other side of the island. This was just so stupid. I was just so tired. Compared to the supposed relaxation and pleasure of "vacation," the grind of traveling for work was a walk in the park.

Even though it was still early, the sun does its work quickly and efficiently in the tropics and the bottles of water I had left in the car were warm. Still, the freshness was a relief after the saltiness of the ocean. Thirty feet from shore, a turtle, a massive honu, poked its head up, as though to check on the ruckus. I chucked a box of gauze and an ACE bandage in Jake's direction. Not so much as a mumbled or grudging thanks. *My responsibility.*

"I knew you would leave," Jake called out as I climbed into the driver's seat and cranked the AC, Iz incongruously singing about rainbows as I flicked on the radio. "I dreamed it, you know?"

It was the only dream he ever shared with me.

∞ ∞ ∞ ∞ ∞

"How did you end up back in Ann Arbor?" Nao Kao texted me one evening.

"So many coincidences," I replied. It was late. *I should have waited until morning to reply,* I thought belatedly.

"You didn't used to believe in coincidences."

I laughed despite myself.

"I still don't. And coming back to Michigan is just another reason why not."

My brother had sent me link to the job posting; he never said how he learned of it, though I strongly suspected that our mother had sent it to him in the hopes of luring him back home.

"You would be amazing!" Theo had written in the email, and when I read the description, I knew he was right. Still, his last line rankled: "You know Mom would be only too happy to pull the considerable strings available to her."

"Would I be amazing or can I only get this job if I ask the great Rachael Zick to run interference for me?" I asked, by way of reply.

"Life doesn't have to be either-or, Liss. Ends justifying means isn't always Machiavellian…"

I debated until the day before the deadline, then took Theo's advice. My mom didn't flinch. I got an interview, then a second one, and then, mere weeks after I'd first learned of the job, I received an offer letter with terms that brought tears of joy to my eyes.

"I'm proud of you, Liss," Jake said when I told him I wanted to accept. If either of us thought it was odd that I waited until I had a firm offer before I sprang the news on Jake, neither of us said so.

"You won't mind moving back to Ann Arbor? What about your job?"

Jake shrugged ambivalently.

"There are schools in Michigan. I can work as a sub until I find something. I don't mind."

"You know I'll be traveling at least once a month. You're okay with that, too?"

"Of course, Liss. It's a great job. You should take it. If you're worried about Penny, don't be. I think I can handle her."

I laughed. Maybe it had been short-sighted to adopt a cat after all.

"And you're sure you won't mind me going back to school, too?" I had applied to the doctoral program even before I received the confirmation that my dream job was waiting for me.

"It's what you've wanted as long as I've known you. There's no time like the present!" Jake enthused, a little too brightly. "Seriously, Liss, I'll be fine.

I don't need a babysitter – I'll keep myself busy while you work and study. I don't mind. And I'm proud of you! Really proud!"

I shouldn't have been surprised. Jake never complained when I stayed late on campus to attend a lecture or audit a course. He encouraged me in my endeavors to learn to paint and draw, and praised my culinary efforts, even if we both knew I would never amount to much in the kitchen. He read my personal statements for a half-dozen doctoral program applications. He commiserated with me when I received the thin envelopes that foretold rejection and cheered the acceptance from Michigan when it came. And now he was all in for us to move back to Ann Arbor so that I could pursue academic and professional dreams. It should have been enough.

Three weeks later, we loaded our belonging into a U-Haul and headed east on I-94, one chapter closing and another opening. As if by a miracle, Nao Kao never crossed my mind.

∞ ∞ ∞ ∞ ∞

AS I LOOKED out the rain-streaked window of the van somewhere near Mbour, at the flooding, the rutted roads, the cattle roaming alongside big rigs, young boys prodding them along, I could not have been farther, literally or figuratively, from the sun-drenched North Shore. The cognitive dissonance in my life was real, the contrasts always fighting for headspace.

"You okay?" Catherine asked, noting the glaze of my expression. It was a lot to take in, even for us, or at least for me. Catherine was at home anywhere. After New York, she had spent two years in the Peace Corps, and the villages of rural Africa were still perhaps her second home.

The communal tub of onions and rice, the shared spoons, the rodents scuttling through the kitchen: she didn't even bat an eye. Catherine had not flinched when confronted with the facilities that afternoon. She had nonchalantly hiked up her skirt and gotten down to business, swarms of flies and filth around the hole notwithstanding. Of course she assumed those were the images I was ruminating on.

"I want a divorce." It was the first time I had spoken the words aloud.

Everyone in the van turned to look at me. Three colleagues, including Catherine, and two representatives from the NGO riveted their gaze on me; even the driver darted his dark eyes from the road to my face in the rearview mirror.

« *Merde,* » muttered François, our fixer. He removed his hat and ran his fingers through his short hair, as though allowing my words to escape that way.

I laughed.

«*Si,* » I responded, «*vous avez bien compris.*»

Of course, he had understood. His English was excellent and the sentiment wasn't exactly Chaucerian prose.

"When will you tell him?" Catherine asked.

"As soon as we get back to the hotel." There was nothing pre-meditated in my plan. I had not thought about it even once before, the idea having fully announced itself to me. But as soon as I said it, there in that steaming, claustrophobic van, I knew it was true.

"You mean when we get back home?" Catherine clarified.

"No, I mean when we get to the hotel. Assuming I can get a strong enough signal to place a call on WhatsApp."

« *Merde,* » she said.

We rode the rest of the way in silence, save for the squeak of the wiper blades and the hammering of the rain.

As I picked up the phone and opened WhatsApp, curtains of water descended from the heavens and beat against the roof.

"I want a divorce," I practically yelled down the line, when Jake answered.

Even if the connection had been clear, the pounding from the rains would have nearly drowned out my voice. I swatted at mosquitos and thought about malaria.

"What did you say?" he asked. "You want what?"

"I want a divorce," I hollered louder at the same moment the rains, those pounding ropes of water, ceased their cacophony. My ill-timed shout echoed off the walls and penetrated the neighboring rooms.

Admittedly, it was not my finest moment.

∞ ∞ ∞ ∞ ∞

"I ALWAYS WONDERED what happened to you. Thanks for finding me, Liss."

The words sat gently in the little text bubble on my screen.

I always wondered what happened to you.

What cause, these gales? An absence, perhaps, known to the heart if not the mind, festering, untended, allowed to billow and build in the space of years? I saw suddenly how much I had missed my friend; the gratitude was mutual.

I sucked in my breath, quieted the storm, and debated where to start.

If a job is worth doing, it is worth doing right. My father's mantra was drummed into my head since I learned to walk. As I review the trajectory of my life, I see I have both learned and applied that lesson well, and perhaps never better than when it all came crashing apart with Nao Kao.

The lesson, of course, is that there can be no half measures. Maybe if I'd believed in coincidence with as much fervor as I believed in fate, I wouldn't have leapt so readily into the void. I didn't believe in coincidence, though. That I'd been presented so quickly, so easily, with the opportunity at marriage – at a new identity – however inadvisable seemed, well, fated. In hindsight, I could see clearly, too clearly, that it was the enticement of this new identity, coupled with the attraction of needling my own mother, the formidable Rachael Zick who believed a woman should keep the name she was born with, that led me to say "I do" even when everything inside me screamed, "You don't and you won't; you shouldn't and you shan't."

I would prefer to think not, that I believed my vows, that I believed everyone who ever stood at an altar suffered from a case of the nerves, that I never could have undertaken such a solemn obligation as marriage so cavalierly. I would prefer to believe that I am better than that. The truth, of course, is more complicated. Maybe I married Jake because I couldn't believe it was a coincidence that we'd ended up in the same area code, if not the same ZIP code. Maybe I married him because he engendered no feeling in me stronger than a cup of warm milk. If numbness was what I sought, marriage to Jake was one way to find it.

Whatever it was, by the time I walked up the aisle, train trailing and my grandmother's veil firmly pinned in place, I had accepted what the fates had in store for me without, I thought, too much of a quibble. Yes, with Jake I could be both numb to the world and completely anonymous. I changed my name, and then for the first time, I felt I could breathe again. Liss Miller disappeared right before my eyes, replaced by Liss Larkin. I might not have known who she was, but neither did anyone else.

What do we know that we don't know we know?

Of course, Nao Kao looked for me.

I like to read books to my nieces over Zoom on Sunday mornings, as they're readying for bed and the week ahead. It's a nice end to their weekend, and good English practice for little girls whose friends and schools and lives are otherwise conducted in Chinese. They are smart girls and their favorite book for several years was *The Brain Is Kind of a Big Deal*. Is it ever. What it can repress, repackage, and reveal is the mystery and essence of life. When I told my therapist that I had not consciously thought of Nao Kao in the nearly two decades that had passed, she gave me a funny look, a look that said maybe I was not being entirely truthful with either of us.

"How is it possible that you obliterated from your mind one of the most consequential relationships of your life?" Stacy asked me once too often.

The question, the entire theme, was beginning to annoy me.

"I wish I could explain it, Stacy. To you, so that you would stop asking, but more importantly to be able to explain it to myself." Or Nao Kao, I added silently. Though he'd never prodded, I could only assume he must have the same question Stacy did.

"In hindsight, I can recognize that subconsciously, I never erased him. In hindsight, I realize that every time I aimed my camera and heard a faint voice remind me about the importance of not centering the subject, of checking the lighting, it was him. But that's the subconscious."

Stacy nodded thoughtfully and moved like she might respond, but I wasn't finished.

"I'm no neuroscientist. I don't know how our gray matter does what it does. But I do know that I could not have possibly spent years – years, Stacy, years! – working toward my doctorate in the same classrooms where he and I had spent so many hours together if I had not entirely eliminated all traces of him from conscious thought."

She looked at me more seriously.

"You win," she said quietly.

AFTER WHAT SEEMED like a year, text bubbles bouncing, stopping, starting again, the words never quite making their way pinging through space and onto my computer, Nao Kao replied to the news I had waited almost two decades to share.

"I don't know what to say." If anything bubbled beneath the surface of his utterly unshakable calm, he wasn't showing it. His equanimity would have irritated me had I expected anything different.

"It's ok. You don't have to say anything."

"I'm sorry. I probably should have written it into an email. Or, better yet, just kept it to myself. Some stories are better left untold, and if ever that was the case, I imagine it is now. It's okay if you're mad."

"Or you can just pretend I never said anything. Telling you now is probably selfish, right? Like what's the point, who does that?"

I was obviously rambling, texts pouring forth from my fingers blindly, my sight streaked with tears, my heart pounding. I couldn't believe I had ever thought that this was the right thing to do. Or, as I had just texted Nao Kao, who does that? Liss Larkin, that's who, and whatever it said about me, it was difficult to imagine him ever wanting anything more to do with me, as a friend or as a colleague.

I saw him beginning to type again, gave him time to consider his words. Looked at the time, and realized I had caught him at the beginning of his work day. Selfish, like I said. Whatever meetings and tasks were on his mind fifteen minutes ago were now most likely consigned to a to-do list for another day.

Text bubbles starting, three dots bouncing. Text bubbles stopping. I waited, trying to give him time to process in two minutes what I'd had two decades to digest. After waiting to see that whatever thought had begun to formulate itself in his head was not one he was prepared to share, I started again.

"It's like this, Nao Kao. All this time, you've never said that you were angry, never said that you were hurt. But none of this made any sense. You were – and likely still are – one of the smartest people I've ever known. Surely you knew there was more than met the eye to what happened. And if we weren't becoming friends again – I think we are, I hope we are –"

I did not know of another word to describe someone with whom so much life had been shared these past few months, but I let it go. Whatever we were, in the past or at the moment, needed no label.

"I just felt increasingly that I was lying to you to try to explain away the past with some vague whitewash of an explanation. So, I'll apologize again, for everything. Especially how I just dumped this on you in the middle of your Wednesday morning."

"Liss. Please. You don't need to apologize to me."

"I might not have known exactly what happened, but I understood enough, understood we didn't have many options. For you to have gone through this by yourself, though, that is devastating."

As I knew he would, Nao Kao understood intuitively. At the end of the day, there was a single option available to me, and I had taken it.

"What can I say, Nao Kao? There was a piper to be paid. A story as old as time, right?" I tried to remember what resentment felt like, but one of the small mercies of life is the way time can smooth even the deepest wounds until the sharp edge of memory is cottony soft. Whatever resentment had once found its home within me had long flown. I bore no grudge against Nao Kao, none.

"Maybe. But the memory of you stayed with me for a very long time."

Perhaps that was the moment the lightbulb fully illuminated, that the fog began to truly lift. All he had said and shared until now, the details he had retained that I had repressed, none of it had fully landed until now. Finally, the full magnitude of what we had experienced landed on me: this was never one-sided. There was always enough hurt for two to share. There were enough ghosts to haunt us both.

"I'm sorry, Nao Kao. I was just so angry, and in that fog of anger, I don't think I could see what it was like to be you. I felt like we had this amazing friendship – and that you had ruined that. And that the only way forward was to erase every last trace of that time."

"But you couldn't?"

"No, I could, and I did. But because the universe does its work in mysterious ways, at the exact moment I was presented with this whole CLMV project at work, I also found myself with time for both existential questions that were better left unasked….and more time still to paw through every last box in my house. The work project and the boxes pointed directly to you and once we started talking again, I realized how long it had been – and how, even across the distance of time and space, I missed your friendship. But also, I remembered. And so."

My screen bled with blue bubbles and I gave it time for Nao Kao to read and digest so many words bursting forth from his screen.

"And so."

"You're not mad, Nao Kao?"

"No, never. Sorry, yes. I am so, so sorry. But never mad. I don't even know what I would be mad about."

"There's no shortage of reasons. That I didn't tell you at the time. Or mad that I'm telling you now. Mad at how it ended. Mad that I reappeared. Or that it took me so long to do so. I don't know. I'm sure there are other reasons, too, that I could think of if you gave me time."

"I just can't believe you went through this by yourself. Entirely alone."

"Well, I started this conversation by telling you that I was stronger than you were. You just couldn't have known what I meant." My intended levity was lost the moment I sent the message.

"No, I didn't."

"In all these years, I've never told anyone. What is it you're always saying – just to live life? How little control any of us truly has. So that's what I've tried to do for all of these years. Just live my life."

I thought about the men who made war from the moment he was born, the treacherous and uncertain paths lain with mines, the myriad tropical diseases endemic in his part of the world. I thought of the men years later who sent him to Michigan and not Minnesota, who decided when he would leave, and under what terms. Of course, Nao Kao understood that a measure of autonomy was just that, a single measure. The rest was but an illusion, no more real than a shining mirage in the desert. Nao Kao's imperturbability – his seeming nonchalance even – was, I suddenly realized, a trait unwittingly cultivated and honed over a lifetime of uncertainty, necessary not merely to thrive, but simply to survive. Learning to live with ambiguity is a privilege denied most of the world. It implies a learned skill to be employed on the occasions that life does not conform to one's designs: the difference between learning *to live with ambiguity* and learning *life is ambiguous*.

"I am glad you told me, Liss."

"You're not just saying that?"

"No, not at all. Thank you. And always, you can share whatever you want with me. And I will not be mad at you."

"I have no regrets, Nao Kao. Whatever else you might be sorry for, I want you to remember that."

"And as much as I have babbled at you just now, I'm certain this was an easier way to tell you than it would have been in person. That was never going to happen."

"Don't underestimate life."

"A girl only has so much courage. Even a strong girl. Anyway, it's late, so I'm going to go to bed. Good night, Nao Kao."

"You underestimate yourself and life. Good night, Liss. Sleep well."

A picture of a blazing red sunset appeared on my monitor.

NAO KAO

I KNEW SHE could see me typing, formulating some thought, but the words would not emerge. Not from my brain, not from my fingers, and not, for her, from the screen. Pregnant.

Every philosophy student is familiar with Occam's razor. It posits that the simplest, the most realistic, the least far-fetched of competing explanations is most likely the correct one. I have forgotten much of what I learned in my philosophy courses, but that I remember. And so, I had taken Liss at her word.

I reassemble the breadcrumbs she has been dropping. She was scared. She felt she had no one to talk to. She was stronger than me. Even knowing the outcome, I do not arrive. Pregnant.

I feel now how I felt when my twins were born. I'd just finished a soccer game when my brother-in-law rode across the field on his scooter to tell me I had become the father of two squalling daughters. Then he slapped my back so hard it knocked the wind out of me, a gesture for which I'd always been secretly grateful.

"I don't know what to say," I managed finally, an honest if underwhelming assessment of the moment.

She started apologizing then, the words on the screen serving the same purpose as my brother-in-law's forceful back slap. Even speechless, I knew this was backwards. She had nothing to apologize for, whereas I, Icarus, had flown too close to the sun. My error was compounded by the conclusions I had drawn. Occam's razor might dictate "when you hear hoofbeats, think of horses, not zebras," but zebras do exist. Liss herself, I was increasingly sure, was one.

"You don't need to apologize to me," I assembled, my heart and my head both racing, my fingers trembling over the keys.

How different it all might have been, I thought. But what a gift to understand.

"The memory of you stayed with me for a very long time," I added, and thought of a Zen teaching about monks I once learned. *I left the girl there,* said one monk to the other, *are you still carrying her?*

LISS

I FLIPPED ON the screen in front of me, checked how much time was left until we reached our destination. 02:13. Of all the crazy things I had done in my life...but there was no sense mining that territory again. I tried to calculate how many hours I had been traveling, what time it was at home, but my brain was soft, and the questions not pressing.

My mind went back instead to the thread it had picked until it was frayed, yet still I could not leave it be. How did this happen? Through the hills and the valleys of life, I had prided myself on my ability to simply power through. My mantra in life was to never back away from a challenge. But now it was my own mind that challenged me, or specifically the stubborn holes that remained, no matter how zealously I sought to fill them. To my great chagrin, thinking longer or harder brought me no closer to the answers I sought.

In the midst of the 2001 holiday season, I began a new journal. I opened it simply enough.

A fresh start. That is what this blank book represents, and God knows I need nothing right now if not a fresh start – clean, white pages free of previous days and previous pains.

I was making lots of fresh starts then. I set aside my particularities to accept a job at the University of Chicago. It was a purely administrative role managing grants, and with not a shred of international work, the type of job that only weeks earlier I had sworn to Nao Kao I would never accept. Circumstances change, the planets spin, and we find we are grateful for that which we may have previously disdained. I boxed up my memories of a lifetime in Ann Arbor and signed a lease on a new, sun-dappled apartment in Chicago. I adopted a cat, Penny, the first pet I'd had since my beloved childhood Labrador retriever expired of old age as I began high school. It wasn't like I would be traveling. I packed Penny and a few suitcases of belongings into my Civic and pointed my car west toward a brand-new life.

The one fresh start I did not make was Jake. It was so easy, too easy, to return to him. Our split had not been acrimonious and our time together blissfully uncomplicated, especially when compared to what I had recently known. I liked Jake then. He was smart. He was funny. And perhaps most of all, he was safe and familiar company. A week after I moved to the city, he showed up with cartons of ice cream and a toy for my cat. What he offered was no less than a lifeline. When I accepted, I sealed our fates.

Impossible though it seems for a girl from Michigan, I had no other friends in the city at the time. And so, it was also so easy, too easy, to spend Saturdays gawping at the giant rabbits at the Lincoln Park Zoo together or riding the Navy Pier Ferris wheel or the escalators at the Crate and Barrel on Michigan Avenue where I could only dream about owning the creamy velvet sofas or buttery leather chairs that occupied floor-upon-floor of that great, glass flagship store. Jake was smitten – still or again – and whether I wanted to have lunch at Gino's or get half-priced tickets to a show, he was always available.

As a bonus, he never asked any questions, not one, though I had steeled myself for the old Ross and Rachel routine: we were on a breakup. A nice boy with a steady job who knew me and loved me and posed no awkward questions. It should have been more than enough. I tried to remind myself to be grateful.

What Jake thought or suspected, I never knew, though my intuition – again, that blasted and blessed sixth sense – is that he presumed the time we were apart was no more than a big, blank space. And I cannot and will not lie. It made it easier for me to move forward that way, erasing all the space in between, until eventually I believed it myself, thoroughly convinced we had hardly broken up at all.

Until the first step, quicksand looks solid, too.

My parents' delight – *my mother's delight* – that I was back with that nice boy Jake Larkin, the one whose parents were also professors, the politest boy I had ever brought home, only sealed the deal. How could I have explained to Rachael Zick that the nice boy with the faculty parents lacked intellectual curiosity and ambition, that our conversations never delved beyond the headlines, that after the initial shock of breaking up with him wore off, all I felt was relief?

I couldn't have, and I wouldn't have wanted to. Jake and I were not the only ones for whom the gap in time sealed shut, for whom the space where Nao Kao had existed simply disappeared. By returning to Jake, I satisfied my mother so completely that she never again mentioned my unfortunate lapse in judgment, that ill-advised affair that temporarily marred her opinion of me. Probably, she didn't even remember it.

After we decided to get married – a subject I say he raised, but Jake claims I broached, and a state of affairs which encapsulates our entire relationship – I wrote vows.

Because you see me for both who I am and who I could be
I choose you
Because you lift me up when I am down
I choose you
Because you love me
I choose you
I choose you to stroll the ancient streets of lands both near and far
To face one million dawns
To share my chores, my sorrows, and my joys
To dance in the glint of the moon and build sandcastles in our dreams
I choose you

I never delivered them. On the morning of our wedding, Jake's best man delivered the news that writer's block precluded him from doing the same. Could we just recite the traditional vows? Relief triumphed over annoyance.

When I stood at the altar paralyzed by what I was doing, the warnings that I was making a mistake echoing through my mind from the far reaches like a ship's horn through a bank of fog – the repeated blasts reminding me that there was more to life, more to a relationship, than stability, security, and serenity – I merely repeated the bland words of the officiant, detached, as though watching a drama unfold in a play. But at least I would take a new name, erasing not only the gap of time in which I had known Nao Kao, but covering my trail so thoroughly that I could at least be certain he would never find me, at least not in this lifetime.

Why was it so important to hide so deeply? Stacy asked me again and again, but I never could give her a satisfactory response. *Why did you feel so intently that he would search for you? And why would it have mattered?* Repeatedly I attempted to explain something for which I did not have words, only feelings, and feelings without names at that. All I knew was that it mattered tremendously. Dense. Because alone at night when I allowed myself to tentatively peel back the layers of the onion that was "denial," I knew the answer. I had always known the answer. As

186

the eel seeks the Sargasso Sea without knowing how or why, so, too, I needed to vanish completely into the shadows of time. The ways of the eel are still mysterious – a mature one has never been found in the spawning grounds, yet scientists are as certain as they can be without proof that the Sargasso is from whence they come. The universe retains secrets it will not give up. *Fin.*

Love is a funny thing. You marry someone, sleep beside them every night for years, think you know them, believe you love them, and then discover it is only a mirage. Or, you cross paths unexpectedly, two ships passing in great, wide waters, but each sending a wake rippling across the ocean, each changing the course of the other ever so slightly, the drops of the ocean leaving a trace of the seas they shared from the bow to the stern even if the ships never sail the same way again.

And so, deep into the pandemic when time and events conspired and conjoined to lead me into the books of my lives, I was seared but not surprised by the words I had written, these whispers from the past. Nor could I claim surprise that in the vows I wrote and then tucked away, more translucent papers in the sun, that in those one hundred little words that were to evoke to the world – or at least three hundred guests – the deep love and commitment we had for one another, I prioritized travel, made two mentions of sorrow, and was prepared to acknowledge for posterity that I chose Jake Larkin because he loved me.

I never said I love you.

∞ ∞ ∞ ∞ ∞

ALL THROUGH THE spring, I felt like a yo-yo sliding up and down the string, my conversations with Nao Kao evocative of the national conversation: when would this all be over, the clarity waxing and waning with the moons. Regularly he sent pictures, but actual words were much rarer, like fairy dust to behold, until unexpectedly a message would appear. The YouTube link to a song whose lyrics were decidedly non-platonic, but for which he offered no context at all. A passage in a book that he wanted to share, or some note about travel he knew I would appreciate. He asked if I had gotten my bike back out, reminded me to be careful not to crash recklessly as I had done the year before. He asked if it was warm enough and light enough for my early morning runs.

187

And then he would disappear, the days between our conversations stretching across weeks. Occasionally I would see the shadows of him on Facebook proper, his name in the list of friends who had liked a new profile picture or some random link I shared. Always I would hear from him before we had a business meeting, a quick request for the Zoom link and the passcode.

"What do you do with the calendar invites I send?" I asked him once. "Outlook tells me you've accepted, but you clearly don't save it in your calendar. I didn't even know that was possible."

I was not surprised when a sticker of laughter is all the reply I received in return.

When we would be on a call the banter would return and I would decide he was not quite so distant. Nor was he, I realized, annoyed by the stream of consciousness I sometimes directed his way. Rather, Nao Kao was tired and busy. He was but a man, and one with an exceedingly full life.

Up and down the string the disks danced.

I teased him that whenever we met over Zoom, that he was always waving a pen around, but I never saw him writing.

"You always did have the world's best penmanship," I complimented him sincerely, remembering that scrap of paper bearing the title *Acts of Faith*.

"Not anymore," he lamented. "It's gone all squiggly."

"Send me a picture," I replied, and he obliged.

If he was fishing for a compliment it worked. If this was an example of his handwriting gone all squiggly, my memory failed to properly recall the shape of his delicately formed writing years before, writing honed by years of practice inscribing the Lao script, that flowing, curvilinear writing that is murder on my western eyes, though beautiful to behold. Proper handwriting is no mere vanity when it comes to such writing systems.

"Send me one," he asked, but I did not. Two could play at this game, whatever it was, whatever the rules were.

"I bet it's gone all crooked, too," he said. "I remember it used to be great. All loops and lines."

"Has not," I replied, but his goading did not work, and I kept my handwriting to myself.

Only later, when I looked at what he sent did I wonder what the fates had in store. Inked in that gorgeous hand of his were the opening lines of the Victor Hugo poem that adorned my office wall.

Demain, dès l'aube, à l'heure où blanchit la campagne,
Je partirai. Vois-tu, je sais que tu m'attends.
J'irai par la forêt, j'irai par la montagne.
Je ne puis demeurer loin de toi plus longtemps.

Someone walked over my grave.

In my finest writing, those loops and lines still strong, I composed the next stanza, the one that ends, when translated, with "Sadly, and the day for me will be as the night," and snapped a picture.

Toward the end of spring, when the crabapples and eastern redbuds were at their peak, the branches heavy with pink and white and fuchsia blooms, when the daffodils had nearly come and gone and the tulips had their turn in the sun, Nao Kao asked me for a favor.

"A tour of campus," he requested. "I want to see it all again. Spring always was the most beautiful."

I sent him a link to the university's official video, drone footage of the Bell Tower and the Cube, South University and State streets and down to the stadium, blossoms galore. I added a few shots from the Law Quad that I took one sunny afternoon, and one of the profusion of peonies in the Arboretum.

"These aren't as good as yours," I wrote when I sent them, "but then, I'm no professional."

No response.

"What the hell?" I fumed to Stacy. "The man asked for photos of campus, I sent them, and he didn't even have the good grace to acknowledge that he received the pictures. They weren't great, but they were Ann Arbor in spring. Was that not what he requested?"

"Liss, do you remember in the depth of the pandemic when, and this is what you described to me, it was like he put you in his pocket and took you on a tour of the city, that one with all the temples?" my ever-patient therapist asked me by way of response.

"Luang Prabang," I corrected, reflexively. "Uh huh." It was never a good sign when she answered my question by posing one of her own.

"Do you know what I'm going to say next?"

"No." I darted my eyes to the tapestry behind her, to my toes, anywhere but into her gaze.

189

"Liss."

"Fine. I think you're going to tell me that maybe he did not just want a picture of flowers in Ann Arbor. That he could find that online without asking me for it. That maybe the tour he hoped for was more akin to the little journey he took me on, a carefully constructed and narrated tour from the wave fields and woods of North Campus to the Union and Diag and everywhere else."

If what Nao Kao had offered me was a brief respite from the ironclad grip of the homebound life, perhaps now, as Laos experienced its first cases of COVID as the virus began to hopscotch through mainland Southeast Asia and the stress level ticked another notch higher, now he hoped I might offer him something of the same.

"Now you are getting it," she beamed at me, and I fidgeted.

"You don't know that. You don't know what he thinks or wants any more than I do, Stacy."

"Right, but I'm taking you at your word in terms of 'high-context,' and I do know people – it's my one skill in life. And I also know, again, that none of this is common. There is a definite subtext, I'm sure about that. And since we have both arrived at the same conclusion –"

I stuck out my tongue.

By a similar token, any email I sent, whether professional or one of the personal notes he had repeatedly claimed to enjoy reading would seem to disappear into a black hole, until finally, my patience stretched too far, I asked him whether he read a single message I sent.

"I read every word," he replied. "I'm just not always great about making sure you know that."

The next week I sent him a note about summer, my hopes for a "normal" summer with swimming pools and sidewalk chalk and a waning of the restrictions on life that had become so ubiquitous. The next time we texted, he switched the Messenger emoji from the generic thumbs-up to a blazing, yellow sun.

Ever mired in denial, I wanted to believe it was merely a coincidence, and not intended as confirmation that he did, as he'd recently claimed, read and reflect on every word I crafted. I already knew that Nao Kao did not believe in coincidence any more than I did.

Once when we were students, I tried to explain to him how often I felt like I was chasing ghosts. I had almost opted to attend grad school at another university, so strong were the phantoms that lurked in the corners of my mind.

"The universe does not make mistakes; it's good that you are here," he replied.

"Maybe. I'm not sure the spirits are always friendly though."

"Ah, but Liss, la. In Laotian culture we believe in spirits. The land, the water, all have spiritual masters. And of course, the ancestor spirits," he began, telling me in detail about the PuYer-YaYer, the guardian spirits at the center of the annual Songkran, or New Year festival.

"These spirits are holy, sent from heaven to save humankind. Even today the Lao worship these sacred spirits who destroy demons and darkness on earth."

How ironic, then, that Nao Kao was to become my own personal ghost, his long shadow quietly haunting my subconscious until, finally, he was forced back into the light.

Despite a career dealing in the currency of cultural difference, I struggled to puzzle out whether this was Exhibit A of said difference, whether our exchanges merely bore the hallmark of affection between friends, and consisted of no more than the normal give and take old friends could share. Always I was conscious of the prospect that whatever tension I sensed was something that felt unusual only to me. Still, I couldn't entirely eliminate the possibility that this was something more, some kind of long game, and that Nao Kao harbored designs on a future encounter I could not even contemplate. I wanted to reach through the screen, through a dozen time zones and across the thousands of miles, to shake Nao Kao and ask him what was going on.

In truth, if I had harbored even the slightest sliver of hope that he would respond, maybe I would have, but I knew beyond all doubt that he would never show his hand, not unless and until he was ready. Sun Tzu might be my hero, but Lao Tzu was his. No matter how badly I wanted to know the game, I could do naught but let it play out. The ball was in Nao Kao's court. If he wanted to run out the clock, that was his prerogative. Or, as my Japanese friends reminded me about virtually everything, you just have to be patient.

The arc of his life certainly lent itself to holding his cards close: a childhood in a war-torn land, possible informants in everyone you met. And whether there had been other women over the years, and whether anyone else on earth was aware, I, at least, knew for a fact that once upon a time he had strayed from his marriage vows.

The one time I asked my therapist directly what she thought he wanted, she had, of course, turned the question back on me.

"What do you want, Liss?"

"I don't have the first clue, if I'm honest, Stacy. Well, I mean, I definitely don't want to disappear, or for him to, for that matter. I enjoy our conversations. But what I want is to know what he wants."

"If you don't know what you want, what makes you think he does either?" Stacy asked me slowly as you might a young child. A young, slow child.

"Well, he did before! He started this!" I knew I sounded like a sullen child even as the words tumbled out.

"Perhaps. But ever since then, you have controlled the board. You say the ball is in his court. Maybe. But you decided the terms under which things ended before. You decided the terms under which to reappear. It might be his ball, maybe they're even his rules, but it seems that much of the court has been under your control."

"You even decided to send him cookies!" Stacy added, before I could respond to the charges she had laid at my feet.

Guilty, guilty, guilty. Silently, I pled the fifth. It was no wonder he'd said I made him nervous. "I just never know what to expect with you," he had finally elaborated after the fourth or fifth time I'd asked. "I never had any idea what you would do or say next. I still don't."

I wondered again if the cookies had made it, if he had shaken his head in disbelief to think what a nut I must be, shipping two dozen cookies halfway around the world. I also wondered whether he ate them, or shared them, or dumped them in the bin. I owed him a sheaf of documents around his birthday, and with what it would cost the college to overnight those – because overnight service was the only guarantee that the papers would not go missing between Ann Arbor and Vientiane – we had decided to toss in a bit of swag for his students, notebooks and pens, and another shirt for him. The cookies were my personal touch. I make a mean cookie. If the man didn't devour them, he's a fool.

Real American cookies are a treasured delicacy the world over, and Nao Kao was no exception, at least the Nao Kao of twenty years ago. Once I made cookies for him at the little apartment on Madison, me as the chef, him taking notes, a real-life cooking show. You have to cream the butter and the sugars thoroughly, I had explained, to make the mixture completely smooth before you add the eggs and the vanilla.

Cracking eggs was not my forte, and I had spent the next five minutes extracting tiny pieces of shell from the bowl with the tines of a fork, causing him to order a commercial break, during which he mimed ads for appliances and kitchen gadgets until I was ready to sift the flour into the bowl.

"You're not supposed to eat raw cookie dough," he told me, as I forked at least two cookies' worth into my mouth.

"How do you know that? You've never even made cookies before!" I was talking around the dough, my hand in front of my mouth, causing him to waggle his eyebrows at the many bad habits I was simultaneously demonstrating.

"I researched."

"Researched making cookies? Why?"

"In case I needed to know."

I laughed, spitting little pieces of half-masticated dough onto my palm. Nao Kao looked away, bemused or disgusted, or probably both.

"I'm telling you, no manna from heaven ever tasted better. Try it."

"It's the salmonella, you know, from the eggs. Also, it's possible the flour could have e. coli."

"Yes, yes, yes, I know. But I'm telling you, death by cookie dough would not be a bad way to go. Now try some."

Every bit of skepticism vanished the moment the spoon crossed his lips. Nao Kao's eyes widened, and he reached for more even as the first taste was still in his mouth. Victory. Sweet, sweet victory.

When the cookies came out of the oven, he almost literally ate his words. He was so thin then I am not sure where they went, but he must have eaten a dozen cookies while they were still hot, the chocolate melting over his fingers as he plucked them from the cooling racks, and I sent most of the rest home with him on the bus, where he gobbled half of them before he arrived at North Campus. He messaged me in the morning that he had taken a page from my book and polished off what was left for breakfast.

In the years since, I have shipped cookies all over the world on birthdays, Christmases, and Chinese New Years too numerous to count. Never, though, had I shipped them anywhere that the ambient temperature hovered near one hundred degrees. I could envision the great, gooey mess that would be my cookies upon their arrival in Laos. Nao Kao would have to settle for peanut butter. Whether they arrived,

I never knew. Maybe the postman got them, maybe he took them to class, maybe, maybe, maybe.

Oh, but this man was maddening!

"Did you ever think about how hard this might be for him?"

"Hmmmm?" I had been lost in my fit of pique about the cookies and was only half-listening to Stacy.

"Earth to Liss, come in, Liss. I said: have you ever considered that this might be hard for him? Or at least not easy?"

"Um, no?"

Stacy sighed.

"Liss, look. From the beginning, nothing you have told me about this situation, nothing at all, is common."

Her favorite word. Therapists are not allowed to tell you that you or your problems are not "normal." I had learned over the years, though, that things that were not "common" were most definitely *ab*normal.

"I have told you before, I don't know this man from Adam and I have never even met anyone from Laos. I'm not sure, honestly, if I'd even heard of Laos before you told me about this guy. But I know people. I get people. And when I think back to all the things you've shared with me, to the details he has shared with you – what I know, Liss, is that people do not retain this level of recall unless they care uncommonly. I don't know what Facebook's algorithms have to say about friends who have exchanged, what – six hundred pictures in fifteen months? Seven hundred?"

"More like nine hundred probably," I corrected her, "but who's counting?"

"Probably Facebook. And I wouldn't be surprised if that's some kind of record. But the point is not the number. My point is that this is not common. I can't tell you what it *is*, but I can tell you what it is *not*. And what it is not is common. What it is *not* is the behavior I would expect from college friends who check back in after a couple of decades to catch up on life. Those people? They send an email or two and then they content themselves with holiday cards!"

"But I don't get it," I said. "Do you know that in all this time, I don't think he's told me his girls' names at all? If he said them ever, it was once. The same thing for his wife. Why be so secretive? Why be so weird?"

I thought again about the months he'd kept me in limbo trying to guess whether he was still married, the studied way he seemed to keep his hands out of the camera's view on the rare occasions he Zoomed with his camera on, the determined avoidance of any mention of his wife, who was always carefully lumped in with the girls and his parents and spoken of only as *family*.

"Liss, look at it this way. This is a man who, whether he would have followed through or not, at least wanted to have a conversation with you about him staying here, making some kind of life here in this country. Did he want that to be with you? I can't answer that, and honestly, neither can you, since you wouldn't even hear him out.

"But for the sake of this argument, I am going to say yes, that for at least a moment in time, he allowed himself to consider what life with you might look like. And your response…" Stacy's voice trailed off as she thought how to chastise me without appearing to do so too harshly.

"I do a lot of work with high school kids, with college kids. I hear it all, the calls and texts that stop as suddenly as they start, the ex who ducks around a corner at a party to avoid being seen, the ones who change their bars of choice or the routes they walk to class. But you – honestly, what you pulled off beggars belief.

"So, he goes home, and he makes a life, a really successful life. Presumably, along the way, he makes his peace with it. With the life he has.

"And then you come barreling in from out of the blue. You are not exactly subtle, Liss. I have told you before that I am certain – certain – that whatever else you may represent to him, you are without question the most jarring thing that has happened in his life. Once when he was a young man and now in middle age.

"And so, you see, it is called self-preservation. He can't tell you everything because he just can't. He has learned with you that he has to be ready, for whatever comes next, whatever that is. It's no wonder you make him nervous!"

I started to respond, but she wasn't through.

"And, in case I have not provided reasons enough, I will add that you are the one who mixed business and pleasure, probably before he even had an opportunity to consider the implications. Not only that, but you've not exactly made a secret of your work advocating for more stringent sexual harassment policies at the university. Where are the lines? Any of them?"

She peered at me intently, her final words hanging between us. The lines. Maybe there weren't actually any; maybe that was the problem. Not with me, not with Nao Kao, but with life. We tried to draw them, red lines, lines in the sand, lines between business and pleasure, between friends and lovers, between flesh and phantoms. Maybe the lines were only a deception. Maybe ambiguity was all there was.

I thought back to the first time my boss laid his meaty palm across the top of my thigh as we drove to the airport, the dawning realization of the slights to my soul I would have to accept in exchange for meaningful work I loved, for my star to rise. The lines I would distort or shift or even try to ignore, but that he would cross time and again. As Stacy had remarked more times than I could count, only my inestimable abilities to compartmentalize, to move and chase and blur the lines, had allowed me to build a career – to keep climbing – in these circumstances. Abilities, I realized with a sudden start, that I had unconsciously first honed in the aftermath of my time with Nao Kao.

Stacy let me sit with my thoughts for a moment, then started again, more quietly this time.

"Liss....Liss... Two questions for you. First, what is his name, this international man of mystery about whom I have heard so much?"

In an echo of Nao Kao's behavior that drove me batty, for more than a year I had categorically refused to divulge his name, encumbering our conversations with such euphemisms as "my faraway friend" or "the guy from grad school." Knowing my penchant for alliteration, Stacy once tested "the Laotian lover," a label that horrified me, and which I quickly rejected.

I laughed.

"Nao Kao"

"Nao Kao," she repeated, his name my gift to her.

"Liss, do you love him? Do you love Nao Kao?"

I sat silent for a moment, considering that loaded word. Love. Try as I might, I could not get my arms – nor my mind – around a concept as slippery and nebulous as "love." It was, frankly and in all contexts, a topic, a feeling even, that I sought to avoid. I considered the fact that for nearly two decades his memory had not crossed my conscious mind, how I had never so much as Googled his name, how alone among past friends and lovers I'd never sought so much as a profile picture of a glimpse into his current life. I had fought tooth and nail for everything I had wanted in life, yet resolutely let him go, all possibility of contact severed as cleanly as an anchor through an undersea cable, the ship sailing tranquilly along by morning. It was as though my mind were a steel trap, and the doors had slammed shut on all sides, sealing him outside – or in – for nineteen years.

Surely none of that equaled love.

"Love is –" I stopped and then tried again, "I haven't proven very good at love, not in any traditional sense, I suppose. So, I wouldn't say I love Nao Kao, no. I would say that I know the world is a better, brighter place because he is in it. And I have a deep and abiding affection for him."

Even before she said it, I knew. Again, it was about the lines.

"And what is the line, Liss, between affection and love? Show me, tell me, where, exactly, does abiding affection end and love begin?"

I squirmed. She tried another angle.

"From what I know, you speak with him often. As often, I suspect, as you speak with any of your closest friends. As often as most people would speak with their closest friends."

I nodded, slowly, waiting to see where this was headed.

"Why do you think that is?"

"He gets me," I replied immediately. "I can tell him anything, and I feel like he understands without me having to explain it. So, when I don't talk to him –"

I paused. How to explain the antsy feeling that developed when we didn't speak for more than a handful of days, as though something were suddenly missing again, or as though the words that for so long had gone unspoken were burbling like molten lava within me. No longer dormant, they bubbled constantly in their cauldron, erupting not violently, like Krakatoa spewing ash skyward, but slowly and steadily like Kīlauea, lava rolling gently, placidly even, on its way to the sea, but nevertheless chewing up all in its path.

She waited, and I could almost see her considering my words. Whatever iceberg she sensed below the surface, I could see her weighing whether to let it lie or probe its depth.

She simply sighed.

The iceberg would sit. My shoulders relaxed with her sigh, freed of the struggle of trying to articulate exactly what it was I felt toward Nao Kao.

"Last question, Liss: what did you decide about the book?"

"I didn't," I said, and for the first time, I knew I had lied to my therapist, as well as to myself.

∞ ∞ ∞ ∞ ∞

I SMELLED THE beginnings of breakfast, the coffee just on to brew, the familiar choices of eggs or fried rice warming in their little trays. I did not need to consult the tv screen in front of me; I could tell from the rhythms of the flight crew, their studied and efficient movements as they moved through the cabin delivering trays, pouring coffee, offering a final pour of water, that we were no more than 90 minutes from landing. This was the muscle memory of a frequent flyer kicking back into gear, and again I felt the familiar sensation that I had come home.

One of the lessons my nieces have taught me is exactly how much you can learn from children's books. One of my favorites was *Dog on a Frog?*

It begins with a frog telling a dog to "get off," much to the chagrin of the canine who, the reader learns, likes sitting on squishy amphibians that making croaking sounds. A cat becomes involved, reciting the conveniently rhyming rules of how and where animals rest their weary bones. Cats on mats, frogs on logs, poodles on noodles, and of course, dogs on frogs.

Eventually, the nonsense rhyming leads us to the whales, who, the frog dictates, are to sit on nails. The dog rather reasonably posits that whales may not like this assignment, only to be informed by his amphibious friend that they don't have to like it – they just have to do it.

So, it was for me in the days before Thanksgiving in that fateful and momentous year of 2001. Any doubt that those little pills in my bathroom had not been beyond reproach fell from my mind with the leaves around campus.

I was pregnant. By a man who was married to a woman on the other side of the planet. Who was home with their twins, nursing them through tropical disease and god knew what else. Whose best chance for a better life had been to send her husband, their father, packing, alone, to the farthest, snowy reaches of the earth. He was her hope for a life beyond what she had dreamed as a refugee, perhaps even what she had dreamed as a young bride, who had herself fallen pregnant almost immediately. And he was legally obligated to return home a few months hence. For the betterment of his country, I reminded myself, as I recited the facts. As long as I kept this all at arm's length, I could handle it. A problem to be solved.

But now this man, whether he knew of what he spoke or not, was increasingly demanding that I hear out his plans to stay, somehow, someway, in this country a little while longer. Internally, I ticked off the options. An extension on time-to-graduation on his master's degree. Admission into a doctoral program. Some other visa type about which I knew nothing – and neither had he before the power of the internet showed him the way.

Whether I had hit on a winner, I couldn't know, for I never asked. Nor did I ask whether America was the appeal – or me. In all cases, it was better not to know.

I had no job, not in early November, and no place to live after December beyond my old childhood bedroom, with its lavender walls lined with the certificates and awards I had accumulated since grade school. There I would be safely again under the watchful eye of my parents, though I was certain my father, at least, was blissfully ignorant of the state of affairs of my personal life. And I had dreams. Personal and professional. Any way I sliced it, my current predicament had all the makings of derailing my entire life.

If I told Nao Kao, I ran the risk that he might dig in his heels further and determine to stay. I could not, would not, be responsible for that. I read once that one cannot simultaneously love and feel guilty. I am still not certain about that, but for me, there was no question. The guilt I had harbored over the past few months had been monstrous enough while I shouldered it. Should he stay, it would consume me, and any burgeoning love we might have.

Years later, that guilt would be one of the first things I tried to explain. Nao Kao had the good grace not to ask whether that guilt only extended toward the wife I never knew, or if I had saved any of it for him, the man who had been both my friend and my lover and so much else besides, before I made my decision. Unilaterally. Without, one could argue, so much as a second thought for what that might mean for him.

For if he was not going to stay – and he was not – I had already ruled that out – then it was best not to allow him to think he should have the least say in what I did. I didn't actually think he would disagree with me. Anyone could see that it was an impossible situation, and he was not much better at denying me than I was him. He would never deny me the chance at chasing my future, unimpeded by this past. Telling him would be pointless, or so I averred. I was doing him a kindness, or so I convinced myself. Ignorance was bliss, and this way one of us, at least, could continue merrily through life without so much as a hint of the shadow of the other.

More importantly, if I didn't tell him, if I didn't tell anyone, I could almost convince myself it simply wasn't true.

I had already decided the last time I went to his apartment. Once I did this, I would not be able to hide it from him. And I couldn't keep rebuffing the conversation he wanted to have daily now, sometimes more than once a day, even, this idea of him remaining here.

I went to his apartment for the last time on the Tuesday before Thanksgiving, in the afternoon, when the sunlight was weak and watery, the yellow orb already racing toward its lowest arc across the sky. It was windy and the naked branches of the trees scratched against one another as they swayed. Great piles of leaves lie heaped in the gutters waiting to be picked-up. Once they had been small and bright and lacy, then full and lushly green before bursting with the reds and oranges and yellows of fall. In the gutters, they were crumbled and brown, their little circle of life completed.

I remember how slowly he undressed me that afternoon, how everything moved in slow motion, whether in reality or just the reel in my mind, from his fingers hooking into the hair tie that held my ponytail to the line of kisses along my collar bone to our bodies fitting together as though they were made only for one another to the final gentle kiss he placed on the tip of my nose.

"You're sure you won't stay? Just a little longer?"

I shook my head, not trusting my voice. We were dressed then and I looked into his eyes, his face, ran my fingers through his hair. With my index finger I made small looping circles on his chest, between the buttons of his shirt.

"Maybe next time?"

I would not let the tears fall. Not here, not yet, not now. I shrugged, noncommittally.

"Liss, la. You ok? What's wrong?"

Life, la.

But this I could not say. More shrugging.

I gathered my bag and walked to my car. I saw him at the window as I left, the little wave he gave, the furrow to his brow. Whether I lifted my hand in farewell to return the gesture or left it slack at my side is one of the details that defies me still.

I drove to my parents' and parked before walking to my apartment. I think I drove that day rather than ride the bus just so I would have to make that walk. I had made it many times, but with tears streaming down my cheeks and my entire body heaving, it had never before felt so much like the proverbial walk of shame. For three miles, the late November air braced my heart for the one last task that lay before me that day.

My building was quiet. Most students had left for Thanksgiving already, and for once there was no bass thumping from behind any of the doors, no shouts, no laughter, nothing but the silence of my tears and the red of my eyes as I followed through on the last, hardest task. I turned on the computer in my bedroom, the one I had been working at the night Nao Kao changed the rules of the game, and signed into AIM. As I had hoped would be the case, he wasn't online.

"Nao Kao, this has to stop. You've become obsessed, and it's starting to scare me."

I told myself I was doing him a kindness, doing us a kindness. I had considered my choices; I didn't like any of them, but this was the right one, of that I was certain. It was for the best. It was the only way. Come what may, I owned this decision entirely, and even in that heartbreaking moment, was grateful for that ray of light, that sliver of autonomy.

I clicked through the settings and blocked his account, then went a step further and blocked anyone with whom I was not already buddies from sending a message request. I flipped open my email and blocked his address.

Casual cruelties hurled through space, and all contact severed. All *possibility* of contact severed. At the time I was certain: it was the best I could do. Lot's wife might have turned to a pillar of salt, but I had no such worries. What the weight of those final words might cost Nao Kao never crossed my mind.

∞ ∞ ∞ ∞ ∞

HOW I MADE it through that holiday weekend, through a Thanksgiving table undoubtedly piled with turkey and trimmings, more classic

201

holiday sides than I could count, and ringed by faces from near and far, international students, many of them, and each a reminder of the man I had just left, I will simply never know. On Sunday night, as the rest of the world dove headlong into the heart of the holiday season, I steeled myself for the inevitable.

«*Je ne dois qu'avaler quelques pilules,*» I told myself mechanically, in French, placing that much more distance between me and what was happening, the same way, since childhood, I tended to inscribe the biggest, hardest thoughts into my journals in my second language. I just need to swallow a couple of pills. My appointment was Monday morning.

I penned the last words into the journal I had kept all year, the one that recorded my conversations with Nao Kao, my newfound knowledge of Laos and photography, of motorbikes and temples, of runaway inflation and cigarettes sold by the penny, of cows that met their end when their hoof struck a mine, and guardian spirits, and everything else he had taught me over the past year.

> *I must learn not to carry the weight of the world on my shoulders. I must teach myself not only to forgive, but to forget. I must remember my dreams. I dream of traveling the world, of earning a PhD, of a lifetime of writing.*

Sometime in the middle of that fitful night, the cramps came, stronger than any I'd ever known, and with them the unmistakable wetness that sent me rushing half-asleep into the bathroom. Relief flooded through me, mingling with those fraternal twins, sadness and anger. Damn. Damn, damn, damn. Even the end had slipped beyond my control, the streaks of red presenting themselves in the small hours as if to mock me despite the solution they presented.

Daylight seeping into my conscience as the past seeped out, I repeated the lesson to myself: I would learn to forget. Ever the star pupil, my brain complied, both effortlessly and aggressively erasing entire patches of my memory. Like floodwaters surging over a dam, sluicing away all before them, so too that night did the blood and the tears stake their claim, their torrent utterly sweeping away territory I have yet to reclaim.

The flood has long receded, but the rocks of my mind remain barren. That last cruel message, for example, the one I forced Nao Kao to carry with him, is but a fuzzy film in my mind. He tells me that is what I wrote, and I trust him implicitly. It certainly sounds like what I would have said at the time.

To his credit, he did not try to find me, not then. I finished the semester in a daze and collected my diploma through the mail.

∞ ∞ ∞ ∞ ∞

I WAS DRAWING stares from the passengers around me. Tears streamed down my cheeks as the flight attendants made another final sweep of the cabin, and passengers stretched their legs or restowed belongings in the overhead bins or used the lavatory one last time.

There are over twenty thousand monks in Laos, a country with a total population of some seven million people that is roughly twice the size of Pennsylvania. To ordain as a monk in a high honor in the Laotian culture, and somewhere in the neighborhood of one-third of all males will, at some point in their lives, do so. Nao Kao did: whence, I believe, his preternatural calm. All boys of the Lao ethnicity are expected to become novice monks for a period of at least three months in their lives, so it came as no surprise that there was a score or more of monks on this flight.

The one behind me gently tapped my shoulder and offered me a tissue. I wiped my eyes, then removed my mask to blow my nose. As I turned in my seat to thank him, I thought of the story of the monks that Catherine shared when I finally came clean with her about what happened all those years ago – and why I was the only one of our circle who changed her name when she married, who didn't even wrestle with the decision of whether to do so.

A couple of monks travel down a muddy road and come across a lovely girl who is unable to cross through the mud. The older monk does not hesitate to pick the girl up and carry her over the mud. Hours of silence later, the younger monk finally chastises his elder, reminding him of their vow not to go near females, and especially not those who are young and lovely.

"It's dangerous," he ranted, "why did you do it?"

The older monk looks at the younger one calmly, quizzically, and replies, "I let her go hours ago. Are you still carrying her?"

It's all very Zen, you see, a lesson in letting go of attachment to the abstract and the importance of making decisions based on kindness and immediate need and not allowing the past to weigh you down.

"Be a monk," Catherine said to me, and then she let me cry.

∞ ∞ ∞ ∞ ∞

"GOOD MORNING, LADIES and gentlemen. We have begun our final descent into Vientiane International Airport. Please make sure your seatbacks are locked and upright and your tray tables are stowed. Flight attendants will be coming through the aisle to collect any remaining service items. If you have not yet received a customs form, you may ask for one at this time. We will be landing shortly."

I lifted the window shade to see the sun just beginning to rise over the curve of the earth. In that moment I was reminded of both how big and how small this planet is. I watched the sky being bled of night, indigo giving way to violet and rose, tangerine and peach. I thought back to the advice a friend gave me as I beat myself up over the debacle with Jake.

"You have to keep looking forward in hope, Liss, not backward in regret. If you keep your face to the sun, the shadows will always fall behind you."

I could not help but wonder, again, for the millionth time, whether he would be there, waiting at arrivals. Despite the promises of months ago to never be mad with any of what happened, and implicitly with me, I knew there was every possibility that I had finally traveled a bridge too far, pushed even Nao Kao's patience beyond the breaking point. I knew Stacy thought it was possible.

"Say that again, Liss. I lost you there for a minute."

We were on FaceTime, and this was at least the third time the screen had frozen. I was back on the road again, spotty internet just one of the hazards I faced. God willing and the creek don't rise, I would be walking down the jet bridge in an hour, wheels up in less than two, bound for a place far, far from home.

"I said I decided to write the book." She looked surprised. For how long had I debated with her whether this was a story worth telling, whether it was fair and right and proper of me to tell it. A measure of autonomy, I had decided.

"Have you told him?"

"Sort of."

"Sort of. What does that even mean?" How much I had put off and how much I had left unsaid: she knew.

"Actually, I wrote it already. It's done. Signed and sealed. So, I didn't tell him I'm writing a book, I told him I wrote one. Forgiveness rather than permission, that kind of thing."

"I see," already Stacy looked concerned, and she didn't know the half of it yet.

"I overnighted an advance copy to him a few days ago. And I sent him an email just before it would have arrived and told him I thought he might want to read it. That he should read it."

Her eyes grew wide, but our time was always short, even when I didn't lob such surprises her way. Expertly she parsed the wheat from the chaff, setting aside her own astonishment.

"What made you decide?"

"I think I always knew. Boys come and go, but books are forever."

A look of sadness replaced the shock of a moment before. More than once she had asked me if I wrote this story and didn't tell him, if I wouldn't simply be repeating the pattern I had established all those years ago, the one where I unilaterally make moves, oblivious to the consequences.

Obviously, my next move was not even to tell her that I had secured an agent. I did not need her reminding me that I was doing my best impression of a below-average human. Or, that I was possibly even slipping from impersonating one into becoming one.

She drew a deep breath, again, and waited for me to continue.

"Ink on paper is a rare form of permanency in an impermanent world. Boys?" I shrugged.

"Will your name on the cover keep you happy?"

"If you mean will it keep me warm at night, we both know the answer to that."

She laughed lightly.

"You ask questions I can't answer except with more questions, Stacy. What is to say what made me happy today would keep me happy next month or next year? And what's a little happiness in the scheme of the universe, after all? The planets keep spinning no matter how those of us pinned to the earth's crust by gravity feel, whether we are living and breathing or serving as matter for the next iteration of civilization. But at the end of the day, we are who we are. At least I am who I am. Unvarnished and flawed, but wholly me."

That part, I am certain Nao Kao understands. We cannot, either of us, any more than most people, change how we are wired. It is what draws us together and pushes us apart, two magnets circling, our poles shifting through time and space. I will not know his secrets; now he cannot stop knowing mine.

"There is something else I should tell you," I said to Stacy. "I'm at the airport, Detroit, in the Club," I picked at some lint on the chair, this last bit arranging itself in my mind.

"I'm on my way to Vientiane. To see him. Sort of. And for work. And vacation. Today. The flight boards in an hour."

Probably I could have waited, but first after so many years, and then after so many messages and emails pinging through space, it seemed enough time had passed. And the world is a big place: I've got places to go and people to see, but I wouldn't have been able to concentrate on any of them until I made this trip.

Silence. Absolute, utter silence.

"Does he know? Is he pleased?"

"I had to tell him. Business and pleasure," I reminded her. "I think he was surprised. I'm not sure about pleased."

Completely and utterly stunned was more like it. I imagine he felt the need for a stiff drink – or two – when that message popped up on his phone. And possibly regretted ever planting the seed in my mind.

"And?"

"He promised not to shout at me."

Stacy looked at me closely, as closely as she could through the screens that were connecting us, perhaps truly appreciating for the first time the depths of the steeliness – the stoicism, even – that I once described to her as my defining characteristic. I wasn't Rachael Zick's daughter for nothing.

"I shouldn't have expected anything else. Good luck, Liss. Whatever that means."

The call ended and I stared and my phone, willing my fingers to punch a number it knew by heart. I breathed deeply as I waited for her to pick up.

"Liss? Is that you? Where are you? Is everything okay?"

Belatedly, I remembered my parents were traveling. Of course, she thought something was wrong.

"Mom, it's ok, I'm sorry, I forgot you were out West."

She waited for me to continue; I paused just long enough to let the sleep fully lift from her mind.

"My flight leaves in a couple hours. For Laos."

"Laos? I thought you were off to Bangkok?"

Oh, what a tangled web we weave...

"Well, I'm not. It's complicated, Mom." Even in middle age she could still make me feel like an adolescent being told off for too much sass.

"Liss?"

"Mom, I don't know what I'm doing. I mean, I'm going to Laos. And it *is* work. But also, I'm going to see Nao Kao."

"Nao Kao?" I could picture her, was certain she was pacing next to the bed now, trying to listen between the lines, beginning to parse fact from fiction. I could almost see her long, lean body wrapped in the lilac-colored, silk wrapper she always kept within reach, even when traveling. Her brain, I knew, to be feverishly working over a lifetime of names and faces.

"Oh. OH."

She had arrived.

"Liss? What do you mean?"

I told her as briefly as I could, the story pouring forth in a torrent. Surprisingly, I felt naught but relief to be unburdening myself to her in this way.

When I finished she was quiet, as quiet as I had ever known her to be. I was about to ask if she was still there when she asked quietly, "Do you love him?"

That blasted, blasted question. Of everything Rachael Zick might have said – *Why were you hiding this from me? Is he still married? What are you possibly thinking?* – these were the last four words I would have expected her to utter.

I looked out the windows of the Club and down into the terminal at the passengers hurrying to the tram, to their gates, to the planes that would take them anywhere and everywhere. Each of them carried a story, and probably more than one. Undoubtedly more than a few were running to somewhere or someone, while others scurried away from friends or lovers, from hurts or hungers. Running to and running from: just as endings are not written with edges etched cleanly, or boundaries neatly delineated, I was no longer convinced of the firm line between the two. Running to or running from: I couldn't even say with certitude which I was doing.

"I don't know, Mom. There are a lot of kinds of love, aren't there? Maybe I feel one of them for him, and maybe I don't. I don't know. And I don't know what he feels either."

Certainly, I thought, but could not make myself say, Nao Kao made me *feel* loved. Not that I would ever presume to think, let alone utter aloud, that he loved me. The feeling of being loved could easily be nothing more than a figment of my mind – something his words and actions engendered deep within my brain, but without any intentionality on his part. An illusion, like so much else in life. Whether I loved him was equally elusive.

"Don't you see?" I continued. "That's why I have to go there. To try to figure it out. To try to understand if there's anything between us, or if this, whatever it is, is nothing more than a mirage in a desert. Because there might not be anything."

"I don't have any advice, Liss. Or maybe only this. Remember: you cannot prove a negative."

Lack of love, lack of feeling, lack of affection, all of these were beyond the linear proofs into which I tried so doggedly to squeeze my life. But people did not work that way, as I was still discovering. Life was far more complicated, far messier, far harder to predict than any mathematical equation. And far more beautiful.

Our words, my soliloquy and her response, hung between us, more emotion than we'd shared since I was a kid still skinning her knees. Maybe it wasn't too late to fix that, either.

"I love you, Mom."

"I love you, Liss. One more thing: the universe works in mysterious ways. You'll have more success if you don't always fight it."

Her words surprised me, calling to mind as they did someone I had once known, holding my hands tightly in his on the beach at Grand Haven, reminding me, even as the sands of time sped along their journey, to savor every moment.

I peered out my window as dawn broke over the mountains and jungles and cities below.

NAO KAO

O F COURSE, I looked for her. Not immediately. That last message, the accusation I was scaring her, was crystal clear. I would have preferred that she spoke to me, that we'd had one final conversation, an opportunity to explain, although I am self-aware enough to realize that Liss would have qualified any further explanations as pleadings, and that route was off the table. I understood the situation we were in, of course I did, but the way it ended was a shock to my system.

Ann Arbor was bleak that winter and Liss would have been impressed by how much time I spent at the library studying and contemplating my future. "It's all planned out for you," she'd reminded me throughout the fall, whenever I marveled at her determination to create a future of her own design, aided by nothing but the sheer force of her will. Liss would never accept a life that had been mapped out by others.

In April I graduated on a raw, gray day that bore no similarities to the spring days we'd spent roaming around campus on a quest for ice cream or locations for photo sessions or merely basking in one another's company and conversation. I missed that more than anything, her bubbling, effusive chatter on anything and everything. Liss was equal parts silly and pensive, unyielding and vulnerable, and always unabashedly herself. I'd never known anyone with her wit or her spirit and her absence left an outsize hole in my final semester. I emailed her once or twice, to no avail.

As I packed up my apartment a few weeks after commencement, I made one final attempt to learn what had become of her.

I visited Rachael Zick's office in Tisch Hall, knocking on the door.

"Come in," her voice rang out, and I pushed the door tentatively.

"Why, Nao Kao, hello!" she exclaimed in surprise, though I quickly realized it was more likely alarm.

"Dr. Zick, Rachael," I began as she stared at me uncomfortably. "I'm leaving Ann Arbor next week and thought to pay my respects before I do." My words were too formal, but it was a start.

"You might have emailed. Or scheduled an appointment with my assistant."

"Yes, I see. I apologize."

"Best of luck to you, Nao Kao. I'm sure you'll do well for yourself back in Laos."

"Thank you. One more thing, if I might ask?"

She arched her back and sat up straighter, like a cat preparing to pounce.

"Please give my regards to Liss."

"Liss?"

"Yes, please."

"I'd prefer not to, Nao Kao. I'm sure you're aware she's left Ann Arbor and she's quite happy now. Work she enjoys and she's back together with that lovely boy, Jake. I'm not sure you met him?"

I stood mutely in the doorway as her words sunk in. Liss spoke of him only once, and then only to tell me they were on the verge of breaking up.

I stared at Rachael Zick, ramrod straight in her ergonomically correct chair and tried to picture her as the warm hostess I'd first encountered. The distance was too great.

"I understand. Thank you, again, for the kindness you showed me in the past. Good-bye."

"Good-bye, Nao Kao. Please give my regards to your wife."

I fled the building then, anger and heartache surging through my veins, bested only by the humiliation of the final knife twist.

Eventually, I felt it may have been a kindness of sorts, for I never wondered if Liss received my message or if she would contact me. I returned home and plunged headlong into the life that was waiting for me. The twins shied from me until their younger sister was born; she made us a family and life proceeded apace. Birthdays and vacations, family dinner, and smiling portraits – on the surface, all was right. Beneath it, we never recovered from the two-year separation, the battles we'd been left to fight individually. The gales.

The wife who, as I'd told Liss once, had been a nice, normal girl, became a nice woman. Still, our lives ran parallel paths more often than intersecting ones. Determined to make the most of my time in the U.S., I grasped for every brass ring in front of me once I returned, accumulating titles, honors, and awards, theoretically fulfilled, but always searching for something that eluded me. A few times I searched for her, Liss Miller, Melissa Miller, Melissa Claire Miller, whatever iteration of her name I thought might yield a trace of her. Nothing. She might never have existed except in my memory.

EPILOGUE

~

LISS

NAO KAO HAD said he would meet me at the airport if his schedule permitted, even if it meant jostling for space alongside the tuk-tuk drivers and cabbies hoping for a fare. I had been told the pandemic thinned their ranks, but that those who survived are more aggressive than in the past. "Schedule permitting" sounded like a get out of jail free card, and particularly given the hours it took to wind my way through the new pandemic protocols – verification of vaccination status in one line, which fed into verification of a negative PCR test in another, which led to an interminable wait for a rapid test on arrival – to say nothing of the usual passport-baggage-customs procedures, I couldn't blame him for abandoning whatever vigil he may have held through the early morning hours.

When I finally stepped into the din of the arrival hall, a man with my name on a placard pushed his way forward as soon as I was visible to the assembled crowd of friends and families eager for long-awaited reunions, and the jostling mob of tuk-tuk and cab drivers. The man with my name on his sign guided me carefully by the elbow out through the airport doors, and I thought again how much of my life was predicated on an inherent trust in the goodness of humankind. So many times had I followed strangers with whom I could exchange not a single spoken word through doors like these, into places unknown. As the glass panes slid open, the dewy air of dawn walloped me, the heat of the early hour holding the faintest clue of what was yet to come. As the waves of steam wafted up from the pavement, I appreciated again the discomforts borne by the millions without complaint. I had arrived at my destination, if ever that was in doubt.

Put it down to intuition, but I knew immediately, of course. Hope and fear are opposite sides of the same coin and, like salt and pepper, you can't pass one without the other. The million times I asked myself in flight whether he would be there, I had been tossing that coin up in the air. In the close, humid air of the international arrivals hall, the coin landed and I had my answer.

Oh Liss: ye, of little faith.

For there, waiting, leaning nonchalantly against his gleaming truck, was Nao Kao Inthavong.

"Welcome to Laos, Miss Miller," he said, more mischief than I could muster at that hour twinkling in his dancing eyes. "Let's enjoy your visit."

I didn't trust my voice, nor the words my brain may foist upon it.

"I already am," I texted him from the back seat; I knew they'd met their mark when I heard him chuckle a moment later.

"I was afraid you would decide not to come," he texted back, and then, "You really did a number on me, Liss."

All of my fears – the knot that had lodged deep within my gut – dispersed.

I'm guessing no happy ends, Nao Kao had foretold when I asked if he wanted to watch *Au revoir les Enfants,* the night my own world would tilt so precipitously on its axis, its rotation around the sun forever altered.

But who are we to judge what constitutes a happy end? Or when or how they arrive? The universe moves in mysterious ways. It cannot, will not, be bent or coerced to conform to the designs of the mere mortals who move through it for their brief moment in time. As the driver conveyed us calmly and competently through a city coming to life, I felt the proverbial page turn. I couldn't yet read the text, but allowed myself to consider that maybe its last words were not what I'd assumed them to be for so long.

∞ ∞ ∞ ∞ ∞

NAO KAO HANDED me off to his team at NUOL, assuring me I would be in good hands, of which I had no doubt. They showed me every inch of the central Dongdok campus, making sure I appreciated the peaks and the red roofs, the pillars with their bases and crowns of gold. We strolled the lush grounds dotted with fountains and toured Buddha Park and Pha That Luang, the Wat Si Saket and the city's sprawling night market. We sought the blessing of the Buddha at the Wat Si Muang, where we honored the spirits of the city embodied – and perhaps, if you believe one of the myths, entombed – by the City Pillar. I thought of Si, sacrificing herself to appease the angry spirits, and now the guardian of the entire city, the PuYer-YaYer never far from my mind. I earned points for my knowledge of those guardian spirits, never revealing their existence to have been one of Nao Kao's lessons to me so many years ago.

Whether by coincidence or design, my hosts ensured a steady supply of factory-sealed bottles of water, each labeled Danone. They plied me with tam mak hoong and sticky rice, khao piak sen and laap. As I ate my rice, the beginnings of a memory came to me, Nao Kao and I making fried rice in his apartment, but bringing it into focus was as elusive as grabbing for a handful of the morning mist that hung over the city each day. For once I understood the currency of memory, understood it was no more expendable today than the old francs or lira or marks, and I let it go. After all, I had only look across the table to see Nao Kao himself, the same but changed, and smiling at me not through the mists of memory, but here, in real life.

"You think too much," he'd said to me once, and so I tried merely to be. In the moment. At peace. *Enjoying,* as he had suggested we should as his driver steered the course from the airport when I arrived.

As I said my farewells and prepared for a few days of much needed and long-overdue vacation in Luang Prabang, he surprised me.

"Can I come with you?" he asked.

I could only nod; inside, I felt like a three-year-old on Christmas morning. The fabled temple city offered much needed spiritual renewal and respite after the confinement of the pandemic. Together, we strolled the banks of the Mekong and the Nam Khan gazing at the golden-roofed wats, admiring the mosaics and murals, enjoying tea on the teak balconies that proliferated the town. We climbed Phou Si to watch the sun slink to its rest beneath the horizon and climbed it again some days at dawn. Being there, I remembered: this is why I travel. This is the reward for the deal with the devil that is so often travel itself; this is the reason I crisscross the skies. This is who I am.

We watched the saffron-clad monks stream through the streets at sunrise for the alms ceremony, and I prayed at Wat Xieng Toung, the oldest and most beautiful of the monasteries, throwing heavenward my prayers for all the world's goodness to descend upon its denizens.

I was grateful to the gods, all of them, in whatever form they may embody, for all that life had offered me. I prayed especially that goodness and peace would descend upon Nao Kao, this man, whom I grasped now, I had loved, and who, I was equally certain, had once loved me – and did still or again – even if neither of us had ever spoken the words aloud.

As darkness descended across the quiet of the hotel courtyard – once bustling, no doubt, but empty of any guests now, like the entire hotel, save for Nao Kao and me – I went for a swim, the surest way I knew to simultaneously think and clear my head of extraneous thought. Back and forth, back and forth I stroked as the lanterns twinkled on and the stars began to peep overhead; back and forth, back and forth until I'd worn out my muscles as well as my mind. Nao Kao was there, as I knew he would be, having come not to watch my laps but merely to be proximate as my time in Laos wound down. Now he moved from his lounge chair to where I rested at the pool's edge and gently draped a towel across my shoulders. Softly he flicked his feet in the pool, sending ripples of water outward in concentric circles. Watching the water pulse around us, I couldn't help but think that we make choices in our lives and we live with them, learning to accept their ripples, the gentle undulations that mark our days.

"I'm so glad you came here with me," I whispered, nestling into his shoulder.

He pulled off my swim cap and ran his fingers carefully through my wet hair, teasing apart the tangles. He brought his arm around my side, scooting me closer and turning me toward him.

"Oh, Liss," he said, as his mouth sought mine, "I have thought about you for twenty years. I was never going to miss this."

ACKNOWLEDGMENTS

I AM FOREVER GRATEFUL for the many individuals who have made this book possible, not least my amazing agent Dani Segelbaum whose enthusiasm for and belief in this novel has been priceless, and whose friendship has been an unexpected treasure. I am likewise grateful to my editor, Kim Budnick, without whom it would never have been published. Thank you, both, for taking a chance on this first-time author.

My parents, of course, who have supported my every endeavor for four-plus decades: Mom, *je t'aime jusqu'au bout du monde* and Dad, if you've instilled anything in me, it's that if a job is worth doing, it's worth doing right. To that end, I have always striven to do right and make you both proud, and can only hope I have succeeded on both accounts.

As they say, it takes a village, and I'm so incredibly lucky that mine is peopled with the finest humans on earth. My especial thanks to Viola, whose friendship is worth more than any degree, and without whom this book never would have happened; Maureen, with whom I have been lucky enough to brave the rains near and far and who shared so generously her Canva talents; Angela, who pushed me daily, for months, to put this story to paper; Loretta, whose friendship is proof that every cloud has its silver lining; and Katy, who has loved me through thick and thin practically since we were in diapers.

My early readers, too, have nothing but my gratitude for recognizing a diamond in the rough and helping me apply the polish. Carol, Mel, Stephanie, Liz, Marie, Meagan, and Kay: you ladies rock – as friends and colleagues, as readers, and as my fellow travelers on the road of life. Thank you, too, to Kristen, who read the revision in a single afternoon and whose guidance proved deeply influential; to Christine, who provided valuable last minute advice; and of course, to Kersten, who read it and told me I might not have to choose.

Your ideas and encouragement have made this feel like the greatest group project of my life, and every one of you has inspired me along the way.

I want to also acknowledge the women on whose shoulders I have stood, especially my high school English teacher, Mrs. Walker, who helped me hone my writing for years, taught me what it meant to develop voice and style and ledes and kickers, and remains one of my hero(ine)s all these years later. If you, dear reader, have made it this far, I know you can read. Thank a teacher.

There are three other women without whom the trajectory of my life would have been completely different: Mrs. Stockard, Dr. Harper, and Dr. Mabokela. All three have shaped my writing, my career, and my life, and especially as a white woman, it is important to me to acknowledge that all three of these remarkable individuals are strong and inspiring Black women for whom I have nothing but bottomless respect, admiration, and appreciation. Diversity matters. Fight for it.

To G, who remains the most resilient and remarkable person I've ever known: thank you for the privilege of being your mom. Your courage and determination inspire me every day and I love you more than words can say.

Finally, for Khemara, who has shared so much with me over the years, and without whom there could be neither a story nor a book.

ខេមរាសូមអរគុណចំពោះអ្វីៗគ្រប់យ៉ាង នឹងគ្រប់ពេល

ABOUT THE AUTHOR

Sarah Magee is an inveterate traveler, unabashed globalist, and firm believer in always eating dessert first. It is never too early for ice cream. She is a master packer of suitcases and lifelong Michigander. *I Never Said I Love You* is her literary debut.

Printed in Great Britain
by Amazon